The Secret Wish List

PREETI SHENOY

w

westland ltd
61, II Floor, Silverline Building, Alapakkam Main Road, Maduravoyal, Chennai 600 095
93, 1 Floor, Sham Lal Road, Daryagani, New Delhi 110 002

First published in India by westland ltd 2012

15 14 13 12 11

ISBN: 978-93-82618-18-8

Typeset by Ram Das Lal

Printed at Manipal Technologies Ltd., Manipal

For Satish, Atul and Purvi
And for Mum and Dad

Heart! We will forget him!
You and I—tonight!
You may forget the warmth he gave—
I will forget the light!

When you have done, pray tell me
That I may straight begin!
Haste! lest while you're lagging
I remember him!

—Emily Dickinson

Prologue

THE CONVERSATION WITH TANU HAS REMINDED me, with startling intensity, of the person I used to be—a person with hopes, ambitions and a desire to live life to the brim. I was just like Tanu—bubbly, enthusiastic and positive.

I think about Ankit. I think about that kiss. I have replayed everything that happened on that day at least a million times in my mind through all these years. I loved him with all the purity and innocence of a sixteen-year-old heart. I was certain at that time that he loved me too. I wonder how he looks now. I wonder what I will feel if I were to ever meet him again.

It is ironic how the years change you and yet you remain the same. Even if you are married, become a parent, deep down you are still the person you were before you became all of that.

Later, as I cook the afternoon meal, Ankit dances around in my head. He refuses to go away when I serve my mother-in-law her meal and make inane conversation with her. He is still with me when I greet Abhay, back from school, and remains there when I help him with homework. And later that night when my husband, after his usual round of television viewing, comes to bed and squeezes my breasts and has sex with me, he is still there.

I lie awake a long time that night, the darkness of my bedroom punctuated by Sandeep's rhythmic post-coital snoring.

I realise with a jolt that Ankit had never really left. He has been in my head all along.

And now that the possibility of reconnecting with him has been presented to me on a platter, it makes me intensely restless. It is as though someone has poured a can of gasoline to the already blazing fire and turmoil within my heart.

Somewhere at the back of my mind, warning bells are clanging, but their sounds are very feeble, almost muffled.

The voice of my heart is too darn loud.

When you cannot get someone out of your head for eighteen years, it has to be true love.

One

THE HEAT AND HUMIDITY DIDN'T BOTHER ME back then. I guess when you are sixteen and in the throes of adolescent crushes (each of which you are convinced is the real thing, with feelings that chug at the speed of a locomotive, with an intensity just as strong), minor things like being drenched in sweat do not affect you as much as they do when you are an adult. You are enthusiastic, full of life and you believe that the world is yours to conquer.

I cycle back home after my Bharathanatyam classes which are thrice a week. I do not much like this difficult South Indian dance form, but Mother insists I learn it. I would much rather prefer Bollywood dancing or even ballet to this.

'Look, now that your Papa is posted here, you should make use of every opportunity available to you here,' says Mother. 'Tamil Nadu is truly the cultural hub of India. You will never get such accomplished Bharathanatyam teachers elsewhere. So you might as well make the best use of it,' she argues.

It has been a year now since we moved from Pune to Chennai. I did not like Chennai initially, but once I got used to the heat, I realised it was as good a place as any, even Pune. In fact, the co-ed school I attend here is far better than the convent I used to go to in Pune. But I will never admit this to my parents.

Some things are best not revealed.

When I suggest, very timidly, to Mother that I want to take up Bollywood dancing, her reaction is far worse than expected. She shouts and raves and promptly calls up her sister who lives with my grandmother in Ernakulam. Both take turns to admonish and lecture me about how great our Indian tradition is and how hard it is to master the Indian classical dances. They go on about how far superior Bharathanatyam is to Bollywood dancing which is crass and crude, only about shaking your booty and wiggling your hips. Like all the western dances which, according to my mother, aunt and grandmother, any fool can do.

'Good Lord! What are you saying, Diksha? How can you even talk about the two in the same breath? Where is Bollywood and where is Bharathanatyam?' Meera Mausi yells so loudly on the phone that I have to hold the receiver away from my ear.

I stifle a giggle at her hysteria, but she catches on.

'Is that a giggle I hear? You shameless girl. What is so funny?' she reprimands angrily.

'Meera Mausi, I just pictured you as Goddess Durga,' I say amidst helpless giggles now, whereupon she quickly changes tracks sensing that being so far away, she cannot do anything and that her anger is not having the desired effect. Her tone becomes gentle and persuasive. She tries to explain the dedication and discipline involved in classical dancing, and that I am fortunate to get admission in Natya Kesari Dance Academy, run by the renowned, Padma Shree awardee, Mrs Subhalaksmi.

Finally, under the weight of their collective persuasion,

I agree and now find myself waiting for the dance class to get over so I can cycle home leisurely along Elliot's Beach, watching the waves as I do. I love this part of Chennai where we live. Besant Nagar faces the beach and I enjoy the tiny garden which our modest middle class home boasts.

I cannot help thinking how unfair it is that my brother, Rohan, is never forced into doing things he doesn't want to. A year older than me, he is the school captain and is on the school debate team. I think my parents are very proud of him and never miss an opportunity to mention his achievements to anyone who visits us.

Being a popular boy, his friends come over to our place often. They lock themselves in his room for hours and plan and prepare for all the upcoming school functions like plays, debates and dumb charades. They are an active bunch, very involved in the interschool cultural scene and have won many laurels for the school. Somehow our home has turned into their hub, probably as Mother is friendlier and sweeter to our friends than most other parents of teenagers.

'At least they are sitting indoors,doing useful stuff, right under your eyes and not loitering about and wasting time,' Meera Mausi had commented to my mother when these meetings had first started. My mother had nodded approvingly.

So far as I am concerned vis-a-vis my brother's friends, I merely say a 'hello' to them when they arrive and a 'bye' when they leave. That is the extent of my interaction with them. I am a junior at school and the senior guys do not really talk to juniors unless they are 'cool', and I have not yet qualified to gain entry into this category.

Sometimes Mother asks me to make chai for them and when I take the tea tray to his room, Rohan opens the door, takes it from me and shuts it again. In those brief seconds, I catch a glimpse of his friends. Some are sprawled on the floor, some having animated discussions, some practicing their lines.

My best friend and classmate, Tanu, thinks I am very fortunate to 'have access' to the senior boys.

'I so wish I had an elder brother, Diksha. You are so lucky! How cool is it that these guys hang out at your place.'

'It's no big deal, Tanu, I hardly interact with them,' I say, but that does not convince her.

Ankit Uttam is one of my brother's many friends. Tanu and I would have never dared speak to a senior, that too someone as cool as Ankit, but for a blue canvas satchel with two large buckle-down flaps in the front and a red-piped border. The bag is what set the whole thing in motion.

One evening, I find this satchel lying by a pot in the foyer at the entrance of our home. I do not remember leaving it there and so I carry it into my room, a little puzzled by its odd placement. Tanu is with me as we meet most days under the pretext of combined studies. In reality, we just giggle, talk, gossip and, occasionally, *try* to study.

Ankit and my brother, Rohan, emerge after an hour or so from his room. They start frantically hunting for Ankit's bag. It does not strike me that the bag I carried in to my bedroom could be his. It doesn't even occur to me that his satchel is exactly like the one I have. I bought mine, choosing it with great care to project just the right amount of coolness and nonchalance so important at that age.

And so Tanu and I help them look.

We search for at least a quarter of an hour. We look in the hall, in all the possible places in Rohan's room, in the dining area and even in the kitchen.

'How can a bag vanish into thin air?' moans Ankit. 'And God! We have a Bio test tomorrow and I so need my notes,' he grumbles.

'Dude, we have wasted enough time looking for your bag. I tell you what, let's study together and then you go home,' suggests the very practical Rohan.

Ankit agrees that it is the best they can do and both return to Rohan's room.

Tanu and I go to my room, still wondering about the missing bag.

'Maybe he left it outside your house and the *kachrawala* cleared it away thinking it was garbage,' giggles Tanu.

'Shut up,' I say, but with a smile.

Then I open 'my' bag and out tumble Ankit's books. It takes us a few surprised seconds to comprehend what has happened. And then the penny drops. Tanu cackles with excitement.

'Quick, let's look at his handwriting,' she hisses.

'No way. We can't do that. Let's go and return it,' I whisper back equally fiercely.

'We will never get a chance like this. Come on,' she insists.

Finally we take a quick peep, our teenage excitement peaking an all-time high at the prospect of checking out a 'cool' guy's stuff, something we would never have had access to but for the serendipitous confusion. We riffle through notebooks covered with his neat handwriting and are amused to see the doodles on the back of the book. Then we shut it hurriedly, giggling away.

Tanu says, 'Hey, I have an idea! Let's scribble a message for him.'

'Are you crazy?' I say, shocked by her audacious suggestion. 'Rohan will kill me if he finds out. We can't just scribble in someone's book.'

'C'mon, Diksha. You're such a scaredy cat. Here, give it to me.'

Tanu snatches the book from my hand and, before I can stop her, opens the last page and begins writing. I watch in fascinated horror as she writes.

'Hey, Ankit. I really, really, really like you. I follow every football match you play, and watch every debate you take part in. Whenever you're around I can't take my eyes off you. I think you are really cool and, let me be honest, I am a smitten-kitten. I won't tell you my name. If you figure out who this is, call me. I know you are smart enough to figure out my name and my number. I will be waiting.'

She then makes a heart and adds some flowers. I gasp at her boldness.

'Oh my God! Tanu! How can you write stuff like this?' I am shocked at what she has done.

'With a blue pen, by forming one letter after another,' she says cheekily.

I shake my head and suggest we tear out the page. But Tanu will hear none of it.

'Look, how can you write something so outrageous?'

'What is so outrageous, Diksha? I do really, *really* like him. Gosh, he is gorgeous! And this is a godsend opportunity to tell him how I feel.'

'Then tell him to his face. Don't write anonymous notes.'

'Noooo way! Tell him to his face? Are you crazy? What if he laughs at me?'

I know she is right. How can she walk up to a guy and admit she is crazy about him? I too have a secret crush on him which I have never admitted to Tanu. We're both probably in love with the same guy. The difference is that she is ready to admit it while I have suppressed it and pushed it aside as though it doesn't exist.

Finally, I give in to her demand and put Ankit's book back into his bag. After which, I rush to my brother's room and knock.

'What?' His tone is curt.

'I found Ankit's bag,' I say, feeling a bit sheepish.

In a trice, Ankit is out. 'Oh! Wow! That is amazing! Where did you find it?' he asks, his eyes dancing.

I blush.

'Er... Actually it is exactly like mine. I am so sorry, I took it thinking it was mine,' I say.

Then I show him my bag to prove the point.

Ankit laughs heartily and Rohan joins in.

'Hey, it's okay. I am so glad to have it back, I could hug you! You know, it seems we have the same great taste,' he says.

Tanu looks at me and mouths, 'Wish he'd said that to me,' and I quickly look away.

That afternoon, we have no idea what lies in store for us in the future. No idea whatsoever how a little joke played so casually will change our entire lives. No clue that we have sowed the seeds for a lifetime of deception and falsehood, woven a web so entangled that even an entire lifetime will not suffice to sort it out.

Two

'DIKSHAAAAA, COFFEE,' BELLOWS SANDEEP FROM our bedroom upstairs.

I glance at the clock. He has woken up ten minutes before than his usual time.

'Coming. Making it. The water's just beginning to boil,' I yell back, suppressing a twinge of irritation. In the fifteen years that we have been married, not once has he made coffee for me. I suppose I must have found it cute, in the early years of marriage, how lost he was in the kitchen. Then the starry-eyed new bride I was, I would gladly make coffee for him which he would sip reclining in an easy chair on the balcony with his newspaper. I would, in the meantime, cook breakfast, lay out his clothes for office neatly on the bed while he showered, and pack his lunch for office.

Once he emerged from the bedroom in his formal clothes, I would rush to make him a toast or a *dosa* or something hot and fresh for breakfast. He would hurriedly wolf it down, praising my culinary skills and I would eagerly lap up the praise. He never asked me to join him. And in the early days, I did not mind it the least bit. As I would watch him eat, my heart would fill with pride at a meal well-prepared and my wifely duty of feeding my husband, done to perfection.

He would then leave and I would have my breakfast, alone.

The pattern that a couple inadvertently sets in the early years of marriage continues even later, unless a conscious effort is made to change it. That never happened in our case. And so, to this day, he and our nine-year-old son, Abhay, eat together and leave. I always eat later. The praise has stopped though. He does not utter even one word in appreciation these days.

I have grown up watching my mother be the dutiful wife and, until recently, I did not even mind being one. But, of late, irritation has begun mounting and not knowing how to deal with it, I deal with it by suppressing it.

I know for a fact that it started after my cousin, Vibha's, visit. When Vibha, who lives in Hyderabad, visits Bangalore for company projects, she stays with us for a week or so, and has observed this routine several times. When Sandeep and Abhay leave, she says, 'Diksha, which century are you living in, girl? Look at what you have turned into. You have totally metamorphosed into a maidservant and cook.'

'Shut up, Vibha. I don't have a high-flying job like you, where your company sends you on fancy trips and all. I am just a housewife, and has it ever occurred to you that I *like* making hot food for Abhay and Sandeep?' I counter her observation, not willing to acknowledge it.

I brush aside her remarks as if they are of no consequence, but deep down I know her words have found their mark. They rankle inside me now like the chains of a prisoner in medieval times who yearns to break free. She has voiced something that I have dared not admit even to myself and her words hang in the air like gloomy mist. Everything that I look at now is tinted with this greyness that had begun to gnaw at my insides.

'Look, Diksha. So what if you are a housewife? That doesn't mean Sandeep can't make a cup of coffee for you! I have seen how much work you put into making their lives smooth. But what about you? You deserve more, girl. You never get to go out. Your mother-in-law being in the same town doesn't help either as you have to spend every single weekend with her. What kind of life is that?' she says gently.

'Vibha, I am happy. I am happy that my mother-in-law lives close by and we get to visit her. Abhay loves spending time with her. Not everyone is like you. I don't have to get Sandeep to make coffee for me in the name of women's lib or whatever. He earns well, he provides us with material comfort and so it is indeed okay if I am the one taking care of cooking and everything else.'

I don't know why I am so stubborn in defending my life.

'Diksha, don't you long for anything more? Are you really happy? Don't you want to go out with your girlfriends, do things for yourself, have some fun?' Her tone changes into concern as she searches my face for answers.

I cannot bear her eyes boring into mine. Of course, I long to go out. I truly do not want to spend every single weekend visiting Sandeep's mother who lives less than two kilometres away. But it has become such a routine now that I cannot even think of spending weekends any other way.

When I had first suggested going out somewhere nice in the early years of marriage, Sandeep had glared at me like I had said I wanted to separate him from his mother. He had reminded me of the time his mother had selflessly helped look after Abhay when he was born. Sandeep never ceased to remind me that my parents hadn't done much by way of being there for us. I had tried telling him that it was only because my mother had fallen seriously ill at the time of Abhay's birth. She had to have a hysterectomy. She had been operated upon and the surgeon had discovered a lump that needed to be removed. There were other complications as well. Then she had been on bed-rest for nearly six whole months. Else, she would have definitely helped. But when I had explained all that to Sandeep, he had just said, 'Bah. What counts is who did the job ultimately.'

How can I tell Vibha all this? How can I admit to her that, yes,I feel trapped with Sandeep. That I long for a better life. The truth of Vibha's words hammers into my brain, hitting me right where it hurts. But I still do not want her to see my pain. After all, she is leading the life she wants. She has a job she enjoys, has good help at home, is independent and smart, everything I am not. So I turn away and busy myself doing the dishes.

We sit in silence, both of us very well aware that the words she uttered are true. I am not entirely happy in my marriage. But I have made peace with my situation and I do not know how to change it. Sandeep is not a bad guy, after all.

These days, however, it feels as though I have to constantly remind myself that. Fifteen years of marriage and motherhood have changed me as a person. I go quiet as I contemplate.

The awkward silence between us now embarrasses Vibha.

'Hey, Diksha. I think I said too much. I know no marriage is perfect. Mine certainly isn't. Mohan constantly complains that I do not have time for him or Monu. Look, I am really sorry to have poked my nose into your affairs. I should first set my marriage right. I haven't done any of the things that Mohan wants us to do together as a family. It is always work and more work for me. Then I come here and see such a contrast in your life and I just couldn't help telling you what I felt. I should have kept quiet. I am sorry.' She is now contrite at having spoken her mind.

'No, Vibha, it is fine. You are lucky to lead the life you want. And I know it is only concern for me that made you say those things. And hey, you're my sis. How can you not be honest with me? I am glad you spoke out. I have been in denial about it,' I finally admit.

And I mean it.

After Vibha leaves, I find myself increasingly thinking about her words. The emptiness of my life has begun to gnaw at me, eating me up from inside. Of course, Vibha is right. I have, over the years, slowly but surely turned into a maidservant and cook. Sandeep and Abhay do take me for granted.

But the fact is, that a part of me feels useful too, doing all this. It gives me a sense of purpose, a sense of 'doing something', as though justifying my existence.

But, for the first time in my life, I have begun thinking about where my life is going. Perhaps the fact that I will turn thirty-five in a few months adds to my increasingly contemplative state. I guess most people take stock of where they are going when they get older, don't they?

It is only two weeks later though that I finally call up Vibha.

'Hey Vibs, you got some time to talk?' I ask.

She *is* a busy person, in a demanding job. As a mid-management level employee in a pharmaceutical company, she has to travel a lot. That is why I never call her during the day. If I have to speak to her, I call on weekends or at night. Vibha is the closest thing I have to a sister and I feel fortunate to have this bond with her. We have spent many summer vacations together in our maternal grandparents' village in Kerala. Our mothers would bundle us off to the ancestral house and, for two whole months, we would laze around, pick raw mangoes from the tree and eat them with salt and chilli powder, play games, go swimming in the river nearby, play pranks on each other, fight, make up and forge bonds and create memories that we now cherish in our adult years.

Vibha had got married long after I had. She had a child much later than I did and went promptly back to work soon as the baby turned three months old. Of course, her in-laws moved in with her and the arrangement suited everyone. I sometimes envy her lifestyle, her career and how she has everything together.

In comparison, I feel as though I am wasting my life. Her words have added to my increasing sense of despondency and today is one of those days when I just have to speak to her, to sort out the chugging train of thoughts in my head that refuses to slow down.

'Of course, Diksha, give me ten minutes. I am reading to Monu. I will tuck her in bed and call you.'

I am clearing the kitchen when she calls back. Abhay has been tucked in bed a long time back and Sandeep has plonked himself in front of the television, his usual unvarying routine on almost all days.

'What happened, Dikku, all well?' she uses my childhood name, a name which takes us back to our roots, our connection, our families, our village and forms a large part of my association with her, reminding me yet again how much a part of my life she really is. I know I can tell her anything. She is the closest I will ever come to having a sister. I know I can never discuss things like this with my brother.

'Hello, Diksha? All well? Can you hear me?' she asks again.

I take a while to answer. I really do not know how to say it, or what purpose this discussion will serve. All I know is that things seem unbearable and I need to speak to her.

'Vibha, I have been thinking. You were right that day when you said my life is empty,' I reply.

'Hey, come on, Diksha. That's really not what I meant,' she corrects me.

I pause again. I am unable to articulate what I feel.

'I know what you meant. See, the fact is that there is indeed a growing discontent in me. I know I am only fooling myself by pretending to be extremely happy cooking and caring for Sandeep and Abhay, but there has to be more to life than that. I feel worthless, Vibha. I really do,' I finally say, the words tumbling out. The bitterness in my voice and the things I have just expressed take me by surprise, as though it is not me, but a stranger, talking.

'Hey Diksha, things are not so bad. You do look after the house and keep it well. Why, your house is ten times more efficiently managed than mine. You know how much my mother-in-law helps me,' Vibha tries to placate me.

But I am in no mood to be consoled.

'She only helps you look after Monu while you are at work. Isn't it you who decides everything in the house including whom to hire as house-help? Isn't it you and Mohan who have done up the house so well? Isn't it you who has decided that Monu is better off in a playschool than being at home with your mother-in-law? Come on, Vibs, you run the show there. Don't give me crap and try to make me feel better.'

Vibha knows all that I have said is true.

'Look, Diksha, you are right, I admit. But hey, why are you suddenly comparing your life to mine? Look, I truly am sorry for all those remarks I made. I spoke because I care for you. I felt you were slaving and slogging and not getting what you deserve. But that does not mean your life is empty or that you are worthless.'

'Vibs, I know that. But you know what? This is something I have been feeling for years. It is just that I had not admitted it even to myself. When you came that day and talked so honestly, it truly hit me like a ton of bricks. I have been thinking about it, Vibha. Look, I took two weeks to call you. I have been fighting this in my head. I did not want to burden you, but today it was unbearable and I just had to call you.'

'Hey, Diksha, you are never a burden. We're sisters, remember? I am always here for you. You can call me anytime, night or day. And incidentally, I have a trip to Bangalore by the end of the month. Let's do one thing, let's talk about this then. I promise we will find a solution. You just hang in there and stop feeling bad. I am coming soon and we will sort this out.'

'Okay, thanks,' I say.

'Come on. What are you saying "thanks" for? Since when did our relationship become so formal? Now cheer up, I am coming soon.'

Once she hangs up, I go to the garden and sit for a long time on the swing with the grass beneath my feet. One of the things I love about this house is the garden which I have lovingly nurtured. In a city where space is devoured hungrily by multistoryed building that rise everyday, this little sanctuary of calm, still standing proud, surrounded by high-rises, gives me so much happiness. The house belongs to Sandeep's paternal grandfather and it is an old construction. Sandeep has got many offers for it from builders who want to tear it down and build flats. They have even offered us four flats in the same building. Artillery Road is, after all, prime location in Bangalore and the property is easily worth a few hundred crores. But Sandeep has not succumbed.

I sit in the silence of the night, listening to crickets, watching a toad hop away and, as I swing, I think about the fifteen years of my marriage. I think about how things have changed. I think about how I have gone along and been a 'good girl' all this while, doing exactly what my parents wanted me to do. I have dutifully married a 'suitable boy', dutifully produced a child and have busied myself raising him. He is nine now. I am quite proud of him, yet why is there this growing sense of discontent in me?

Then it strikes me that it is because, in all these years, I have completely lost track of what I want. I have played the role of wife and mother to perfection. So much so that I have forgotten what I want as an individual. My identity is truly Sandeep's wife or Abhay's mother.

It is as though I have been living in a dream all these years and, like Rip Van Winkle, have suddenly woken up. What is it that I want? (Apart from raising my child well and keeping house). I know I want something more from my life. I want to do something about it. But what? I really don't know.

It is a frightening feeling. I sit in the darkness and stare at the starless sky. The darkness stares back at me. I have no idea what I want anymore. What have I done with my life? Where am I headed? I feel miserable and sorry as I sit there and take stock of my life.

I have everything, yet I have nothing.

And I have no idea what I am going to do.

Three

THE TELEPHONE RINGS AND I AM HAPPY AT THE distraction. I have been studying really hard and need a break. Mother is watering the plants in the garden and Rohan has shut himself up in his room.

'Hellooooo,' I say as I rush and answer it.

'So. I knew it all along. You did take my bag on purpose, didn't you? You little witch!' says the voice at the other end.

It takes me a few seconds to register that it is Ankit and a few more to understand what he has just said. I stand there with the receiver in my hand, my jaw almost dropping to the floor. I am gobsmacked, outraged and embarrassed, all at the same time.

'Hello, it is Diksha, isn't it?' He sounds a little unsure now.

'Ankit, yes. It is me.' I finally reply.

'Oh, thank God. I thought I had shot off my mouth to someone else. And you know what, I really like you too. But I never spoke up. Heck, I did not even admit it to myself. But boy, am I glad you did,' he says, a visible relief in his voice now.

I squirm further in embarrassment. A part of me goes, 'Oh-my-God, Oh-my-God, Ankit likes me!'

I do not know what to do. I know the right thing would be to tell him that it was Tanu who wrote the note, not me. But fact is, that he has just admitted he likes *me,* not Tanu. I am too happy to think. My heart sings a million symphonies all at once. I smile a huge smile.

And finally, I say, 'Yes, I am glad too.'

'Meet me tomorrow for coffee? After school?' he asks.

I quickly calculate the time it will take me to cycle back home, change and then go to dance class. I know I will have less than ten minutes with Ankit. My mother is really strict about my dance class.

'I do so want to. But I have a dance class tomorrow.'

'What time does it get over? And where do you go for dance?'

Ankit lives in the same residential area and I am certain that he knows all the lanes well, just like any other teen living in Besant Nagar, is one of the nicer localities of Chennai, close to the beach.

'Five thirty. I go to Natya Kesari.'

'So I will meet you outside dance class then at five thirty.'

'No way, Ankit! My other friends will be with me. Mrs Subhalakshmi herself may call up my mother and tell her that she spotted me speaking to a guy outside dance class.'

'Hmmmm. Okay, meet me at Infinity?' he asks.

Infinity is one of the many coffee shops that dot the beach. It always has a lot of young people hanging out.

'Okay. Will meet you there tomorrow around five fifteen,' I say and, as I hang up, I realise I have bagged myself a date with none other than Ankit Uttam, one of the coolest dudes in school.

Ladies and Gentlemen, I, Diksha Balaram, will be going on a date with Ankit Uttam, a senior, that too one of the smartest guys in school. I want to stand on rooftops and announce this. I am elated, excited and so happy.

Finally, when my excitement subsides a little, I realise that I have to break the news to Tanu. I have no idea how she will react. Things have happened so fast that I can barely believe it myself. Now I begin to feel guilty over my lie. Well, not really a lie, but a concealment of the fact that it was Tanu who wrote the note and not me. But the fact is, he likes *me*, and has asked *me* out, not Tanu. At the very least, I have saved her the embarrassment of being rejected by Ankit.

Yet, I dread telling her, but I know I must.

So I tell my mother that I am going over to Tanu's house to study. I hoist my bag over my shoulders and cycle as fast as I can. I am breathless when I arrive.

Tanu looks at me and knows instantly that something is up, in a way that only the closest of friends can know. She steers me into her room and shouts out to her mother that we are going to study, and asks not to be disturbed.

And by the time she has shut the door, I feel myself wanting to escape and not having to face her. How in the world do I tell her that her little trick bagged me a date?

'So, what's up? What are you trying to hide?' her eyes search my face and I feel she is looking into my very soul.

I am unable to meet her gaze. I turn away and sit on the bed and idly stare at my toes.

'Tanu, I don't know how to put this to you,' I start hesitatingly.

'What? You are getting me worried. Whatever it is, say it fast. Don't make me tense,' she says.

That makes me even more nervous.

I clear my throat and say, 'Ankit has asked me out for coffee.'

Tanu gives me a look that says, 'You're pulling a fast one on me, right? It's only a joke, huh?'

I am unable to say anything.

'Look, I am sorry,' I say. 'He thought it was me who wrote that note. I did not get a chance to explain to him that you wrote it.'

And then I repeat the whole conversation I had with Ankit and tell Tanu in detail what has happened. I can see how hurt and disappointed she is.

She doesn't say anything.

'Look, Tanu, I am awfully sorry. I will tell him that I can't meet him,' I finally say as I put my arms around her. I don't know how else to make her feel better. I am not able to bear that forlorn look on her face.

'Don't be silly, Diksha. He has asked you out. He clearly likes you. Forget explaining anything. Just go ahead and enjoy yourself. I will be fine,' she says.

I love her for saying that. I know she is miserable, yet she wants me to have a good time. While one part of me desperately wants to go on a date with Ankit, the other part wants to stay back and be with Tanu. Tanu senses my hesitation.

'Hey, listen, that note I wrote in his book… it was just a joke. I didn't even really mean it. I truly don't care. I just wrote it for fun,' she says.

And we both pretend that the statement she uttered is true. It is the easiest and kindest way to deal with it.

Then we try talking about the things we usually talk about, but there is an awkward feeling now. A sense of discomfort hangs over our heads like a grey cloud which can pour rain any time. This wasn't the case earlier. The easy camaraderie that existed between us is gone and seems to be replaced by a forced jovial banter. After about ten minutes, I am not able to take this charade anymore and I tell Tanu that I have to leave. She too seems relieved.

As she sees me to the door, her mother asks why I am leaving so early.

'Just remembered that I have to be home early today, Aunty. We have some relatives coming over,' I quickly lie. Her mother seems satisfied with my explanation and goes back into the house.

As I leave, I am acutely aware of the wedge that has been driven between Tanu and me. I ask once more, 'Are you sure, Tanu. I truly do not mind not going on this date.'

'I told you it's okay,' she says with steel in her voice and it feels as though something between us has changed irrevocably that summer afternoon.

I cycle back slowly, reflecting on the fickle friendships of adolescence. Tanu and I have shared so many secrets, have had such good times together and truly forged a strong friendship—or so I had thought until now. And all it has taken is just one date-request from a boy—we have not even gone on a date yet—to have caused this gap.

The more I think about it, the more awful I feel. I really like Tanu. I remember all the times that she has taken down class-notes for me, all the times that we have giggled together, studied together and discussed boys, movies and books. I think of the countless afternoons we have spent in each other's houses, trying on new clothes, applying nail polish and having a whale of a time, without a care in the world. I am overcome with a feeling that is hard to describe—all I know is that something doesn't feel right and it is because of Ankit.

By the time I cycle back home, I know what I must do. I cannot go on this date with Ankit. I have to call him up and tell him the truth. I wait for a chance to have the house all to myself so that I can make the call. I certainly do not want Mother overhearing this conversation. The chance comes around six forty in the evening when Mother goes to the next street to visit a friend.

Rohan isn't at home and I know he will be back only after seven thirty when his cricket practice gets over. My father is travelling and is out of town. I thank my lucky stars for this chance and call up Ankit.

'Hello, Precious,' he says with a smile.

'Ooooh! Precious? Have I graduated to "precious" so soon?' I smile at his audacity.

'Okay then, Gorgeous. Does that suit you better?' he asks boldly.

'Hey listen, Ankit, I have something to tell you,' I say before he can go on.

'Something more to what you wrote in my book? God I have read it so many times now. I loved it, Diksha,' he says.

'Ankit, this is about that. I can't hold it in anymore. I have to tell you, I did not write that note,' I finally manage to spew out the words that have been festering inside me ever since I left Tanu's.

There is silence at the other end for a while.

Then he says, 'Ha ha, you are kidding, right?'

'No, Ankit, Tanu wrote it. I would never dare write such a thing,' I say.

'Oh,' he says.

And then we are both silent.

'I feel really bad about it. And look, I did want to have coffee with you tomorrow. In fact, I was looking forward to it. But I don't think it would be right on my part to do that now. I called to tell you that I can't meet you tomorrow.'

'You've got to be kidding me! I would have asked you out for coffee, with or without the note. I was planning to. But the note just made it easier.'

'You are just saying that, right? You just want to make me feel better.'

'Of course not, Diksha. I really would have, but I felt guilty asking you. I have visited your house so many times to study with Rohan and I didn't want him thinking that I was friendly with him only because I liked you. You are, after all, my friend's sister. I would have to, umm, how do I say it, kind of get an okay from him, you know. Hence I hesitated, that's all.'

I do not know what to do with this new piece of information that Ankit has hurled at me. I am hugely flattered and excited at the same time. My sixteen-year-old heart is thudding away with all its might. I find a large grin spreading across my face and I barely recognise my own voice as I whisper, 'Oh, Ankit. I had no idea.'

'How would you? I never told you. But now I have,' he whispers back and my heart does a somersault inside my ribcage and makes an expert landing for a perfect ten that Ankit has scored with that statement. Though he has not said the exact words, but what he has said is almost as good as confessing his love for me.

I continue smiling and Ankit says, 'So the meeting at Infinity is on, right?'

I am still hesitant as I remember my earlier resolve of not wanting to hurt Tanu. Ankit seems to be able to read my mind.

'Hey listen, I can explain to Tanu, if you like.'

'Oh no! Don't be silly. She will hate me for it and she would be mortified if you did. Right now she is just pretending that it was all a joke.'

'Then say a yes and meet me tomorrow.'

After that I have no choice but to agree. I definitely don't want to hurt Tanu anymore than she already is. But Ankit will not take a no for an answer.

After a very long pause, I say, 'Okay, will see you tomorrow at Infinity. Don't keep me waiting, okay?'

'Promise I won't,' he says.

That night as I crawl into bed, I think about the dynamics of friendships, crushes, love and infatuation. I wonder whether I have been unfair to Tanu. I decide that I haven't. I have even confessed to Ankit that it was Tanu who wrote the note, but all along Ankit had been nurturing a crush on *me*. I still can't believe it. I feel plain lucky. I have read enough books that describe whatever I am feeling towards Ankit as just hormones playing up. They say that it is puppy-love, an adolescent crush, that will soon pass.

But it definitely doesn't *feel* so. My heart sings, there is a smile on my lips and my face glows at the mere thought of Ankit. Whoever wrote all that stuff about hormones playing up is definitely wrong.

I know that, for me, this is the real thing.

And even though I hate to admit it, I do know for a fact I *am* indeed in love with Ankit, regardless of what the experts say.

Four

'ABHAY, HURRY UP. YOU WILL MISS YOUR BUS. Eat this quickly now,' I say as I place piping-hot, aromatic, soft idlis and sambhar in front of the sleepy reluctant child. Idli-sambhar is one of my signature dishes and I pride myself on the fluffiness of the idlis I make. I can almost picture my mother and Meera Mausi nodding proudly as I pile the idlis on my son's plate.

'Maaa, I don't want breakfast,' he mumbles as he pushes away his plate and slumps on the table, closing his eyes.

I know now why parents send their children to boarding schools. I have woken up at five thirty am to cook this traditional, nutritious and delicious meal. The easiest thing for me would have been to dump a bowl of cereal in front of the child. But I would rather that my family have fresh, hot home-cooked meals.

I muster all the patience that mothers have on tap in secret reserve for such situations and say, 'Darling, you have to eat. You know the rule, right?'

'Breakfast like a king, lunch like a nobleman and dine like a pauper,' he parrots the words he had heard me uttering a few thousand times by now, his eyes still closed.

'Yes,' I smile at how he imitates my tone and stern expression.

'But kings don't eat idli-sambhar,' he says.

'*Accha*! How do you know? King Ashoka always ate idli for breakfast. In fact, his mother ensured he did,' I say quickly. Years of parenting a smart aleck child has taught me to think on my feet.

'No, he did not. He had a choice of a thirteen dishes that were cooked exclusively for him. Also he did not have to go to school. He went to *a gurukul* and learnt archery and fun things like that. Not boring lessons like we have. Also he did not take a school bus. He rode a horse.'

I stare in surprise at the little speech Abhay has given. He is now tucking into his breakfast solemnly. I wonder when he learnt words like 'exclusively'. I realise Abhay is no longer the little baby he used to be. He has started reading voraciously on his own without, other than enrolling him at the local library, much effort on my part. He is one of those naturally bright children that need very little effort to learn new things.

My heart fills with maternal pride as I watch him finishing his breakfast after which I hurry with him to his bus stop. Then I rush back and Sandeep is now reading the morning newspaper.

I know this is the moment when he will ask for his tea. He always likes to be woken up with coffee in bed and then a couple of hours later, he wants a cup of tea, while he reads the newspaper.

'Diksha, can you please make a cup of tea?' he asks predictably. I can almost time it to perfection, that exact moment when he will ask.

Of late, his requests for tea too have begun to irk me. Vibha is right. They do treat me like a maid. I never get to read the newspaper in the morning. All these years, it is he who reads it first. In the early years, the pattern had been established. As he had to leave for work, it seemed only logical. I was anyway at home the whole day. I could read it later.

But after Vibha's visit, I have begun to notice these things a lot more. In the larger scheme of things, perhaps a tiny thing like who reads the newspaper first will have no significance, but when the weariness of a fifteen-year-old marriage is beginning to run you down, it is these little things that prick the most. The tiny little things are not big enough to break marriages and yet they are cracks that have been neglected. They stand out now like cacti on a barren desert-scape that is my marriage. Funny how Vibha's little comment has acted as a catalyst to aggravate things to the point of them becoming unbearable.

'Making it,' I say as I hurry to the kitchen.

Vibha is right. I *am* conditioned to wait on Sandeep and Abhay and serve them day and night. I hate my life as I dully hand over the cup of tea to Sandeep who takes it without even an acknowledgment and goes back to reading his newspaper.

It is always little things like this that build up. Often there is no dramatic reason for discontent in marriages. It seeps in slowly over the years. You don't even notice it creeping up. It happens, trickle by trickle. You do not realise when or how the easy familiarity gets replaced by a 'taken-for-granted' attitude over the years. By the time you do, it is often too late. Habits have been formed, patterns have been set. And a comfort-zone has been established. A zone that is hard to get out of.

I know now that there is only one word which sums up my marriage perfectly: Boring.

I watch Sandeep blissfully oblivious to the thoughts

racing inside my head. I cannot bring myself to talk to him about this. He is not a new-age metrosexual male that one reads about in magazines or sees in movies, the type in front of whom the wife can pull up a chair, tuck back her designer hair-do, prop her perfectly manicured legs up and say, 'Darling, we need to talk.'

Oh no. Ours is a conventional Indian marriage. And good Indian wives don't do things like that.

Which century are you struck in, Diksha? Go on and tell him you need to talk.

But when I look at him again, my courage fails me. He would probably stare at me uncomprehendingly like I have gone mad.

Finally, I just do what I always do.

Get his breakfast ready and wait for him to leave for work.

Once he leaves, the whole day stretches bleakly in front of me. I stand and stare at the messy breakfast remains on the dining table. He has not even bothered to put away his plate. It is nothing new. On normal days, I would have cleared it without a second thought. But today, I just stand, wanting to rebel, wanting to pick up the plate and smash it dramatically into the wall and send the remnants flying in all directions. I breathe hard as I stare at it. I clench my fists. I know I am working myself up into a rage. I feel like exploding now.

Unable to bear it any longer, I pick up the plate, march into the kitchen and fling it angrily into the sink where it lands with a clang. Then I wait for the house-help to turn up.

I am filled with a restlessness that is hard to describe. I sit with my cup of tea and contemplate on what my life used to be and what it has become. I think about Vibha and me. Circumstances were not similar for both of us, but both had ultimately bowed down to parental pressure in the great Indian marriage system and had arranged marriages, me much earlier than her. I had got married when I was nineteen, even before my graduation results were out. My parents had been over the moon to find a guy as suitable as Sandeep.

My mind hops skips and jumps down memory lane as I remember how shy and awkward Sandeep and I had been around each other when we were ushered into a room to 'talk' while the rest of the family waited outside.

'Hi, I am Sandeep,' he had said.

I had burst out laughing and said I already knew that.

Whereupon he has said without any preamble, 'I like you. You are sweet and nice. I am a simple guy and it doesn't take much to keep me happy.'

I was taken aback by his forthright attitude.

Thinking back now, I recall with a small pang of pain that he had never talked about making *me* happy. It was about keeping him happy. I had beamed with pride in my nineteen-year-old naïvety and had mumbled that I would do my best. I had hoped that agreeing to this marriage would win me some redemption in my parents' eyes and they would forgive me for what I had done when I was sixteen.

It is funny how, even after these many years, I am still trying to do my best. He is, of course, happy. But I am definitely not.

Fact is, he never promised to make you happy, Diksha. It was never about you. It was always about him. You were content then. You agreed, knowing what you were getting into. You have made your bed, now lie in it.

I have tried to lie in it and be content. But it pricks now and is no longer comfortable. It is a tired, old worn-out bed. I know I have to do something to alleviate this feeling of disquiet.

When Sandeep comes home that evening, I wait for an opportune moment. The dinner plates have been long cleared, Abhay been read to and tucked to bed. Sandeep is watching a war movie and I know it is a movie he has seen several times. I cannot comprehend what he finds so fascinating in all the violence, gore and blood. How many times can one watch that? I wait for a commercial break to tell him that I want to talk to him.

'Hmmm, what about?' he asks distractedly.

'Sandeep, we never talk,' I say.

'What is there to talk about?' he asks again, not taking his eyes off the television. I grab the remote from his hand and switch off the TV. My hands are shaking with nervousness, but I try to mask it.

He looks at me as though I have slapped him. I have never done anything like this before.

Soon the surprised shock on his face is replaced by annoyance.

'Can't you see I was watching that?' he says, the pitch of his voice a notch higher than usual.

My heart beats really fast. I have never really stood up to him before. The meek little doormat that I am, I want to take back all that I have said. I want to curl up and apologise and grovel. But now I have taken the plunge and if I do not at least try to sort out this issue, it will blow up and explode.

'Sandeep, I just need fifteen minutes of your undivided attention,' I say, mustering up courage and exhibiting a bravery that I do not feel at all. I try to not let my nervousness show and, by the look on Sandeep's face, it seems like I am succeeding.

'Okay. So now you have it. What is it?' he says.

I feel like an amateur boxer in a ring who has won a first round entirely by fluke against an opponent who is a world-class champion.

'Sandeep, I feel this growing sense of discontent in our marriage,' I say.

He looks at me as though I have just confessed my desire to become a strip dancer.

He blinks a few times.

I stand and stare back at him.

Finally, he says, 'Sit down.'

I sit opposite him, like a child who comes late and has been given permission by the teacher to enter the classroom. I sit and wait for him to talk.

'What do you mean by discontent? Am I not doing all my duties as a husband?'

Sure, as long as 'duties of a husband' mean earning for us and providing for us, you are. What else do you really do other than that? A big fat nothing.

'Yes, Sandeep. But surely there is more to a marriage than that,' I meekly say, suppressing all I am feeling inside.

'Diksha, I am a simple guy. I do not understand what more you want? '

I squirm.

'Sandeep, I want some conversation. I feel a bit taken for granted in this whole deal here. I feel I want to do something with my life. Other than being a wife and a mother, I truly am nothing.'

'Have I ever stopped you from doing what you want to do, Diksha? Didn't you go for your interior design course after marriage? Did I ever stop you? Wasn't it you who decided not to have a career?'

'Yes, but I wanted to give the best care I could to Abhay. How would I have done that had I gone ahead and had a career? We would have had to send him to a crèche.'

'So it is a choice you made, Diksha. Nobody forced you. Not me. Not my mother.'

'I know, Sandeep. All I am saying is that I now want to do something of my own. Abhay goes to school during the day. You travel so much on work and keep long hours. After that you just come home and watch TV. We hardly ever even talk, Sandeep.'

'How many couples do you know, married for as long as we have been, who have conversations? We aren't dating or newlyweds for God's sake. What conversation are you talking about? We are talking now, aren't we?'

'It wasn't as though we had great conversation even when we were newlyweds. But don't you agree, it was so different then, Sandeep?'

He does not know what to say. I have stepped across an invisible line here. I have expressed, for the first time, how I have felt. I feel triumphant, almost emancipated for having stood up for myself.

Finally he says, 'I think all the new-age mumbo-jumbo which these women's magazines feed you have influenced your thinking. I don't think I am such a bad guy. I earn enough, I am a good father and husband. I have never questioned the choices you make, and I think I have given you reasonable freedom and allowed you to do what you want. You made a choice to stay at home. Now you regret it. And you are blaming me and making me the scapegoat for what you think is your boring life. How am I responsible? You act like a martyr here while living in luxury even as I work my balls off. Don't you ever forget that.'

His little speech has crushed me like a ten-ton truck. All my newfound bravery vanishes swiftly.

I wince at what he has stated so plainly. He has thrown at me a fact—that it is he who has been earning while I live in the lap of luxury. It hurts as there is an element of truth to it. Heck, not just an element, it is the entire truth.

And it is bitter and hard to swallow.

So I bite back the tears that are threatening to spill over and with an intense self-loathing, mutter a 'Sorry, you are right. I don't know what came over me.'

Then I retreat into the kitchen and I sob and sob and sob, even as Sandeep turns the television back on and goes back to watching whatever it was that I interrupted.

Five

ANKIT AND I MEET AT INFINITY AFTER MY DANCE class. I am still in my dance uniform—a plain pink *salwar kameez* and a plain yellow *dupatta*. It is as unglamorous an outfit as can be for a first date and on top of that I am covered in sweat after a very hard dance practice. Yet I am happy even if somewhat conscious of my appearance. I am a bit nervous too. But Ankit seems to neither mind nor notice any of it and even if he does, is too polite to say. He waits just outside and helps me park my bicycle, though I tell him I am perfectly capable of parking it myself.

'I know you are, but allow me to do at least something for you, Diksha,' he says, his eyes twinkling. I find it hard to avert my gaze from him. He is handsome. His eyes are a deep brown and his straight hair falls across his forehead. He flicks it back with a slight toss of his head. He is nearly six feet tall or at least a five eleven and a half. I feel puny next to him.

'Ankit, we should have met another day. I am all sweaty and I am wearing this stupid salwar,' I say.

'You look lovely, Diksha. Just relax,' he replies as I

follow him into the coffee shop. He asks me what I will have and we both settle for cold coffee.

We make small talk for a while.

Then he says, 'Listen, you heard of this Environment Awareness exhibition happening at the Air Force School next month, right?'

I nod. I have already seen the notices and heard the announcements about it. We were all asked to make models and the best ones would get selected. But I wasn't interested in it. But now that Ankit has mentioned it, my interest is piqued.

'Take part in it, Diksha. It involves an overnight stay and my whole group will be there,' he winks.

'Oh!' I say. I wasn't aware about the overnight stay. Actually, I hadn't even given it a thought. But now, getting a chance to spend one whole day outside school with Ankit is too wonderful an opportunity to pass up. I am very tempted and excited at the prospect.

'But what in the world will I present? What environment awareness project can I do?' I ask.

'Look, I will help you with it. You need to go and speak to Mrs Rao and tell her you are keen. You can rope in some of your classmates if you want. But don't miss this opportunity,' he commands.

I smile at how he has taken charge of this whole situation and decided for me that I am attending.

He tells me to make a low-cost model farm. He has done research on it. He seems to know a lot about it. He says he will help me with everything. I am surprised at the level of detailed planning he has done. By the end of our coffees we have agreed on a grand plan. Only six best models will be chosen and Ankit says that my model has to be really good in order to get selected.

He and his gang are making a working model on

rainwater harvesting and explaining the concept with charts and impressive statistics. Rohan is of course a part of this group.

That evening I explain my model to Rohan and my parents over dinner. I leave out the part about Ankit's involvement in all of it.

Rohan is quite impressed. So are my parents. I beam with pride.

'Not bad, Diksha. I never knew you had it in you. I hope yours gets chosen. I know our model already has. I overheard Mrs Rao speaking to Miss Bindu in the staff room.'

'I hope so, too. Let's see,' I answer.

'So are you working with Tanu on this one?' asks Rohan

'I will ask her. But I don't know,' I reply.

I know for certain that Tanu will not want to be a part of it. Especially if she hears that it is Ankit who is behind the whole idea. But I do not want to leave her out. So I ask her the next day. I explain my project in detail. I tell her that it is actually Ankit's idea and that he is masterminding it.

To my surprise, Tanu is excited and wants to be a part of it. She also asks me about my date with Ankit in detail. I downplay it all and tell her it was just okay. I don't tell her how madly my heart was racing. Or that Ankit and I have planned the whole project so that we get time together away from school. Instead, I tell her that Ankit casually mentioned this idea and I thought I would give it a shot. Tanu has no reason to disbelieve me and she says she will throw herself with full gusto into the project.

We have several weeks left for the final exhibition in our school from which the best models will be chosen for the exhibition at the Air Force School.

Ankit and I meet almost every single day now. It has become a kind of ritual. It all started when I called him up to tell him that Tanu had agreed to work on it with me. He asked me to meet him after school to discuss the project model in detail. I told Mother that since I was working on the project with Tanu, which isn't exactly a lie, I needed to meet her every evening, and this is how our (Ankit's and mine) regular meetings came about.

I usually cycle back and reach home in fifteen minutes. But these days, Ankit waits for me around the corner two lanes away. We cycle together to Elliot's Beach and sit watching the waves and talking about almost everything under the sun. I enjoy his company immensely and I discover that he loves the Arts. He wants to do a degree in Fine Arts after his Class Twelve, but his father is keen for him to join the family business. He also knows he will probably never end up doing Art. Not much money in it, he says. I tell him about how my mother forces me to learn classical dance. I tell him about my taste in books and we discover a common ground. He loves reading too. We talk and talk and the hours feel like minutes.

Ankit opens up to me and tells me about his family. They are very wealthy and the Uttam Group of Industries is well known. They have tons of money. But things at home are not so fine. He is a single child and his parents are on the verge of a break-up. He hates going home as his parents fight all the time.

'It is so peaceful here with you, Diksha. I feel really good with you. I hate the constant fights at home. I just can't wait to be independent and lead my own life. My parents—I am really tired of them,' he says.

I feel tender towards him. I hear the pain in his voice and I see, behind his 'cool dude' façade, a child who is begging to be loved. I badly want to hug him right there but we are in a public place and that too in conservative Chennai. So I slide my hand over his and I squeeze it. He holds my hand tight. Time stands still in those few moments.

We watch the sunset together. Finally, only when it is beginning to become dark do we head home. He cycles with me till the end of the street where my house is and waits till I reach my gate. Then I wave and he leaves after that.

It is strange how one can feel so close with another person just after a few regular meetings and long chats. I feel as though I have known Ankit all my life. He says he feels the same way.

At school, I can't wait for the last bell to ring so I can be with Ankit. On the days that I have a dance class, we meet at Infinity. I know that I am head over heels in love with Ankit. I have no idea whether it is a crush or whatever it is the experts call it. All I know is that I feel so alive, so happy and so good about myself when I am with him.

I meet Tanu during the weekends and we work on our project. I am happy that we are back to being friends again, the old awkwardness seems to have truly vanished. Who knows, maybe Tanu did not really have a crush on Ankit, after all. We plan out the project in detail. I have made some rough sketches with Ankit's help. Tanu loves my layout and design. Of course, I don't tell her that Ankit has been helping me. We get a large wooden tray from her attic. Then her mother helps us pile red, fertile mud which she has got in sacks for planting a lawn. We get small plastic houses from the Monopoly set. Tanu raids her attic and comes up with tiny plastic farm animals that she used to play with as a child. Her mother helps us plant mustard and says if we water it regularly, we will have an impressive little green field on the day of the exhibition. She says this is just for trial and we will have to repeat this a few days before the exhibition as the mustard plants wouldn't thrive for that long.

Tanu and I water it diligently and work on it every day, adding elements like canals, a self-irrigation system, a well, a barn, miniature signboards and many other little details. We even put in tiny people from her doll house. Finally, on the day of the selection of models for the final exhibition, we are rewarded with a splendid-looking model farm, complete with real little green plants. It looks extremely impressive and all the students as well as teachers gather around us to examine it.

I catch Ankit beaming with pride and our eyes meet across the crowded room. We do not exchange a single word but the look in his eyes says it all. We communicate such a lot without even talking. I feel as though I am floating on air.

Of course our model gets selected.

'Well done, Diksha, I am so proud of you,' says Rohan as he thumps my back when the announcements at school are made.

'Hearty congrats,' says Ankit and gives me a knowing little smile. We hug our secret to ourselves and I do a tiny jig in my head as I think of all the time I will get with Ankit.

We wait eagerly now for the exhibition at the Air Force School at Avadi. The mustard plants which we planted in our model farm will die by then, but we now know what to do and tell Mrs Rao that we will replant them a few days before the actual exhibition so that we still have a grand model on the final day.

That is exactly what we do.

There are about eighteen children chosen to go to Air Force School with their models. Tanu and I are over the moon to be a part of this. All arrangements have been made for spending two days and one night at the host-school. There are more than fifty-five schools, including ours, taking part and the event has been organised on a rather large scale.

It is a two-day exhibition and we will be returning at the end of day two. The best models selected here would then represent the south zone and will get to go to Delhi for the grand finale.

Our school has made arrangements for a mini-bus and three teachers will be accompanying us. Mrs Rao, Miss Bindu and our sports teacher, Mr Paul, are our escorts. My parents are totally relaxed about sending me on this field trip as Rohan is on it too. They have proudly informed all their friends as well as Meera Mausi and my grandmother that both their children have been chosen to display their models at the exhibition.

Tanu is as excited as me. It is the first time we will be spending the night away from home.

'I wonder where we will stay. I wonder what it will be like,' she says as we clamber onto the bus. All our models have been arranged very carefully right at the back.

'Yeah, I wonder too,' I say, my eyes searching for Ankit all the while. Finally, I see him making his way along with his gang to the bus and I relax. His eyes catch mine and I quickly look away guiltily and smile. I catch him smiling too. I have never been happier in my life.

Tanu is oblivious to the chemistry between Ankit and me. To me, it seems so obvious. I can almost hear my heart sizzle each time he catches my eye. He has positioned himself in such a way that from where he is standing, he has a clear view of me. The accompanying teachers arrive and make everyone sit down. Ankit is seated in the aisle seat, just a row in front of me. I too have chosen the aisle. From where I sit, if I extend my hand, I can touch his hair. The physical proximity to Ankit gives me a heady rush. It is nothing like I have ever experienced before. He is with Rohan and his gang and yet, any chance he gets, he glances at me. Tanu is busy gazing out of the window. I desperately want to tell Ankit to not look at me so much. I am terrified of being discovered. So I pull out my notebook from my satchel, turn to the last page and slowly tear out a piece of paper. I furtively look around. Everyone is busy chatting and doing their own thing.

I quickly scribble:

Hey—don't look at me so much! You are making it so obvious.

The next time Ankit catches me eye, I hold the note with my thumb and forefinger and slowly wave it. Then I drop it and slide it with my foot towards him. My heart races furiously. Ankit manages to bend down and pick up the note. He reads it and smiles.

I look away. I hope to God he listens. But to my horror I see him pulling out his notebook. He has torn out a whole page too. I see him scribbling and, a moment later, he passes the note to me by dropping it and kicking it back with his foot. In a jiffy I have retrieved it. It reads:

Don't worry. Nobody will know. Can't take my eyes off you. I love you so much (there, I have said it). Meet me tonight after everyone has slept? Please?

I blush furiously and crumple the note and stuff it in my bag. He looks at me and smiles and raises his eyebrow.

I mouth a NO. How can I creep out and meet him? What if we get caught? I am too scared.

He mouths 'Please' and makes a puppy face.

I suppress a giggle and quickly pretend to cough and look away.

Then I see him scribbling a second note.

'What in the world are you writing?' asks Dhiraj who is next to him.

'Some notes about the talk I have to give about the project,' answers Ankit without missing a beat.

I am amazed at how quickly he has made up a story and that too on the spot. I would have probably fumbled and mumbled something and been caught out had Tanu asked me about it. Ankit is totally unruffled. He finishes the note calmly and slips it to me.

I am too terrified to even open it.

Finally I do and I read it.

There is an open auditorium at the back of the school. Look around when we arrive and you will find it. Meet me there at 12.30 am. I will be waiting. Do not disappoint. Please.

I quickly crumple that note too and stuff it in my bag. I wish there was a way to calm my racing heart. Even though one part of me is too frightened and too terrified of this audacious plan, the other part of me knows with certainty that I will definitely meet him.

It is at that moment I realise that I truly cannot say no to Ankit.

Six

WE REACH THE SCHOOL ONLY BY FOUR THIRTY PM. We are greeted by the student committee and teachers of the Air Force School. We all fall in love with the lush green campus.

'It is beautiful, Diksha! Tanu exclaims. 'How lucky these kids are to be studying here!'

I glance around at the natural surroundings, the rather modern-looking interiors and nicely done-up classrooms. This school is no doubt much better than ours which has old walls with peeling paint. Two students are assigned to show us around. We are first taken to a classroom which has been converted into a dormitory with neatly made beds—just like the ones in hotels—clean white sheets tucked in neatly, a pillow and a blanket. The room has turquoise-blue curtains!

'Our school has hired these beds specially for the event. Hope you have a comfortable stay with us,' says our student-guide proudly.

'The arrangements look very nice,' I respond. 'Do you really have these curtains in the classroom?' I ask

'No,' she laughs. 'These were also hired for the event,' she says.

Tanu and I look at each other and are very impressed. I didn't expect the staying arrangements to be this nice.

She then takes us around to see the school grounds. They have been attractively landscaped with trees, bushes and flowering plants. They even have vast green lawns. I think of our school which has a concrete entrance with a cycle-shed right in front and no greenery whatsoever. This school has a music room, an audio-visual room, a large library, auditoriums and very well-equipped laboratories. Tanu and I feel like poor cousins visiting a rich relative's house.

Our guide takes us to see the basketball, volleyball, tennis and badminton courts as well as the football ground. It is a huge campus indeed. Finally, she takes us to the outdoor amphitheatre. The beauty of it makes me inhale sharply. There are very large circular steps in gradient slopes, carpeted with carefully manicured grass. Right at the centre is a raised wooden stage. The whole arena is surrounded by softwood trees and eucalyptus whose branches seem to be doing a slow dance in the gentle breeze. It looks more like something that belongs in a luxury resort rather than at a school.

'Oh, wow! Look at this!' exclaims Tanu.

Our student-guide is clearly used to such reactions.

'Yes, it is nice, isn't it? This is where all the graduation ceremonies and informal functions are held,' she says a matter-of-fact voice.

So this is where Ankit wants me to meet him and he couldn't have chosen a lovelier spot, I think to myself. I make a mental note of how to reach here from our dormitory.

We are escorted back to our dorm and told that dinner will be served at eight pm. Our student-guide asks us if we need anything else. We don't. Girls from other schools have arrived by now. Three dorms have been assigned to the girls. The boys' dormitories are located on the first floor of the building.

The school is soon bustling with about two hundred and fifty participants from various schools. There is a buzz of activity as groups are shown to their dorms. Tanu and I go and sit on the school lawns and watch them arrive. The other girls from our school are all seniors and hang out with each other, leaving Tanu and me by ourselves.

My eyes scan the school grounds quickly to see if Ankit is around. Then we spot him. Rohan, Ankit and their gang are walking towards us. I pretend to not see them and make inane conversation with Tanu. Tanu spots them and tells me that my brother is heading towards me along with Ankit and the others.

Seeing the senior boys walk towards us, the group of senior girls joins us and soon there is a small little conference of students from our school.

'Hey, Diksha, how are your sleeping arrangements? All comfy? Are we all good?' asks Rohan, assuming the typical elder brother role.

'Yeah, it's very nice. How are yours? And by the way, where are the teachers being put up?'

'Bindu Ma'am and Mrs Rao have a room on your floor. Paul Sir has a room to himself on our floor. And their rooms are really like hotel rooms,' answers Alok, one of the senior boys.

'Awesome. Their school is much better than ours, isn't it?' says Anusha, the school vice-captain.

'Yep, they do have better infrastructure than us, but watch out, we will win tomorrow and beat them hollow,' says Ankit sounding confident.

'Let's just hope. Let us not be overconfident. You never know what they come up with,' says Tanu.

'We had a sneak peak at some of their models. They are just so-so. Ours definitely look better. But anyway, let us not slip up. We have to do a splendid job on the explanations. And for that we need to be fresh and bright tomorrow morning. So, I suggest, all of us go straight to bed. No staying up late and chatting,' instructs Rohan. He has completely taken charge and I recognise his authoritative school-captain voice.

Everyone agrees.

'Aye, Aye, Captain,' says Ankit and salutes smartly clicking his heels.

I am certain if this were a cartoon movie, there would have been hearts in place of my eyes. I gaze at him in fascination. It is as though I adore every single thing he does—the way he speaks, the way he walks and how he just saluted. I cannot stop the tidal wave of admiration I feel for him. He makes me so happy. He makes my heart sing. I know at that moment, he can ask anything of me and I would give it happily.

The dinner arrangements too are very well-taken care of. Fresh food is being cooked on the school premises where a large makeshift kitchen has been set up. There are long rows of tables and chairs. We form queues and everyone chatters excitedly. The atmosphere is one of great camaraderie, but there is also an underlying element of rivalry. Everyone sticks to their own school group and we all sit with ours, eating a sumptuous meal of steaming hot *aloo, rotis*, rice, *dal* and salad.

Tanu and I are totally enjoying our first experience of staying away from home along with the school group. This is such fun! Ankit, Rohan and their group sit opposite us and Ankit manages to catch my eye and wink at me. He mouths a 'meet me' and I quickly look away guiltily. I do not look at him for the rest of the meal even though I am dying to. I am so afraid of being caught.

'Okay then, good night, girls. See you tomorrow. Straight to bed now,' orders Rohan after dinner, and all of us bid a bye to the boys.

My heart starts its customary drum roll again. I wish I could remove the damn thing and throw it away. We all get into bed. There is a light on at the other end where three girls from another school with whom we are sharing the dorm, are chatting, but they do not mind that we want to sleep early. They are cooperative and soon the lights are all off.

Tanu and I lie next to each other, a distance of one foot separating us.

'Diksha, isn't this just like the Enid Blyton books?' Tanu whispers animatedly. 'I wish we were in a boarding! What fun it would have been! Imagine having this experience every day.'

'No talking, girls. You heard what Rohan said. Go to bed,' calls out Anusha.

Tanu is quiet for a while and then whispers again about how excited she is, and how happy she is.

I pretend to sleep and do not answer back. I want everyone to fall asleep quickly. I can't wait for it to be midnight to creep out and meet Ankit.

I keep looking at my watch. I have to press a button for the light to come on so I can see the time. I have turned my back to Tanu so she cannot see what I am doing. I keep my left arm under the pillow and turn the watch around so it faces me. Each time I want to look at the time, I press the button which lights up the watch. I cover myself with the blanket up to my head so nobody can see the glow of light. I am surprised at how naturally stealth comes to me. It is the first time I am doing anything like this in my life, but the way I do it seems to be with the practised ease of a professional.

'Hush my beating heart. Calm down. We will meet him together, you and I.' I change the words of the Emily Dickinson poem that we have learnt at school and smile to myself. I have suddenly begun understanding all the love poetry we have studied. I now comprehend the desperation of Romeo and Juliet as they waited to meet each other. Our English teacher had told us that Juliet was just fourteen and Romeo was probably a few years older. At that time I had giggled and wondered how someone so young could be so desperately in love. But now I know.

At sixteen, a good two years older than Juliet, I know now how she felt. I feel and completely relate to all those emotions that I had so far only read about. If this is love, I am gloriously submerged in it. All I can think of is Ankit.

Thoughts of him swarm around me all the time. I wonder if it is the same for him. I want to ask him.

How can it be that only three months ago he was a peripheral figure in my life, whereas now he is at the centre of it?

I wonder what Ankit is up to. Is he too watching the clock, like me? I listen in silence to the breathing sounds of the girls. They are fast asleep. I glance at Tanu and in the dark I can make out the outline of her chest rising and falling. I am wide awake and alert to the slightest of noises.

Finally, when it eleven fifty, I cannot wait anymore. I quietly creep out of bed. My eyes have got used to the darkness now. I slip my feet into my rubber-soled sandals and make my way out of the dormitory. I am terrified of waking up someone. In my mind, I already have a story ready, just in case one of them wakes up. I am going to say that I was, of course, going to the restroom and lost my way. Surely that is a perfect excuse.

I walk slowly down the long corridor, feeling like a thief. I know exactly which turn to take as I have made a note of it earlier. But what I missed seeing earlier were the iron shutters at the end of it leading outside. I go closer and see a huge lock on them. I feel so let down. I do not know what to do.

'Damn, I should have known that they would lock them,' I think to myself. How will I tell Ankit that I am stuck? I feel terrible when I think of Ankit waiting in vain for me.

Right then, I hear my name being called out in a hushed tone and nearly jump out of my skin.

I am astonished to see Ankit on the other side. 'Diksha, look outside, it's me,' he says.

'Oh my God! Ankit! How did you get there? Have you been waiting for me?'

'Of course. I knew you would come and wouldn't know how to get out. Go upstairs and take the first left. There is a balcony which faces outside. Go there and I will be waiting downstairs. I'll help you get down,' he whispers urgently.

'Okay,' I manage to respond.

I go upstairs and, in my nervousness, take the right and nearly walk into the boys' dormitory. I am so frightened that I beat a hasty retreat. My palms are clammy with sweat now. I go back to the stairs and calm myself and then realise that I have to take the left, not the right. I go left and see the balcony that Ankit mentioned. I walk to the edge and, true to his word, Ankit is waiting patiently.

'You have to climb on to the ledge, Diksha. Once there, lower yourself to the window sill. Hang on the ledge of the window. I will hold you and lower you. Don't worry,' he whispers confidently.

I look down and I feel even more terrified that I already am. My hands and legs turn into quivering jelly. I have never ever before climbed on to a window ledge and now not only do I have to climb one, but I also have to hang down it. I am thankful that I am wearing my track pants and not my skirt, else Ankit would have got a nice view of my knickers, when I swung from the window ledge, I think to myself.

I precariously cross over the railings of the balcony and balance on the ledge. This feels exhilarating! The view of the tall trees in the schoolgrounds takes me by surprise. The gentle night breeze hits my face and my hair flies in the wind. It is marvellous to stand in the window ledge unbound by grills or railing. I look at the ground. It must be a drop of twelve feet, and therefore I am certain it is not too dangerous.

'Oh my God, Ankit, this is amazing!' I say and I forget for a moment where I am.

'Shhhh, Diksha, keep your voice low. And get down here. Don't stand there. Let's go! This is too close to the boys' dorm,' he says.

His warning kind of shakes me out of the spell and I sit on the ledge.

'How do I get down from here now? What did you do?' I ask.

'I jumped down. But I would not recommend you to do that. Look, you just turn around and hang from the ledge like it's a monkey bar. I will help lower you down.'

I look at the distance and contemplate jumping. But the thing is, if I hurt my limbs or, worse, fracture my hand or feet, I will have a tough time explaining what I was doing jumping from the window ledge. So I decide that the option Ankit is suggesting is indeed the best. I turn around like he says and grip the edge of the ledge tightly with my left hand. Then I place my right hand next to it. It takes a bit of twisting, but I manage to lower my body. I am hanging now from the window ledge and this is a terrifying feeling, though I know the drop isn't probably steep. Before I can think too much and psyche myself out, Ankit is beside me.

I look down and I see him facing me. He puts his arms around my thighs. His touch feels like a thousand volts. It seems like an electric shock has hit me. He is hugging my thighs tightly now and he says, 'Okay, let go now. I've got you.'

I release my grip and am in Ankit's arms. He is strong and catches me effortlessly and lowers me to the ground. All the pent-up passion, adrenaline, and weight of the emotions that I was reeling under so far, come in great floods and submerge me completely. I hug Ankit as tightly as I can, half in relief, half in the excitement and happiness of being with him.

Ankit seems to be taken by surprise but recovers in a jiffy and hugs me right back. I nuzzle my neck in his shoulders. I feel wonderful with him. Then he begins kissing me and it feels like the most natural thing in the world. He kisses my forehead and cups my face in his hands. He looks into my eyes and I am entirely lost in them. He bends forward, his lips meet mine and his hands begin to play with the buttons of my shirt as he kisses me. I am ecstatic and so taken aback by how natural it feels. I am frightened too but not frightened enough to want him to stop.

It feels like heaven has been revealed to me. Ankit's arms slowly creep around my waist and the contact of his bare hands on it is a sensation that takes me by complete surprise. It feels like some molten lava has exploded inside me. I am unable to think and we begin kissing each other passionately. I forget everything but his lips on mine and his arms around my waist. His kisses are so hungry, so demanding and I cannot help but be carried away by the urgency and fervour of this all-consuming passion that has engulfed us now.

So wrapped are we in each other that we do not hear the crunch of gravel behind us. It registers as a sound coming from some great distance. And then, suddenly, there is a light shining right on our faces and we hastily pull apart. I blink a few times and look in the direction of the light.

My blood freezes when I finally make out the forms.

It is Mrs Rao, Rohan, Tanu and Anusha standing there and glaring at us.

Rohan's face is black with rage. Tanu looks aghast. Mrs Rao looks thunderous and Anusha looks shocked.

I stand there, staring dumbly at them, feeling horrified, guilty and so ashamed, not knowing what to say.

I have no clue then what is to follow.

I want all of this to stop. I want to turn back the clock. I do not want to be discovered like this with Ankit, that too by Rohan and Tanu. My head is spinning at the implications of it.

But to what extent and to what degree, I have no idea. My life is about to take a nasty U-turn with a bend so sharp that everything else goes out of focus. I am hurtling down a slope at full speed without any breaks.

All I know is that I am doomed.

Seven

I HANG MY HEAD IN SHAME. I REALLY DO NOT know what to say or do. Ankit looks embarrassed. He stares at the ground. He isn't able to meet Rohan's eye.

Rohan walks up to him and, before my horrified eyes, punches him so hard in the gut that Ankit swaggers and doubles up in pain. This cannot be happening. It is like a scene straight out of a movie. Rohan then says to Mrs Rao, 'I want to talk to her in private. Ma'am, please excuse us.'

All of us are too shocked to react.

He holds me by my shoulders and marches me off towards the amphitheatre.

I feel like a criminal being led to jail. I do not want to face Rohan. I want the ground to swallow me up.

The amphitheatre is lit by the moonlight, and the tall trees surrounding it make it look almost magical. I can't help thinking that it is ironical that my brother is confronting me in this place where Ankit and I were supposed to meet.

'What the fuck is this?' asks Rohan without any preamble.

'I am sorry. I didn't mean to. I... I... We got carried away,' I stammer.

'You s*tupid* girl. Do you have any idea what you are doing? What were you thinking? Sex in the moonlight? You *fucking slut,'* he spits out the words.

They hit me like a hundred needles shot straight at my chest.

I am speechless at the language my brother has just used. He has never ever spoken to me like that.

There is a lump in my throat and I am not able to speak. Tears stream down my cheeks.

'What the hell are you crying now for? What is your fucking excuse? That you *love* him? How foolish can you be? Don't you know, guys will say anything to score with a girl? I am so ashamed of you. And that bastard Ankit. I am his friend. Arrrgh,' he roars and kicks the ground hard.

I do not know what to say. I am utterly ashamed.

'We will deal with this when we get back home. You have let not only me down but also Dad and Mum. How could you behave like this, Diksha?'

I am sobbing so much that I am unable to answer.

We march back in silence.

Mrs Rao, Tanu and Anusha are waiting to escort me back. Ankit is nowhere to be seen.

Mrs Rao looks at me with eyes that seem to have turned into stone and says, 'Diksha, you are in serious trouble. This is most irresponsible behaviour. How could you sneak out like that? Disgusting.'

She succeeds in making me feel like a worm.

She escorts us back to the dorm and I see that the shutters are now open and there is a security guard staring curiously. Mrs Rao asks Anusha to keep an eye on me.

They are treating me like a criminal who will escape. How did they get to know? Who told Rohan?

Who woke up Mrs Rao? How did they know where to find us? Who opened the shutters? All these questions are swarming in my head but I am too shamed, too frightened to even speak.

'Diksha. Listen,' whispers Tanu.

But I do not reply back. I do not want to talk to anyone. I bury my head under the pillow and yank the blanket over my head and sob, replaying my brother's words over and over. I wonder what Ankit is doing. Can what my brother said be right? Was Ankit just saying stuff to me to 'score' with a girl? Was all the time that we spent together false? It definitely didn't feel so. It felt so wonderful.

Till then the possibility that Ankit could have been lying just to get into my pants (even as I think about it, I wince at my thoughts) had not even occurred to me. But the way Rohan put it is making me think about it. But more than that, I am terrified about what is going to happen once we get back home.

'Hey, Diksha. Are you okay?' Tanu whispers again. I pretend not to hear.

I lie quietly in bed, but sleep eludes me. It feels like the longest night in my life. Sometime towards dawn I doze off.

The next thing I know, I am being woken up by Tanu and I am still in a daze.

I sit up slowly, feeling completely disoriented. Then the memories of last night's happenings come back to me all at once and I don't ever want to wake up. I just want to go back to bed.

'Diksha, I tried to protect you. I did. But Anusha found the notes crumpled in your bag,' says Tanu.

What she says takes two whole minutes to sink in. Anusha *searched* my bag? *How could she?*

'How? And why did she search my bag?'

'She saw you and Ankit passing notes to each other in the bus. I think she waited for the right moment to strike. Personally, I think she has some kind of a crush on Ankit and was jealous of your exchanges. That is what I think.'

'God,' I groan. This was worse than I thought.

'She saw you go out, Diksha. Then she woke me up and asked me where you were. I said you had gone to the loo. She said she knew I was lying and then she started going through the contents of your bag. It seemed like she knew exactly where to find the notes. She read them and insisted I go with her to Mrs Rao's room. Mrs Rao marched to the boys' dorm and woke up Rohan. The rest you know.'

I sit on the bed with my head in my hands. I don't want to get out. But Tanu urges me to forget it for a while and accompany her for breakfast. We also have the exhibition today. There is work to be done, we have to set up our model and prepare to explain our project to the visitors.

As we go and join the queue for breakfast, I feel all eyes are on me. There is a sudden silence when Tanu and I appear. My ears burn and I go red. Instinctively, I know that the news about last night's happenings has spread and that they are all talking about me. I see many students turning to look at me as though to say, 'There – there is the girl who was caught kissing that guy.'

But what I do not know then is the power of rumours. They spread like wildfire. I somehow get through the day, hiding behind Tanu for most of it. She handles our model and does all the explaining. I am in no mood or state to do so.

Ankit is with the other boys at their exhibits. I catch him looking at me several times, but I turn away.

Our school wins the overall trophy for the best exhibits.

Tanu's and my display also wins a prize for the 'Most innovative and well-constructed' model. But I feel no happiness. The events of last night have cast a big black shadow over everything. All the success at the exhibition pales, withers, shrivels up and becomes meaningless as my brother's face and words keep coming back to haunt me. The more I try not to think of it, the more those thoughts rush in and surround me, drowning out everything else.

That evening, we leave for our school. It is almost as if I have become an outcast overnight. None of the girls other than Tanu want to even talk to me. They stare and whisper among themselves.

Mrs Rao watches over me like a hawk. She orders Ankit to sit in the last seat and I am made to sit right in front. As though Ankit and I will begin to kiss in the bus or something.

I feel miserable and scared, but a part of me is angry too. Is kissing a guy you like so wrong that I am being treated like I killed somebody?

Tanu reminds me that I have to accept that we live in a very conservative city like Chennai. It is definitely against Indian culture. She says it may be okay in the West. But even in the West, it is most certainly not permitted when you are on school time. What you do outside school is perhaps your business. She says that what I did was undeniably wrong.

I know that she is perfectly right, but am too upset to accept it yet. I ignore what she is saying and tell her that I am sorry and do not want to talk. I thank her for being a great friend. Then I bury my head in a book for the rest of the journey.

But the worst is yet to come.

Once we get back home, Rohan narrates the entire

episode to my parents in detail. My father is furious with me. My mother starts weeping.

I feel even more miserable than I already am when I see her crying.

'Ma, please don't cry. Nothing happened,' I try to console her.

'How can you even say that, Diksha? How could you behave like this? I feel that I have failed in raising you. If I was not able to instill a little bit of culture in you, what was the point of all these years of my parenting? I have really gone wrong somewhere. And you have the guts to say nothing happened?' My mother's voice comes out raggedly, as though saying it all hurts. Perhaps it does.

'Ma, everyone is acting like we had sex or something,' I say and at that moment my father steps forward and slaps me hard across my face.

'DON'T YOU DARE SAY A WORD. Look at her guts. She dares talk back after all that she's done. Didn't you think of your family even once?' His eyes are blazing and he is breathing hard.

His is burning wrath. I am terrified just looking at him. His voice is ringing in my ears. This man standing in front of me does not seem like my father at all. It is as though he has transformed into a beast.

I am stunned by the slap. My cheek stings with pain. My father has never hit me as far back as I can remember.

My hands begin to tremble and tears roll down my cheeks again.

'We are pulling you out of that school. No more co-ed for you. We will see what can be done,' he says with an air of finality.

I am shocked by this pronouncement. What are they going to do? Where are they going to send me? I do not want to go to a different school. I like my school and my friends. The thought of not seeing Ankit again makes my heart go heavy.

Later, that evening, I beg and plead with my mother. I apologise a thousand times. I tell her I am terribly sorry and to please not send me to another school.

But her heart is as hard as stone and she does not melt. No amount of pleading or apologising works.

'Diksha, sixteen is an age where you have to be careful. You don't even know what you are doing. We are your parents. We know what is best for you. Leave it to us,' she says with an edge in her voice that is alien to me.

My parents' attitude towards me has completely changed. Rohan is told that none of his friends can come home now.

'Like I am going to call that bastard home anymore,' mutters Rohan under his breath.

When I go back to school the next day, it seems as though the whole school is talking about me and Ankit.

All the seniors, the juniors, and even the staff. Everywhere I go, there are hushed whispers.

'Tanu, what am I going to do?' I ask her

'Don't worry, Diksha, it will die down soon,' she says and squeezes my hand. I feel very grateful to her. I tell her what my parents said about sending me to another school.

Tanu is shocked.

'Surely, they can't mean it?' she asks in disbelief.

'I don't know, Tanu. My mother sounded as though she did. They have even banned Rohan from inviting his friends home.'

'I feel so bad, Diksha. If I hadn't written all that silly stuff in Ankit's book, all of this would never have happened.'

'No, Tanu. It isn't your fault. Ankit and I met many

times after that. I knew fully well what I was doing. Or at least I thought I did. I downplayed it as I thought you might get hurt. I like him so much, Tanu. In fact, I love him. I feel so happy when he is around. But I should have controlled myself. I am so silly. I deserve all this,' I say

'Hey, don't be so harsh on yourself. He too pushed you into meeting him, didn't he? Why should he be excused? Just because he is a guy? That is so not fair. You can't blame yourself alone.'

I don't know what to tell her. So I hug her and she hugs me back.

I just think to myself, how lucky I am to have her support.

Within the very first hour of school, I am summoned to the Principal's office. I am jolted to see both my parents sitting there.

'Diksha, whatever happened is unfortunate. You have fine parents and you come from such a cultured family. Your parents have decided that sending you to another school is the best option. We will be completing all the transfer formalities within this week itself. You have a bright future ahead of you. Do not get into bad company like Ankit. His family background is not too good and that boy is nothing but trouble. I personally think your parents are doing a wise thing,' says Mr Shetty, the school principal.

This is so unfair. I feel like screaming. How can Ankit's parents fighting with each other be *his* fault? I agree I have made a mistake. But does it warrant this big a punishment? I want to say I am sorry. I want to ask to be allowed to continue in this school. I really cannot bear the thought of not seeing Ankit every day. I like my school and have been a very good student. This is the only time I have slipped up. Please give me one chance, I want to beg.

But no words come. The look in my parents' eyes breaks me down.

A plethora of emotions washes over me in those few moments. I feel anger, bitterness, regret, helplessness, sadness.

I don't know what to say or do. So I stand there, hanging my head in shame, scrunching my toes inside my shoe and making a fist so hard that my finger nails dig into my palms and leave a red mark.

This one incident is going to change the course of my entire life. But I have no idea to what extent and, for the moment, all I feel is this huge heaviness in my heart and the horrible feeling that life as I know it is about to change forever.

Eight

IT IS ELEVEN THIRTY PM. SANDEEP IS FAST ASLEEP and I am reading in bed when the phone call shatters the silence of the night.

Sandeep, a creature of habit, always stops watching television at eleven pm. If he is in the mood for sex, he initiates it. There is no foreplay, no conversation, no sweet-talk. He claims it like it is his right. He reaches straight for my breasts and I can predict exactly what he will do next. But I have learnt, over the years, to just give in to whatever he wants. He is usually in a better mood then the next day. I look at the fan rotating and think of the next day's chores as he finishes his act, grunts in satisfaction, rolls over and falls asleep.

I usually read after that to take my mind off the niggling feeling that if our society was as conscious of women's rights as they were in the West, what Sandeep did would probably be construed as marital rape. But, here in India, where people hush up even rape and do not speak about it, how do things like 'marital rape' even stand a chance to be discussed. Fact is, I hate sex with Sandeep. But I do my duty as a wife. How can he have no clue as to what I really want? How can he be so insensitive to my needs?

The phone call puts an abrupt end to all these thoughts racing through my head and it also wakes up Sandeep, who sits up in surprise, rubbing his eyes. He is beginning to go bald and without his glasses or shirt, with a burgeoning potbelly, looks so comical I almost laugh.

But when I answer the phone, any mirth I am feeling dissipates. It is Vibha.

'Diksha,' she says haltingly as though she finds it hard to speak. I know instantly from her voice that something is wrong. Terribly wrong.

'It's all over,' she says.

'Huh? What are you saying? Mohan wants a divorce?' I ask puzzled. As far I knew, things between her and Mohan weren't that bad. Sure, he had been complaining that Vibha was always busy and barely had time for anything other than her work. Vibha herself had mentioned this to me many times. But that definitely didn't warrant a divorce, that too so suddenly.

'No. He passed away an hour back,' she says and I can hear her breaking down.

'Oh my God. How? What happened?' I ask.

But she is unable to answer. Her father-in-law comes on the line and says that the funeral will take place the next day at three pm. It was a cardiac arrest, he says.

I am too stunned to ask for any more details.

The phone rings almost as soon as I hang up. It is my parents calling from Dubai where they now live with Rohan's family. They tell me that Rohan will be flying to India to attend the funeral. My father and mother will not be able to travel. Mother's arthritis has been plaguing her and Papa's treatment for prostate enlargement has just started, due to which he is constantly tired, has spells of dizziness and pounding headaches. For them to travel from Dubai to India for the funeral and fly back is difficult.

Also Rohan's wife is expecting their second child and they help her look after his first who is a year old. Mother explains to me, at great length, why it is not possible for them to come.

I haven't asked for any explanation. But perhaps she feels guilty as Vibha is her niece and wants my assurance. But the way my parents have treated me over the years—never forgiven me for my one stupid silly slip-up at sixteen—has left in me an enormous bitterness towards them. Every action of theirs over the years, ever since the day they pulled me out of school and sent me to an all-women's college in Kerala, away from Tanu, away from Ankit, as though in exile, and then the way they forced me to get married even though I was only in the second year of college, has killed something within me.

Their act has created a permanent fence in my heart, with Rohan and my parents on one side, and me on the other. Even after all these years, I have never ever really come to terms with it and the scars of that hurt still manifest themselves in my lonely moments, though I pretend outwardly to be fine. I have tried to compensate for my childhood mistake by doing all I can to please and placate my parents all through my adult life. Really, I have led my entire life as they have wanted me to lead it.

For, it is as though they have constantly judged me for that one mistake, never allowing me to even raise my head for anything I wanted. It is hard for me to now reassure my mother and so I just say an okay and keep listening to her till she hangs up.

'What happened?' asks Sandeep.

'Vibha's husband passed away. Cardiac arrest. I don't know the details. My parents aren't coming for the funeral, but Rohan is. I have to fly to Hyderabad tomorrow,' I say.

'Oh,' he says, the news slowly sinking in.

I expect him to offer to come along with me. I wait for him to say that we will fly to Hyderabad together.

Instead he says, 'I have a presentation tomorrow. You know the team from Korea is coming. I cannot take leave. What are you going to do about Abhay?'

I feel angry. The person closest to me, someone who is almost like my sister, has lost her husband and he is more bothered about his presentation and about Abhay. But this is no time to pick a fight with him or point out his insensitivity. Besides, years of marriage has already conditioned me to his black and white approach to most things.

'Well, your mother can look after Abhay, surely? I will be gone for just a day. I will be back after the funeral. I simply have to go,' I say.

'Yes, yes. I will ask her tomorrow morning. You book your tickets now,' he says to my relief. Then I stare in disbelief as he rolls over once more, adjusts his blanket and is snoring within seconds.

I am in shock. I badly want to talk to someone about it. The only 'friends' I have are the mothers of the children in Abhay's class. And I am not that close to them that I can call them late in the night for a chat. I have always been too busy raising Abhay and catering to Sandeep to make any deep friendships. Vibha is the closest friend I have and, of course, she is in no state to talk.

I book my tickets to Hyderabad using my add-on credit card which Sandeep has made for me. I never use it except in emergencies like this one. I usually pay for all the groceries in cash. In the early days of marriage, I had been excited about a credit card. I had shopped like crazy. But at the end of the month, when the credit-card statement had arrived, Sandeep had given me a pasting for overspending and lectured me on the value of money. Somehow after that, I had never ever spent money on myself, preferring to use cash whenever I shopped. The cash too was 'rationed' and strictly governed by Sandeep. There was a designated amount which he had calculated as 'fair spending' and all the household expenditure had to be within this limit. He also insisted that I maintain accounts for everything I spent. I found it all very stifling. Sometimes, when I could not for the life of me remember what I had spent on, I would make up stuff to write in the account book. Once, when that had happened, I had put down: 'Five packets of sanitary napkins' and filled in the amount to match the money I had remaining. Sandeep's reaction had been typical and hilarious.

'*Five* packets?' he had bellowed. 'Why?'

'I have a rather heavy flow. Maybe I have cysts. I might have to go to the gynaecologist,' I had lied.

He had quickly closed the topic after that, his mind perhaps calculating the doctor's fee. And I had giggled later at the cheap thrills I got in getting back at him this way.

Today is not the day to wonder if plane tickets to Hyderabad amounts to 'fair spending' in Sandeep's books or not. All I know is that Vibha needs me and I will move heaven and earth to get there.

I toss and turn and am unable to sleep. Scenes from Vibha's marriage keep playing out in front of my eyes. The trip we made together to Darjeeling—Vibha, Mohan, Sandeep and I—when Abhay was a baby, barely eight months old, flashes before my eyes. I had really enjoyed myself. Vibha and I had giggled and chuckled as only cousins can and she had helped me manage Abhay. That was the only trip we had made together.

I cannot believe that Mohan is no more. How is it possible that a person who was perfectly okay yesterday, no longer *exists*?

I call my mother-in-law as soon as I wake up the next morning. She is shocked to hear the news. Whatever be the state of my marriage, one thing I have lucked out in is having an extremely understanding mother-in-law. She has indeed helped me out with Abhay whenever the need arose. She asks me to pack Abhay's clothes and to give the bag to Sandeep who agrees to drop it off at her place on his way to office. I instruct Abhay that he has to get off at his granny's house when the school bus drops him off in the evening.

I tell him that Vibha Mausi needs me as Mohan Mama is sick and I have to go to Hyderabad for a day. Abhay is very excited at the variation in his routine.

'Don't worry, Ma. I am a big boy now. I will tell the bus driver where to drop me off,' he says confidently.

Nevertheless, I write a note to his teacher explaining the circumstances. Then I instruct the house-help to arrive before Sandeep leaves for work. I take care of a hundred other things in the house. This is the very first time I am travelling without Sandeep or Abhay and it feels strange. But it definitely feels reassuring to have my mother-in-law in the same town, that too so close by. I know that Abhay will be well-looked after and Sandeep can get his mother's cooking. I feel grateful for one less thing to worry about.

Throughout the journey on the flight to Hyderabad, I keep thinking of how unpredictable life can be. How can Vibha's life turn upside down like that? While I am at the airport, my mother calls once more. This time she has more details.

'He was fine last night. Then after dinner, he said he

felt uneasy and wanted to go to the loo. He collapsed before reaching the loo and he passed urine on the floor. They immediately called the doctor. He died instantly. Nothing could be done,' says my mother.

'I am on my way. Sandeep had some important work,' I say. I am too shocked to comprehend and process the details of how it could have happened. Mohan was just forty-one. He was even younger than Sandeep. It seems so unfair. That too he was a complete teetotaller.

'So what about Abhay? Is he with you?' asks my mother.

'No, Ma, I saw no sense in taking him along. My mother-in-law will look after him.'

'Okay, yes, it's better that way. What will the child do there anyway? Poor Monu. I wonder how Vibha is coping. I wish I could come. But your father as well as Seema need me. Seema's due date is anytime now. Rohan will be reaching there around the same time as you. Please explain all this to Murali Mama, okay? Rohan won't open his mouth. You know how he is,' she says.

'Yes, Yes. Don't worry. I will tell them,' I say.

Nothing prepares me for the sight of Mohan's dead body lying wrapped in the white shroud with cotton stuffed up his nostrils and a pile of incense sticks lit at his head.

There is a large group of people who have gathered around. My eyes fall on Rohan who is seated next to the body. Mohan's mother is inconsolable.

As soon as Monu sees me, she runs up to me and hugs me. 'Can you make me wear some nice clothes?' she says. 'So many people are visiting us and I am still in my old clothes.'

I hug her tightly and choke back my tears. But then, when I see Vibha, I cannot hold back my tears anymore.

I embrace her and we both weep.

Nine

DEATH IS A GREAT LEVELLER. IT CHANGES THINGS. It makes you confront your mortality. It shakes you up. It changes your perspective completely. The weight of it is usually so much to bear that people who face it, do things they normally wouldn't.

Mohan's death does not even feel real. It seems as though any moment now he will appear and greet the gathering, even though his dead body is right before us. On the face of it, Vibha is making an attempt to appear calm. But, I know, she is completely broken inside.

Once the body is taken and everyone has left, the loneliness becomes oppressive. It is hard to even sit in the drawing room as just hours ago, the body was there as were all the people. The furniture had been moved around and I now help Vibha move it back. Once it is back in place there is not even a hint of the tragedy that has occurred there. Everything *seems* so normal.

Except it isn't.

We sit in silence and I hold her hand. Monu has been told that her father has gone away to sleep and will not be coming back. What can a child of three comprehend about death, really? She answers that she too wants to go go to sleep like Papa. Vibha breaks down once more and hugs her.

I take her inside, try to make her eat some dinner (which has been got from a neighbour's home, adhering to the Hindu tradition of not lighting a fire in the home which has housed a dead body, which means one cannot cook) and read her a story and put her to bed.

My return tickets are booked for the next day, but Vibha begs me not to go.

'Please, Diksha, I need you,' she pleads. The sorrow in her eyes and the plea in her voice gnaw at my heart.

I call up my mother-in-law and tell her what the situation is. My mother-in-law asks me to stay as long as is necessary. I am worried about what Sandeep will say.

'It is okay, Diksha. I will explain to him,' she assures me. I feel like hugging her.

How did a person who is so sensitive raise someone like Sandeep who seems to have no consideration for my feelings? Then again, perhaps it is partly my fault as I have always played 'the willing doormat' role in this relationship, right from the start.

Sandeep calls me up shortly.

'Mother spoke to me. How long do you intend to stay at Vibha's? What in the world can you accomplish by being there?' he asks, coming directly to the point in his characteristic blunt style.

'Hey listen, Vibha is totally devastated. Her husband's died, for God's sake. I will return soon as I can. Your mother did say it was okay.'

What I really want to tell him is that my sister needs me. That there is something called 'family support', something perhaps he will never understand as he does not have siblings.

I am, however, unable to explain to him why I need to

stay back. Sometimes, when the outlook and wave-length of the other person is completely different, it is best to keep quiet. After all, he hasn't really objected to my staying with Vibha and neither has he demanded that I get back. He has merely asked me a question, the answer to which is obvious and comes instantly to me. How can I *not* stay back when Vibha needs me and has asked me to?

I spend five days with Vibha. We go over all of Mohan's financials arrangements and sort out everything. For the first time in my life, I feel I am doing something useful, other than being a mother and a wife. I sort out all the papers, the loans pending in his name, the mutual funds invested in, the shares he holds, the PF, the insurance policies. I even help her get the death certificate. In college, accountancy was always my favourite subject. But it is the first time in my life I am using it practically. Finally, I manage to neatly organise almost everything and tie up the loose ends.

Every night, after her in-laws and Monu have gone to sleep, Vibha and I sit and talk. Our need to communicate seems to be endless and even though we have been talking for four nights now, we still have so much to say to each other. We talk about the uncertainty of life, reminisce about old times, the future and everything else in between.

Tonight, Vibha is very grateful for all my help and for my presence there. 'You are good at this, Diksha. You should be working in the financial sector, you know,' she says.

I smile at the compliment she gives me despite her grief.

'Then again, it is good that you never had a career. Look at me, Diksha, I have never really lived my life.'

'What do you mean, *you* haven't lived your life? You

got married when you *wanted* to. You are working, you have a career. You are successful. If anything, I should be the one complaining. I was forced into marriage at nineteen, Vibha. Nineteen. Then I got pregnant and became a mother. I know I am grateful for Abhay and I adore him and all that. But it is me who hasn't lived her life, Vibha. I got married in the second year of college, for God's sake. I made one silly error at sixteen and was branded for life. It changed my whole life. You have at least lived life on your terms, unlike me.'

'Yeah, Diksha, But look at us now. Abhay is nine and does not need you around so much. My Monu is just three. You were wise to have a child early. You are so young and you have your whole life ahead of you.'

'What young? I will be thirty-five soon. And what do I have to show for it? Nothing whatsoever, Vibha. I feel my life has been a total waste. Never have I had a chance to do the things I've really wanted to do,' I say bitterly.

I have always felt cheated, pushed around by my parents. It is all pouring out now—the frustration, the pent-up hurt. I am unable to stop myself. I have been made to feel guilty my whole life for that fateful night. I have been constantly reminded of it. Everywhere I go, it is always with a grey cloud hanging over my head, reminding me of the dishonour I have brought to my family. I have been made to feel as guilty as a cold-blooded murderer for what seemed to me to be a not-such-a-terrible thing. I have never lived my life according to my wishes. My whole life has gone in trying to make amends and please my parents first, and catering to Sandeep and Abhay after that.

'So change it. What is stopping you?' says Vibha quietly.

It takes me a few seconds to comprehend.

'How can I change it? You know how Sandeep is. He is

a conservative, conventional guy, eight years older than me,' I say.

'So?'

'What do you mean "so"? How can I change anything? He is a very different sort of a guy, Vibha. We agreed, right at the start of the marriage that he would earn, while I stayed at home. I opted to be a housewife. And to be fair, I wasn't forced into it. It was a mutual decision as neither Sandeep nor I wanted to put Abhay in a crèche. See, Sandeep's outlook is very different from Mohan's.'

Then I realise that I have referred to Mohan as though he exists. I bite my tongue.

But Vibha has a strange faraway look in her eyes.

'Look, Diksha, even if I *want* to do the things I really want to, I can't. Do you know, for the past three years, Mohan had been hounding me incessantly for a holiday, but I never took time off for him? I went back to work when Monu was barely three months old and have worked continuously ever since. Today, if you ask me what it is I really want, I would say, it is to spend time with Mohan and Monu. But it is too late for that now, isn't it? See what I mean? We all must really *live* our lives, Diksha. We should do what makes us happy. I kept pushing myself in my career, as I wanted to prove that I was as good as any man. I didn't want to be seen as one of those women who neglects work and goes home early just because her child is ill. You know, Mohan had pleaded so many times with me to come home early and go to the movies. But, it was always work and more work for me. I have hardly *lived,* Diksha. And, in a strange way, I don't think you have either.'

The pain, depth and honesty in her voice go straight to my heart.

I fall silent, thinking about everything she has said. I know she is right.

'Yes, Vibha. I know what you mean,' I finally say.

'If you do, then what are you going to do about it?'

'Eh?'

'It is not enough to *know*, Diksha. You have to *act*. I am going to take a year-long sabbatical now. I know what I want. I want to spend time with Monu. I want to take her to places, I want to show her the zoo, the museum, do all the fun stuff that I have missed out. I want to be there for her when she comes back from school. I am clear what I want, and I know I will go for it. But what is it that you want for yourself, Diksha?'

I think hard about it. I am surprised to discover that I do not have an answer to that.

'Vibha, I have done all of the things you want to do for Monu, for Abhay. I was there for him throughout. In fact, I have been a mother for so long that I really don't know how to do anything else. You ask me what I want, about my desires and dreams, and I can't think of anything.'

'Okay, let me rephrase that. Presume you don't have Abhay or Sandeep to hold you back. Presume all the decisions are your own. What then would you like to do?' Vibha prods.

I can see that she is in no mood to let go of her line of enquiry. Perhaps this conversation is helping her to not think about Mohan's death. After his funeral, we have talked so much about him and all the memories associated with him and wept. This time, the conversation is veering towards something serious. It is definitely making me think.

What do I really want?

For so many years really, I have suppressed my desires.

I have not even allowed myself the luxury of dreaming. Now Vibha's prodding is making me contemplate.

'I would like to do some fun things. I have never had what people call "fun" in my life, and would like to experience that. I want to try all those things I never got a chance to,' I finally say.

'What fun things? Be specific,' demands Vibha and she snatches up the writing pad which I had been using earlier to make notes about Mohan's loans and other stuff.

'Hmm... I will have to think,' I reply, not wanting to commit and feeling suddenly vulnerable and exposed.

'So think. We have the whole night. I will write down what I want from life and, here, you do the same as well,' she says, tearing out a page from the writing pad and handing it to me.

'I don't know, Vibha. I really haven't thought about such things in a long time,' I reply.

She thrusts the pen at me.

'Is it important to you or not? Just a moment ago, you were complaining bitterly about having lived your life so far as per your parents' or husband's wishes. So I want you to write down what is it that YOU want on this piece of paper. Put down everything that will make YOU happy,' she speaks slowly as though speaking to a child.

'What is the point? Are you going to make it come true?' I feel the resentment creeping back into my voice.

'Maybe. Maybe not. But if you don't even know what you truly want from life, how can you ever hope to obtain it? How can you give up on LIFE, Diksha? Do you want to continue to resign yourself to your so-called fate? Sure, you got married early. Sure, you paid a heavy price for a silly thing that you did when you were sixteen. But, can you change the past? No, you can't. Your future is in your hands. Our hands. I know what I am going to do and I am writing it down. When you write down something, it intensifies your intention. There was this training programme I attended at work where they made us write down our goals for the next five years. That is what we need, Diksha. We need goals. Write down yours. No matter how crazy they seem or how unachievable. Do you have anything to lose by doing so?'

Vibha is emotional now. There are tears in her eyes. It is as though she is determined to squeeze out the best bits of life and do all that she feels she has missed. Her quiet determined manner is beginning to affect me.

I take the paper from her hand and think.

It is a first for me.

What is it that I really want? I rack my brain for answers.

I see Vibha furiously scribbling. She looks up as though on cue and says, 'Go on! Write it down. Pretend Sandeep and Abhay aren't there in your life and it is just you and nobody else.'

That gives me a starting point. I pick up the pen and I write:

Things I badly want to do.

Then I pause and close my eyes. How would it be if Sandeep and Abhay weren't around? How would I design my life in that case? I haven't gone on a vacation since a very long time. So I put that down.

Ideas begin to flow and I quickly jot them down. When I am done, my list looks like this:

1. *Take a vacation alone, without family, but with a friend.*
2. *Go snorkelling.*
3. *Get drunk!*

4. *Learn salsa.*
5. *Wear a bikini.*

   I pause and think. I let my imagination run riot. The thought of wearing a bikini is giving me ideas. And then I add:

6. *Have sex with a guy other than husband, just to know what it feels like!*

I am surprised at what I have written. Where have all these wishes come from? I am married to an extremely conventional man and have led a sheltered, protected life. I have never had alcohol, never gone on a vacation alone and never worn a bikini. I realise that my list is pure fantasy.

I am about to scratch it out.

But before I can do that, Vibha who has stopped writing, snatches my list from me.

'Nooo, I am not ready to share it yet,' I shriek in horror even as she reads it and I try to grab it back from her.

Suddenly we are not grown-up women anymore, but a pair of cousins fighting, just like when we were kids.

'Why in the world would you want to hide it from *me*? Come on!' she says as she reads.

I expect her to laugh. Especially since the whole list seems so ridiculously impossible.

She doesn't. She nods solemnly instead.

'You know, Diksha. Your list, it is not so hard. You should just go for it. I have done everything on this list except the last thing.'

'Wow! Lucky you! I guess it was easy for you. I, on the other hand, have never gone anywhere without the family. I have always dressed conservatively and that last wish about sleeping with another guy, it is just a silly, totally wild fantasy. Forget I wrote all this. I did it just to please you. I did not mean it,' I say, trying to cover my embarrassment.

'See my list,' she says and hands it to me.

I am surprised to read it. Everything that I have been doing with Abhay—ordinary mundane things like being there when he returns from school, reading him a bedtime story, packing lunch for him, taking him to the park, teaching him to ride a bicycle—are on Vibha's list.

'You know what, Diksha? You *must* do the things on your secret wish list. You really must. We don't know what tomorrow will bring. See, whoever anticipated this? I really wish I had spent some more time with Mohan. And now there is nothing I can do to bring to change that,' she says and breaks down again.

I hold her for a long time as she sobs and gradually quietens down. I think to myself that the list I have made is indeed a secret wish list.

That night, l am awake for a very long time. The more I think about it, the surer I am. I feel light and happy and also excited and frightened. It is as though a weight is off my shoulders and I suddenly know what I want. I haven't felt this way in a long time.

As I fly back to Bangalore, back to my normal life the next day, I make up my mind that I am going to strike off each and every item on my wish list except perhaps No. 6 which will remain my secret fantasy.

No matter what it takes.

Vibha is right. I have never really *lived* my life. But, now I want to.

But there is only one thing: I have no idea how I will do it.

Ten

So that is how it is born. My secret wish list.

In the darkness of the night and the suspended isolation of the plane's interiors where your life is on pause mode, my wish list seems to be believable, achievable even and, most of all, perfectly sane.

But the moment I land in Bangalore and take a prepaid cab home (Sandeep does not come to the airport—his team from Korea is still visiting), the vacuity of my wish list begins pressing down on me, like a phantom ghost whose weight you feel but cannot see.

I wonder what has got into me. Why did I ever listen to Vibha? What a crazy thing to do—write down a wish list which I don't have a hope in hell of achieving. And how foolish was I to feel determined about achieving it. How could I? Ordinarily, I should have been able to dismiss it as just as something I did for a lark. Just something I did to please Vibha. But the wish list seems to have taken on a life of its own. I am unable to dismiss it. It is as though the words I have written on paper have transformed themselves into a coil of rope which has wrapped itself around my neck and is pulling me towards my desires.

I open the paper once again. As I look at it, my heart begins to beat faster. The words beckon me, taunt me, mock me, ask me to *live* my life, and bring my wish list to fruition.

I sigh, fold the paper neatly and put it away and pull my thoughts towards what I will cook for dinner, and how happy Abhay will be when I pick him up from his grandmother's house. It is almost as if I have shoved the list into a bottle, shut it tight, thrown it into the sea and returned to my normal life.

To my surprise, Abhay does not seem to have missed me at all. In fact, he looks mildly disappointed at my return.

My mother-in-law gives me a knowing smile as if to say, 'See, this is how you raise children. See how happy he is?'

I do not mind at all. I am relieved that he has been happy in my absence.

'You should do this more often, Diksha. The child is very comfortable here. This apartment complex has so many more facilities than your house. So many children to play with. We have a pool, the park, tennis—everything. I really don't know what Sandeep sees in staying in that independent house, when I myself prefer an apartment. People have to change with changing times,' she says.

She is truly modern, my mother-in-law. She is so practical and correct in her thinking. But Sandeep loves the independent house with the tiny oasis of greenery that surrounds it.

'Ma, you know how he is. He hates "living in mid-air" as he calls it,' I answer.

'I know. It is not that we haven't had this conversation so many times before. Anyway, I do enjoy having Abhay over. He is such a lovely child. You really should do this more often, you know. Get away from the husband, kid,' she winks and there is a twinkle in her eye.

I smile back at her, thankful for having such an understanding person in my life.

'And how is Vibha coping?' she asks.

'She is being brave. She is holding up remarkably well. But this has come as such a sudden shock. She now wants to take a sabbatical from work and spend more time with Monu,' I answer.

'And rightfully too. These moments with children, they never come back,' she says.

On the way back home, Abhay quizzes me about my trip. I tell him that Mohan Mama has gone to heaven. We talk about death. He is at an age where the adult world doesn't completely make sense, but he is beginning to understand that certain things are irreversible. I feel a bit awkward, so I change the topic deftly and ask him to tell me all about his school and his stay with his grandmother. He is still not old enough to realise when the topic is being changed. He happily chatters about all the delicious food that his granny fed him, the new friends he made, and how he even took a free swimming lesson at the apartment pool without the coach realising.

'Oh my God! How did you manage that?' I ask in surprise.

'He doesn't even know who the students are, Mummy. He should know better. Else he will get cheated of his money,' shrugs Abhay.

I smile inwardly but nevertheless do my motherly duty and tell him not to do it again.

When Sandeep returns in the evening, it does not occur to him to ask me about Vibha. He merely hands over his briefcase (like always) and waits for his customary cup of tea.

I long to talk to Sandeep all about it. To tell him how difficult it has been for me to be the strong one and cushion Vibha's shock. To describe how I sorted out the finances and what a big difference my being there has made to Vibha. My eyes beg him silently to ask me how it all went. My heart begs him to show a little concern. I want some conversation, some understanding from his end. I do need him—can't he see that?

But he is so immersed in his BlackBerry, furiously replying to mails or whatever it is that he does on his phone, that he hears neither my heart's whispers nor notice the plea in my eyes.

We continue to sit and sip our respective cups of tea and even though we are sitting close together in a serene beautiful garden, we are a million miles away from each other.

It hits me with a sudden pang of realisation that I have never ever felt lonelier in my marriage of fifteen years.

I feel like lashing out at Sandeep, telling him we need to talk, or rather I need to talk and I want him to listen. But, remembering the last showdown I had, I say nothing and I continue sitting there and watch him fiddle with his phone, increasingly resentful of my relationship with the man I married and the path that my life seems to have taken.

❦

The next day, I wait for Abhay to leave for school and for Sandeep to leave for work. I desperately want to talk to Vibha and find out how she is coping.

I call her as soon as the house is empty.

Her phone keeps ringing but there is no answer. After a few seconds, I get a text from her:

With neighbours. Check mail.

I rush to the computer and log in to my email account. There is a long mail from Vibha.

Hey, my lovely sis,

Just want to give you a huge big thank-you for being around when I needed you most. I am deeply grateful. I know how it must have been for you to leave Sandeep and Abhay behind and stay on for so many days. You have no idea how much it meant to me.

I wouldn't be lying if I said I couldn't have coped without you.

My decision to take a sabbatical has left me with copious amounts of time. My home is in perfect running order, as I had organised everything in clockwork precision to cope with my absence from it due to the demands of my career.

Diksha, I am so used to being busy all the time that I am finding this sudden change a little strange. Of course, I do not regret it, but it just struck me that I am actually writing a personal email after ages! I have written nothing but work-related mails.

I spend every waking hour with Monu when she is around. But when she goes to playschool, I find time hanging heavy on my hands. It is still so hard to accept that Mohan is gone. I have discovered that the best way to pull myself out of the grief mode is to immerse myself completely in something or the other. I try to switch off, Diksha, and try to think of other things.

Ever since you left, I have been thinking of your wish list. Just do it, girl! Don't dwell too much on it. I am going to make it my personal mission to see that everything you wrote on it is ticked off. Every single thing. Okay, not the last one. I do not approve of extramarital affairs, but everything else on that list is doable. Life is indeed so short. Consider it my way of saying a thank-you to you for all that you have done for me.

And before I forget, I took the liberty of registering you at this really cool site I discovered called 'Blast from the Past.' An office colleague had recommended it to me. It lets you list all the places you have worked at, lived in, studied at and helps you find common friends. You would have got a confirmatory email in your inbox. Check it out please, and if you do not want to, you need not accept. But do look.

And hey, let's video-chat soon.

Love you, my beautiful sis. I feel so lucky to have you in my life.

Stay blessed and beautiful,

Vibha

I read her mail one more time and feel ridiculously happy. She does sound like she is coping. I am happy to help her in whatever way I can. I am glad that she is ticking off stuff on *her* wish list, stuff that matters to her most, like spending time with Monu.

I take out my wish list from my bag and look at it again. All my wishes seem outrageously impossible given my current circumstances. How will I go alone on a vacation, do snorkelling, wear a bikini? Yet here is Vibha urging me to complete them. And to top it, she says she will make it her life's mission!

I check the mail and, sure enough, as Vibha said, there is an email from the site asking me to click on a link and confirm my email id.

I click on it and it opens to a site which shows some people smiling happily apparently in the company of long-lost friends. There are testimonials and success stories of how people found friends they had lost in touch with forever.

There is a profile form to fill.

I look at it and think for a minute. Then I decide to fill it. After all, what do I have to lose?

I complete it fairly quickly, filling in all the details, listing the school I studied in, the college I went to. I wonder if anyone from school will even remember me now. Eighteen years is a long time. I highly doubt the possibility of someone *actually* contacting me. I have never worked anywhere and so that entire section is blank. I list my hobbies as 'art' even though it has been ages since I have held a paintbrush or painted.

Then I click 'register' and an icon pops up, thanking me for registering and asking me to wait by my mail box. 'You never know who will get in touch with you,' it says.

I smile and close the site and then I compose a mail to Vibha.

Hey Vibha,

I love you too! Deeply. But you are mad!

You have way too much time on your hands, woman! What is this? You are making it your life's MISSION to see that I achieve my wish list which I wrote on a lark and because you forced me to!

You are hereby certified MAD.

And by the way, I did register at the site you asked me to. It cheekily said, 'You never know who is going to get back into my life.'

Yeah! Right! Like my life is going to change because someone from my past gets in touch.

I am really glad that your sabbatical is going well and that you are enjoying having time with Monu. I do know I want something more from life, Vibha. But I am not sure what.

It gave me great pleasure to help you look after Monu, and likewise to have been of use in sorting out Mohan's financials. I felt needed for the first time in years and I must admit, it was a great feeling.

You're holding up awesome, girl. I am so proud of you and the way you are coping,

We will video-chat soon.

Love,

Diksha

I think about Vibha and how remarkably well she seems to be holding up. I think about how she is pushing me to achieve my wish list. Maybe she does have a point. Life is indeed short. Even thinking about the things on the wish list fills me with joy. Is it because it seems like a forbidden fruit bringing some excitement to my otherwise dull and mundane life?

Or, is it because I have finally listed what I want, as opposed to what my parents, or my son, or my husband want for me. But whatever it is, even if I acknowledge that I do want to do all the things on the wish list, how in the world is Vibha going to help me achieve it?

She did sound determined and sure in the mail.

And even before I log off, her reply to my mail pops up in my inbox. I realise that she must own a BlackBerry or one of those fancy phones which allow you to access your mail instantly.

> Diksha!
>
> You say you want something out of life. And you do not know what!
>
> Well, I know. You just need to *find yourself*. It is not some new-age women's lib mumbo-jumbo I am feeding you.
>
> You need to do the things YOU want, Diksha. When was the last time you did that?
>
> Now open your wish list and go!
>
> Do it, girl!
>
> Live your life. Take it from someone who really knows.
>
> Will call you soon.
>
> Lots of love,
>
> Vibha

Is it really possible? I read my wish list again.

The easiest item on it is, of course, to learn salsa. I can do it without leaving town. I can do it without anyone's help.

I have no idea how Sandeep will react if I express my desire to learn dancing to him.

On an impulse I google 'salsa classes in Bangalore' and I am stunned at the options it throws up. There are at least more than twenty options. There is Salsa, Jive, Cha-cha, Fox Trot, party dancing, Bollywood dancing.

One of the classes is very close to my home.

I stare at it like a child who has been shown a room full of candies and sweets. All these years there was a class happening so very close to where I live and I had no clue at all! How could I have been existing in such a cocoon?

On an impulse I pick up my mobile and dial the number of the dance studio.

Eleven

THE PERSON AT THE OTHER END INTRODUCES himself as Gaurav and he is one of the instructors. He sounds friendly and welcoming. He says that a new batch is starting in eight days and I can come for a free demo session before that, provided I confirm to him and register for the same. The demo session is on Friday. I tell him that I am not sure if I want to join at all. I merely wanted to gather some information as I live in the neighbourhood.

'Oh that is perfectly fine. Most people do that. There is no obligation at all to join after the demo class. You can try it out and see if this is your thing,' he says.

'That suits me,' I reply. 'I would like to register.'

He sounds suave and sophisticated on the phone, like one of those radio jockeys with perfect diction, and knows exactly what to say. I wonder how he will look in person. I already like how he sounds.

He notes down my name, address and phone number and tells me to come for the demo session on Friday at eleven am. He says that, if for some reason, I am cancelling my attendance, could I please let him know as they can then allot the place to someone else. He stresses that they take only ten people at a time.

All he has said so far sounds promising. I also learn that theirs is one of the oldest dance studios in Bangalore. He says that it is a dedicated dance studio unlike other places which are primarily fitness centres offering dance classes.

I think, ever since I got married, I haven't felt this excited about anything. This is the first time I am doing something in secret. I debate whether or not I should tell Sandeep and ultimately decide against it. I am not sure how he will react if I announce a sudden interest in salsa, after all these years.

Also, I am a little apprehensive. I may not like it and decide against joining at all. So I do not see any point in telling him about it. I also wonder whether or not I should inform Vibha about my little salsa expedition. In the end I decide not to. She might just insist that I join and force me to enrol. And I want it to be my decision, not hers.

I am so thrilled about it that I can't seem to contain my feelings. I desperately wait for Friday. My whole face seems to reflect my excitement and happiness. So much so that next day at the bus stop, when I am dropping off Abhay, the other mothers comment on it.

'Hey, what's up, Diksha? Did you join a new workout or something? You are really glowing today!' says Jyoti whose daughter is a year younger than Abhay.

'Or are you in love? Some secret *chakkar*, some extra-marital spice?' asks Rachna whose son is in grade two.

'Ha ha, nothing like that. I lead a boring life,' I reply.

I am grateful when the bus arrives as it means I can dodge their questions.

When I return home, I quickly glance at myself in the bathroom mirror to see if I am that obvious. There is indeed a strange kind of eager anticipation in my eyes. They seem to be blazing. It is like I am hugging a great secret to myself. I am, but I did not expect to be this transparent.

I think a lot about what to wear for my first salsa class. I have stopped wearing skirts after marriage. I mostly have only salwar kameezes. I own just two pairs of jeans and one pair of tights. Sandeep hates any kind of 'modern fancy clothes' as he calls them and so my wardrobe is mostly limited to slightly subdued salwar kameezes and churidars.

Finally, I settle for my sole pair of tights and a loose flowing white cotton shirt, and I tie my hair back in a ponytail. It has been ages since I wore this outfit and, as I glance into the mirror, I am surprised to see how it seems to have taken ten years off me. Always on the slimmer side, I have fortunately not put on weight over the years. Whatever I gained after my pregnancy isn't too much. I realise that in this outfit and hairstyle, I don't even look like a mother anymore. I can easily pass off as someone on the threshold of a career.

I feel good to see how smart I look. It surprises me to discover what a huge difference clothes can actually make to the way you view yourself.

As I take an auto rickshaw from home to the salsa class, for some strange reason the words that Neil Armstrong said when he landed on the moon come to my mind: 'That's one small step for man, one giant leap for mankind.'

I feel as though the distance between my home and the salsa class is very little, yet I seemed to have crossed a huge barrier.

Stop it, Diksha—do not over dramatize. You are here just for a demo class, that's all.

I try to calm my jittery nerves which seem to have a

life of their own. I have half a mind to call this off, get down from the auto and run back to the safety of my home. But I don't. I force myself to act normal.

I reach the dance studio and climb the stairs to the first floor where our class is to take place. From the outside it looks quite unimpressive, but the moment I enter, it is a different world altogether. There is some really catchy Latino music playing. It is something I have never heard before. The studio is fairly large, about four thousand square feet easily with a wooden flooring throughout. Just outside the large hall with a glass door, which let you see what is going on inside, is the reception area done up entirely in white. This is where Gaurav greets me.

Gaurav is muscular and tall and *very* good-looking. He can easily pass off for a model. I am mesmerised by his looks. My mind does a 'wooo-hoo' inside my head and I ask it to shut up and behave itself. He has a confident manner about him and he extends his hand, 'Hey there! I am Gaurav, and you are...?' he asks

'Diksha,' I reply as I shake his hand. I get a whiff of cologne and it adds to his sex-appeal.

'Oh, Gorgeous. Charmed to meet you,' he says and I cannot help smiling a rather large grin at the words he has chosen.

He then ticks off my name and takes me inside where there are about six students, four guys and two girls.

'Diksha, these are the others who will be in the demo class with you. We will wait for about ten more minutes. A few others are yet to arrive.'

I nod. Then I see a petite woman dancing by herself in the corner. I am amazed at her movements and grace.

'Hey, Lorraine,' calls out Gaurav and she turns towards us, waves and continues dancing.

'Diksha, that is Lorraine, one of our senior instructors. We will have a mix of experienced people and beginners for this class. Varun, our other instructor will also be joining us shortly. Now feel at home and we will start in fifteen minutes,' he says as he leaves me in the studio.

The other six look as lost as me. It is clearly their first time and we all stare in fascination at Lorraine who seems to be oblivious to us, as she sways her hips and practises the most complicated moves with ease and panache.

I am not sure what conversation to make with these people and so I keep quiet.

One of the guys approaches me and extends his hand.

'Gagan,' he says.

'Diksha,' I offer and realise as I shake his hands that they are clammy with sweat. I do not like it at all.

'First time?' he asks

'Yes,' I reply, trying to avoid conversation.

'Me too. What do you do, Diksha? Nice name by the way,' he smiles.

I do not want to be drawn into a conversation with Gagan—the clammy-pawed-man (as I have named him in my head).

'I am in between jobs,' I lie and am surprised at how easily it comes to me.

'Ah ha! Laid off, eh?' he asks.

'Between projects, actually. Thinking of switching and weighing my options.'

The lies easily roll of my tongue and I wonder where in the world they are coming from. This seems to be a new avatar of me and I barely know myself anymore.

By now, the others too have gathered around us and we all introduce ourselves to each other.

Janie and Nitya are the girls. Janie is engaged and

will be getting married soon, and before she does, she wants to learn salsa. Nitya is in college and finds salsa a fun activity to pursue.

I catch only one guy's name. He is Pavan and is a techie. He looks fit and is about five feet ten inches. Among the other two whose names I have failed to remember, one is engaged to be married. He is short and balding and has the beginnings of a potbelly. The other guy is about six feet tall and lanky.

'I thought this would be a good place to meet singles like me,' he says and grins at Nitya and me, revealing perfect teeth.

I shudder inwardly. I cannot make up my mind whether I like him or not. Maybe he is a nice guy but I don't like how he has so blatantly announced that he is here scouting around for a girlfriend. Perhaps, this is the accepted norm among people who are single. I have no idea as I have never been in the 'dating-mating' game, having proceeded straight to matrimony and later to motherhood, all whilst in college.

I want to tell him that I am not single and I even have a child, but before I can say anything, Gaurav comes back.

He claps his hands to get our attention.

'Welcome people. So this is our batch. Looks like we have had some last-minute cancellations, but that's okay. Seven is a good number. Three of us are your instructors for the day—Varun, Lorraine and me. So that makes us ten in all, and all of us will have a partner. Gentlemen, since there are only four women, we will have to take turns to dance with the ladies. Initially, we will be doing only the basic steps for which you do not need partners,' he says.

Then he arranges us in rows. There are end-to-end mirrors in the hall. It is the first time I have been in such an environment and I stare at the multiple reflections, fascinated.

'Now, Lorraine and I will do a quick demo to let you all get a feel of salsa and what you can hope to achieve at the end of sixteen lessons,' he says.

Lorraine turns up the volume. The Latino music is infectious and makes one want to dance. Gaurav and Lorraine dance like they are possessed. All of us watch with our jaws dropping. In deft moves and with perfect rhythm, Gaurav has spun Lorraine around, like a top. Then, just as swiftly, he pirouettes her back towards him, drops her down and pulls her back in spring motion. He does some amazing lifts and jumps. They dance as one and when it ends, all of us break into spontaneous applause.

'So this is what you can do with practice,' he says and we all look at each other and laugh nervously.

'If I manage to do that, you can charge me double,' says Gagan and everyone burst out laughing.

'Have patience. You have sixteen lessons and also a whole lot of practice sessions. We will be teaching you step by step, but first things first. I must tell you all a few important things and I want your full attention,' says Gaurav.

He goes on to tell us that we will be rotating partners. Salsa is a form of dance, he says, fairly new to India, where you dance closely with a partner. Given that fact, he says with a grin, everyone has to be extra careful about body odour and general hygiene. The upshot is, that guys must shave, shower and brush their teeth before class. 'Sorry to bring this up, guys, but it is very important that you be considerate to your partner, and ensure your hygiene is impeccable. I've had guys come to class straight after gymming and I've had to actually tell them that they smell atrocious! I don't want to repeat that experience with you guys,' he laughs, then adds, 'Women are usually cleaner by nature and smell good too.' All of us smile.

'Also, there is this whole thing about rotating partners. Please remember, folks, you are only dancing, not having sex.' He emphasizes. 'Okay, at least not in class. What you do outside is your business,' he adds and winks and everyone chuckles.

He talks about why it is important to rotate partners and how the guys have to 'lead the woman' in salsa. He tell us that there is a certain basic etiquette in salsa, or in any other form of dance, which when followed, makes dancing more pleasurable. He goes on to explain with examples from his previous classes.

The next forty-five minutes are spent learning the three basic salsa moves.

Lorrainne and Varun demonstrate and we all follow.

'One two three, back. Five six seven,' goes the count.

Gaurav walks up and down and comes to each of us individually to see if we are getting the moves right.

'Do not worry if you do not get it the first time. Do it as slowly as you can and keep at it. You will eventually learn,' he encourages.

The teachers break down the moves into easy bits and I pick up the basics very easily.

'Excellent, Diksha. You are getting it fine,' Gaurav says as he stands next to me and watches me do the steps.

I glow with pride.

I know then that I want to join the course. This experience has been such a high that I want more of it.

I want to dance with these people. I want to learn all the moves. I feel really wonderful here in this studio. In fact, I feel young, vibrant and carefree—something I have never felt before, at least not for a long, long time now.

After the demo session, Gaurav asks how many of us want to enrol.

All of us do. There is not a single drop-out. Gaurav smiles in satisfaction, but isn't surprised.

He tells us that the sessions will be held twice a week—Fridays and Tuesdays. He asks what time best suits all of us. The majority votes for one thirty pm as that's the lunch hour. Most of the guys are on flexi-time. Both the girls are free as they have their semester break.

The afternoon time-slot, as well as the classes being on weekdays, suits me perfectly too as then Abhay is at school and Sandeep at work.

I feel light-headed as I make my way back home. It is as though I am walking on air. All my apprehensions about whether or not I should learn salsa and whether I would enjoy it have vanished. I know that I *badly* want to learn it.

There is only one problem.

I do not know how to break it to Sandeep.

Twelve

VIBHA CALLS ME UP THE NEXT MORNING BUT Sandeep is still at home. Whenever Sandeep is around I know better than to talk on the phone. Talking on the phone without any specific reason is another of his peeves, topping the list of activities he considers a waste of time. I have never heard Sandeep talk on the phone for more than what is absolutely necessary.

In the early years of marriage, it had surprised me.

'Don't you have friends you want to chat with?' I had asked

'Chat? We are not in college anymore. I have work to do,' he had said and dismissed it.

Sandeep disapproved of smoking, drinking, western clothes, pubs, socialising—in other words any of the activities that most normal young people would enjoy and find relaxing.

He played golf on weekends in the morning and the evenings were always spent at his mother's. He liked routine and hated any kind of change. I had, in the initial years, tried suggesting that we could perhaps go to a movie or eat out, both of which I loved to do.

'The noise in the cinema hall gives me a headache

and do you know how unhygienic the food at most restaurants is?' he had asked.

I was so taken aback that I had nothing to say. How can a person *not* enjoy movies and eating out?! Soon after, I had got pregnant with Abhay and then there had been no question of going to the movies or eating out anyway. Sandeep's mother had narrated in great detail about a friend's daughter who had eaten out during pregnancy and contracted jaundice, as a result of which the baby that she was carrying had been affected and was now mentally challenged. She had mentioned it so many times till I finally assured her that I had no intentions of eating food from outside.

'Who called?' asks Sandeep as he waits for his breakfast.

I hurry to serve him dosas and chutney as he does not like waiting and gets annoyed if I take too long. His manner reminds me of a feudal lord's and most times I feel like a chambermaid scurrying around as I wait upon him. I wonder if this has ever occurred to him. It has crossed my mind many times, but now I kind of accept it in the name of 'adjustments married people make'. After all, it is not like he does it deliberately, I try and justify to myself, suppressing anything else that I feel.

'Vibha,' I reply, answering his question.

'And what did she want?' he asks in a demanding tone as though to say 'what-the-hell-does-she-want-now-don't tell-me-you-are going-away-to be-with-her-again.'

I find his question gratingly annoying. I control my irritation and say, 'Nothing. She doesn't want anything.'

'Why did she call then? What are you hiding from me? What is so private that you cannot talk in front of me?' he asks

His words sting and smart. He *is* insensitive, my husband, the father of my child. No matter how many excuses I make for him, this is the stark truth and it is staring me in the face now.

'Nothing. I am not hiding anything from you. She just wants to talk,' I answer.

'Hmph, *talking* never got anyone anywhere. You have to *take action*, not talk,' he says.

That is precisely the reason I am taking a salsa class. See, I am taking action. And not talking about it.

'Will you have another dosa?' I ask, hoping to distract him, and it works.

Some days, I really hate Sandeep. Actually, of late, I hate him most days. Being with him increasingly seems like a huge burden. His boorishness, insensitivity and lack of interest in what really matters to me have only increased over the years. I have kept putting up with it, pretending it does not exist and forgiving him (after all I have my faults too), but these days it is becoming harder.

As soon as he leaves, I call up Vibha. She asks me to log in to the computer so that we can video-chat. It is new to me and though I know the option exists, I have never video-chatted before. It takes only a few minutes to set up. She guides me through the process and when I finally see her face on the screen, I feel like reaching out and hugging her. She has obviously been crying. She is all teary-eyed. Her eyes are red and swollen. I hate to see Vibha like this. She tells me how hard it is to cope with everything and she sobs.

I listen to her patiently. She talks about Mohan and how much she misses him. She talks about how much she regrets not spending time with him. Even though she is repeating herself (she has mentioned this to me so many times before), I do not interrupt her, knowing instinctively that all she wants is to get it out off her chest.

Sure enough, she calms down after she has vented and wipes her tears.

'So sorry, Diksha. I did not mean to cry. Thank you for listening to me patiently,' she says.

'Hey it's fine, Vibha. You don't have to thank me. I know you are always there for me and, trust me, this is the least I can do.'

'You have done so much already. Anyway, that is enough talk about me. You tell me about yourself,' she says.

I have actually been really dying to tell her all about my salsa demo class but had controlled myself, knowing she needed to talk and not sure if it was the right time to tell her.

Now that she has asked, I say, 'You'll never guess what happened, Vibha. I am so happy about it.'

'What is it? Say! Is it something in Abhay's school? Has he won something?'

'No. This is about me. I went for a salsa class!'

'What?! Oh my God! Wow! So my words do have an impact on you. This is great, Diksha. Now tell me all the details,' she says eager to listen.

I tell her about how I called them up on a whim and how I attended the demo class. I tell her about Gaurav and Lorainne and the others in the class. I tell her how eager and excited I am. I tell her how good I felt dressing up in clothes that made me look smarter and younger. I also tell her that I have not told Sandeep about it yet.

'Hmmm. I really don't think you should mention any of this to Sandeep,' says Vibha finally.

'How can I not, Vibha? He is bound to find out at some point, right?'

'Not if we are careful. Your class timings are in any case while he is at work.'

'Yes, but how can I hide such a big thing from him?'

'You should learn to. Don't tell him. If you do, he might forbid you from going. You know how he is. When you know his nature, why do you want to risk it? Besides he does not have to know everything.'

Vibha definitely has a point. If I tell Sandeep about it, there is no saying what his reaction will be. It is easier to just not tell him a thing. But there is a small problem. The fees (which amount to nearly a thousand rupees per session) have to be paid in advance. It isn't really a small sum. Sandeep would definitely come to know if I withdraw this amount from the bank.

'I too don't want to risk it. But the thing is, I will anyway have to withdraw money for the fees. How can I justify such a huge amount as household expense? And you know how he tracks every penny.'

'Sweetheart, what am I here for? I will pay your salsa fees. Just get the bank details of the institute and I will transfer the money immediately. It is really not a problem for me, Diksha and, to be honest, I have earned so much, it really isn't that a big a sum either. Just consider this a gift from me.'

For a few seconds I am unable to speak. My eyes have filled with tears at the sweetness of Vibha's gesture. I really do not know what to say and so I am quiet.

'Are you going to say something or are you just going to sit there?' says Vibha, trying to make me feel less emotional and overwhelmed.

'But how can I take it just like that, Vibha?'

'Why can't you? Come on, Diksha, don't keep track like that. Didn't you help me when I needed you most?'

'Yes but...'

'No buts. Just allow me. I will feel so happy to do it for you. Now get the bank account details. And, hey, tell me what you wore to the class.'

We spend the next ten minutes, chatting about clothes. We talk about how our style of dressing changes after we get married, but how essentially we are the same people.

'Suddenly your in-laws and spouse dictate what you can wear and what you can't wear and you are expected to conform. It's just not right,' I say.

'But, darling, you conformed didn't you? Why didn't you speak up? Why did you set the pattern? See, I wear what I like. And, honestly, I do think it is every woman's right to dress up in the clothes she likes. Not the clothes that her husband or in-laws think are appropriate for her.'

'Vibha, you know how my situation was. I was not even twenty when I got married. And then I got pregnant soon after. Where did I have the time or inclination to think about clothes? And after Abhay was born, I just fell into a pattern. It was different for you.'

'Yeah, babes, that is right. I am sorry. It's just that sometimes I feel you have been given no freedom, no choice to live your own life. It really feels you are dancing to everyone's tunes but you have forgotten to listen to the music in your own heart. I feel for you and I deeply care.'

'I know that and I appreciate it. Am glad I have you Vibha,' I reply and I mean it.

Vibha says that I need to go shopping for new clothes.

'You can't possibly go to salsa class wearing your salwars. Well, technically you can, but we don't want you to, do we?'

'No, of course not. What will Gaurav think?' I say and smile.

'Click a pic of this guy. I want to see how he looks. Is he really that good-looking?'

'He looks like a model, Vibha. Ooooh, he is gorgeous. All the girls he teaches must be falling for him. What a guy! And he talks so well, too.'

'Look at your face already lighting up at the mention of Gaurav. I wonder if you are learning salsa just because of him?' teases Vibha.

'Yeah, yeah. The only reason I want to learn salsa is so that I can eventually have sex with him,' I retort back.

'Bet he will be better than Sandeep in bed. But no extramarital affairs, okay. Behave and control your urges,' says Vibha and smiles.

'Shut up! What outrageous things you say!' I exclaim.

But I am happy to see Vibha finally smiling after so many days, perhaps the first time after Mohan's death. I realise then that, for her, the involvement in my life is also partly an escape mechanism to help her cope with the tremendous shock-card that life has dealt her. I am glad that I am there for her, cushioning her blows, making it a little bit easier for her.

I text Guarav as soon as I finish the call with Vibha.

> **'Kindly let me know the amount to be transferred for the salsa beginners' course along with bank account details. Diksha'**

When there is no reply even after ten minutes, I decide to go shopping for new clothes like Vibha suggested. I hurry the house-help and urge her to finish fast.

Shopping for clothes that I really like, is something I haven't done in a very long time. Most of my shopping sprees are restricted to twice a year, once invariably on Diwali, and once on the eve of *Gokulashtami* when Sandeep's mother has a special pooja and insists on giving me money to buy new clothes. She is not a very traditional mother-in-law, and this is one of the very few rituals she follows. Of course, I don't mind obliging. On both these occasions, I have naturally shopped only for ethnic clothes. I have not even considered buying westerns. The prospect of actually shopping for some excites me a great deal.

I take an auto rickshaw to one of Bangalore's posh malls on Residency Road. Victoria Hotel, which was established in 1845, used to stand here. Sir Winston Churchill, it is said, used to read his morning newspaper here. It was a beautiful ancient structure surrounded by green gardens and the setting definitely transported one back to the Raj. Architecturally I had admired it many a time. I had been saddened to see it pulled down. Each time I used to pass it, and see the new building being constructed, I would wince and lament that it marked the end of an era. In its place now stands this gleaming shining mass of glass and concrete which is where I am headed to shop. Funnily enough, today I don't even care about Victoria Hotel. It feels liberating to be going out on my own, shopping for clothes of my choice.

About two hours later, I am armed with a new wardrobe of very smart clothes (two well-fitting pairs of jeans, one T-shirt, two fitted tops, a smart knee-length skirt and a capri). Over the years I have squirrelled away a tidy sum of money in a little box in my wardrobe. It is the leftover of the money that Sandeep doles out from time to time for household expenditure and also from the money his mother gives me each year to buy clothes. I have no idea why I did it, but I am suddenly glad that I did. It has come in handy now and I still have almost half of my stash left.

I am elated with my shopping spree and my purchases. I have been so engrossed that it is with a jolt I realise that it is nearly two fifteen pm. I haven't even thought of lunch. My stomach begins to rumble now and I decide to grab a quick bite at an eatery near the mall, as well as get something packed for Abhay who will be reaching home in an hour. There is no time to cook now.

As I am busy choosing which sandwich to eat, I feel a tap on my shoulder.

'Hey Diksha, what a pleasant surprise,' says a deep masculine voice. 'Come, join me for lunch. I am eating over there. I recognised you from the back and came to say hello,' it drawls.

I turn around and my heart starts skipping madly. It is Gaurav.

Thirteen

SEEING GAURAV HERE IS SO UNANTICIPATED THAT I stare at him for a few seconds before I am able to speak.

'Oh. Hi,' I say. 'I didn't expect you here.'

'Ha ha. Is there any rule on places that salsa instructors are not permitted to go to?' his eyes twinkle.

'No, No, I did not mean it that way, I meant…'

'Just kidding. Come, let's sit down and chat and let me get you a drink. Iced mint tea?' he interrupts me before I can blabber further.

I nod and he wastes no time in getting the drink. I follow him and, pulling up a wrought-iron chair, sit facing him. This is indeed a nice place with a lot of plants and a casual 'let's-chat-over-coffee' ambience. I had never noticed it before. But now I do. I can also see that he must have been just about to begin his lunch when he spotted me and came over. He offers his fries but I refuse and thank him.

'Don't tell me you are on a diet,' he says

'I am not, but as a rule I eat healthy,' I reply.

'Me too, but hey, sometimes you break rules too. It is fun.'

'Of course, it is. It is forbidden which is why it's fun,' I smile.

'So, have you broken any rules?' he asks as he sips his iced tea, and gazes straight into my eyes.

His eyes are brown and he is so darn attractive that I find it hard to concentrate on what he is saying. I wonder if he knows the effect he is having on me. I force myself to snap out of the dreamlike state I seem to be entering.

Stop it Diksha and tell him you have a son who will be home soon, that in your other life you are a conventional housewife, that today is an aberration, for you normally don't shop at malls and have lunches with men you have just met.

'Hell yes. And I have got into a lot of trouble too,' I reply and am stunned at my glib reply. Why in the world am I talking like this with Gaurav?

'Oh wow! What kind of trouble? I love to hear stories,' he says with a wink. He stares into my eyes and takes a sip of his tea.

I am unable to meet his gaze.

'It's not what you think,' I mutter nervously. 'It is nothing really, and it was a long time ago,' I plod on, a bit horrified now that I have said more than I intended to. I shut up and look down into my drink.

'I would love to know, nonetheless. Do tell. From the moment you walked into class that day, I knew there was something about you. And, hey, I must say, you look gorgeous in Indian clothes too,' he says.

I blush furiously. This is truly one of the dowdiest salwars I possess. I feel stupid to blush in his presence. After all, I am a married woman and a mother at that. He must be chatting up girls far more attractive than me every other day.

'Thank you. Someday I will. But I have to rush today. I have to be home by three thirty,' I reply.

'Why? What happens if you are late? Will your coach turn into a pumpkin?' he asks in an amused tone.

'No, my son will have to wait outside the house till I return. He comes from school at three thirty,' I reply.

His jaw drops.

I smile at the effect of my words.

'Oh! You are a mother?! You don't even look married,' he says.

I laugh heartily. 'Thank you! I don't hear that often, but it is good to know,' I say.

Which is the truth. I have never even thought of whether or not I look like a mother till I joined the salsa class.

'Really? I would have thought you hear it all the time. Meet me here for lunch tomorrow? I really want to get to know you. You are fascinating,' he says.

I am stunned by his directness. He is a fast operator. I am unable to think of an excuse quick enough and, before I realise what is happening, I have agreed to meet him at the same place for lunch. He says he eats here often as it is just walking distance from the dance studio. Come to think of it, it actually is, when one takes the back road.

'How have you come? Do you have a car?' he asks

'No, I took an auto. Don't worry. I live close by. I will get plenty that will take me home.'

Gaurav insists on dropping me but I refuse. I tell him that I will manage just fine. Coming on a secret shopping spree is bad enough, if someone sees me with a drop-dead gorgeous guy like Gaurav, it will definitely cause a stir in my quiet neighbourhood. Of course, I do not explain all this to him. He insists on seeing me off till the auto-stand.

'So, we'll meet here tomorrow then? Same time?' he asks as I get into the auto.

'Yeah, see you,' I say with a bravado that I am not feeling.

As I make my way home, I wonder why in the world

did I agree to meet him tomorrow. Why in the world didn't I just refuse? What was I thinking?

Actually I wasn't thinking at all, and that is how I, a much married mother of a child, is going on a date with a great-looking salsa instructor who says he finds me fascinating and wants to know all about me. I can't stop smiling all the way home and I can't wait to tell Vibha.

I do not get a chance till late at night as Abhay reaches just seconds after I enter the house. I rush to hide my new purchases at the bottom shelf of my cupboard and greet him as usual.

Abhay gives a whoop of delight and a bear hug when he sees the burger I've got for him. It is so easy to please a nine-year-old. My evening flies as I supervise Abhay's studies. He has a geography test the next day and also has to make a collage of famous English authors for his English class.

Abhay has already read Charles Dickens, Oscar Wilde, R L Stevenson and Mark Twain. I search for their photos on the Internet and print them out. He looks up information about them and condenses it. Then, very neatly, he writes out their life histories next to their pictures. He is such a clever boy, my son. He winds up making a very professional-looking chart full of fascinating details. Abhay loves doing this kind of work and thoroughly enjoys this particular assignment. Most children his age would groan at such a task but he revels in it.

Sandeep does not even notice me as I take his briefcase and give him his customary cup of tea. But, for the first time in ages, I am actually glad about his indifference. Abhay brings his chart proudly and shows it to Sandeep and even Sandeep cannot help but admire Abhay's handiwork.

'Well done, son. But see these lines here, they should

have been written a bit straight. They are a little crooked,' he says.

I squirm as I see Abhay's face fall. I clench my fists under the garden table. I really feel like slapping Sandeep. Can't he be a bit more forthcoming with praise and go easy on the criticism?

'Come on, Sandeep, He is only nine. I think it is a wonderful effort for his age,' I defend Abhay.

'Age is no excuse, Vibha. What's true is true,' Sandeep pronounces sanctimoniously.

I feel like emptying my tea on his head. But instead grit my teeth in silence.

Then I ask Abhay to pack up the chart carefully and to prepare his school bag for the next day.

'I might have to travel to Korea,' announces Sandeep after Abhay leaves.'The project I am handling seems to be gathering momentum,' he says.

'Oh. When are you going and for how long?' I ask.

'Nothing is fixed yet. It is all very fluid right now.'

'And for how many days will you be gone?'

'Don't know yet. It will be for a week initially. But I might have to go back there often. I am spearheading this whole thing. The senior management doesn't want to take any chance, you see,' he says and I can almost see his chest puffing up with pride.

I am not really interested in his work. I have tried to understand it in the past but, truth is, Sandeep discloses very little. Once he gets back from work, all he wants to do is have his tea, his meal and plonk himself in front of the television till he is ready to drop off. I know better than to interrupt his TV time.

I can't wait for Sandeep to go to bed, so that I can tell Vibha all about my shopping expedition and this 'date' with Gaurav. I do not want to say anything in front of him.

I wait till Sandeep's breathing is even and I wait till he begins to snore. Then I take out my phone and text Vibha:

'Can't talk. Can you come online?'

'Twenty minutes, babe. Monu very restless today. Just not sleeping,' she texts back.

'Okay. I'm online. Ping me when you come online,' I reply as I slowly sneak into the guest bedroom where the computer is kept.

When I log in, I automatically check my emails first. I usually get nothing interesting apart from newsletters from an art forum I had joined a long back. Mostly I get mails from our residents' welfare association regarding various issues. I also get forwards sent by the mothers I meet at the bus stop. I read them all and chuckle at a few. But today, one mail takes me by utter and total surprise.

Diksha!!

Is it really you? Where have you been, girl? I couldn't believe it when I found your name in Blast from the Past. Have you changed your surname after marriage?

It's been eighteen years since we last spoke. Eighteen whole years! What the fuck happened to time?!

I live in Gurgaon now, but am moving to Bangalore soon. Yeah! To your city ☺

Give me your contact details the moment you read this mail.

You will never believe who I managed to track down!

Call now!

Tanu

I cannot believe that it is actually Tanu. Tanu whom I last saw when my parents unceremoniously pulled me out of school and sent me to Kerala to stay with my grandmother and aunt.

I can see from the mail that she now works with an investment bank and is Group Vice President. I have no idea what that means, but the logo of the bank, her designation, the address with her phone and fax numbers, as well as the website, intimidate as well as impress me.

I cannot believe this is 'my Tanu'.

This is too much excitement to handle in one day. First, being asked on a lunch date by Gaurav and then, getting a mail from my closest friend with whom I have had no contact for eighteen long years! These events have suddenly dropped into my life like bitten hand-grenades waiting to explode.

If Tanu has managed to track down someone and is saying that I will never believe it, it has to be one person. Ankit.

The very mention of his name makes my heart beats go crazy. Oh my God. This truly cannot be happening. I glance at the clock and it is nearly eleven fifteen. It is definitely too late to call Tanu.

I want to text her immediately. I want to know who it is she has managed to track down. I want to know all about her—is she married, single. Divorced? Nah, she cannot be divorced, I think to myself. I wonder how she looks now. I am dying of curiosity and decide that I will risk calling her anyway.

Just as I pick up the phone, it buzzes and it is a text from Vibha.

'Online, babes. Log in,' it reads.

I log in immediately to the instant messenger and ping Vibha:

Me:	Hey! Too much happening. I so want to talk to you.
Vibha:	What? What happened? Do one thing. Go to your garden and let's talk on the phone.
Me:	At this time?
Vibha:	So what? Sandeep is asleep, isn't he?
Me:	Yeah. He is snoring away for Bharat Mata.
Vibha:	Ha, ha. Then what's the problem?
Me:	Okay. Going. Will call you.

I walk softly into the garden like a thief. It is the first time I have been outside my home this late in the night. I call Vibha and talk in whispers to her, afraid of waking up Sandeep. It terrifies me to think of what he will say if he finds me outside the house, sneaking calls to Vibha in the middle of the night.

I tell Vibha about Gaurav asking me out for lunch.

'Oh my God. What fun. Lucky girl. Go meet him!' she says.

'This is definitely cheating, Vibha. How can I meet him without telling Sandeep?'

'What cheating Diksha? Are you planning to sleep with him?'

'Shut up! Though I must admit the prospect is attractive,' I giggle in the darkness.

'Hey. Why do you even have this tiny little iota of guilt? Doesn't Sandeep go out on lunches with his female colleagues ever?'

'Yeah, he does. But that is work-related, right?'

'As though they talk about work *all* the time. Surely, they talk of something other than work? Stop feeling so guilty. You are finally doing what you want to do.'

'Yeah, but I am a married woman, Vibha.'

'So? Why are behaving like you live in the Taliban era. Can't married women meet men other than their husbands for lunch? Anyway you are hiding the fact that you are learning salsa. How then is hiding this any different?'

Vibha does have a point.

Then I tell her about Tanu's mail. Of course, Vibha remembers Tanu and every single detail of our friendship. Vibha had been my confidante and my main support system during the time I stayed with my grandmother in Kerala. It was Vibha's support alone that had seen me though those dark days.

And even when my parents had pressurised me into getting married, it was Vibha who had comforted and consoled me saying things weren't that bad, and anyway everyone gets married sooner or later. In my case, it just happened to be sooner, so how did it really matter? Vibha was my rock, my pillar of strength. She still is.

'Oh my god, Diksha. Do you think it is Ankit she could be talking about?' Vibha asks.

'I don't know,' I say.

But I am dying to find out.

Fourteen

The next morning, I am so cheerful that the women in the bus stop once again comment on it.

'Come on. Spill the beans. You really are up to something. What is your secret?' Jyoti bursts out as though she cannot hold back any longer. I noticed that she had been studying me from the moment she saw me approach.

'*Kuchch toh chakkar hai,*' adds Rachna. In my head I name her the '*chakkar* woman'.

'*Arre,* no *chaakar-vakkar*. Really, it's nothing. An old classmate of mine got in touch with me and I am happy. That's all,' I say.

'Ah-ha! Guy or girl?' asks the inquisitive *chakkar* woman.

'Girl. Best friend,' I reply.

'Oh,' she says clearly disappointed as though she was expecting to hear a juicy morsel of gossip and I have let her down badly.

'I saw you coming home in a rick yesterday. I was on my balcony sipping tea. Is there a sale going on? You had shopped right?' she prods on.

Both Rachna and Jyoti live in the apartment

complex overlooking our home. I am suddenly very glad that I refused Gaurav's offer of dropping me home. Rachna would surely have wanted to know who he was and how I knew him and why I was getting dropped by him.

The school bus arrives and I am saved from answering her questions.

When I reach home, I find Sandeep standing at the door, instead of in his usual spot in the garden.

'My mother has had a fall. Hurry. We have to rush there,' he says.

'Oh no. How?' I ask

'I don't know. The neighbour called. She slipped in the bathroom. Just hurry and get into the car,' he says.

Once in the car, Sandeep says, 'This is why I don't want her living alone. See what has happened. Why can't she live with us?'

'You know how fiercely independent she is, Sandeep. Besides, even if she lived with us, she could still have had the fall. That has nothing to do with her living alone, right? She does have good neighbours and friends there,' I point out.

His mother has lived in the apartment for several years, first with her husband and now on her own. She has an active social network, is comfortable and happy. She does not want to live in a large home and even though Sandeep has insisted time and again that she move in with us, especially after his father passed away, she has steadfastly refused.

In my heart of hearts, I completely empathize with Sandeep's mother. I too prefer living in an apartment, and not this bungalow. But then I do so enjoy the little garden we have here, an impossibility in an apartment. I really am a bundle of contradictions.

'Yes, it's a good thing she has friends there to help,' Sandeep says, breaking my reverie.

When we reach her place, we find her in great pain. She is unable to walk. She has fallen on her left side and there is a large angry bump on her forehead. She is holding an ice-pack to it with her right hand. She is unable to move her left arm.

Sandeep and I help her into the car with great difficulty and rush her to the emergency section of Manipal Hospital, one of the best in Bangalore. She is immediately attended to and the doctor advises us to admit her for a day. He wants to keep her under observation, as well as conduct a few tests and X-rays to rule out the possibilities of a fracture or any other problem. Since she has fallen on her head, the doctor wants to monitor her in case of an internal concussion. We have no choice but to agree. Sandeep books a private room for her.

'I have this really important meeting today. The head of the team from Korea is arriving. Damn. What rotten timing.' Sandeep is agitated.

I assure him that I will manage and, besides, there is no point in two people hanging around. Sandeep gratefully accepts.

I wonder how he can even think of his office at a time like this. I feel sorry for my mother-in-law. She is very quiet and looks almost frightened, so different from her usual chirpy self.

'Ma, I have to go. Diksha will be here to look after you,' says Sandeep.

She does not talk and waves him away with her hand. He leaves quickly without so much as a backward glance, as though relieved to get away.

My mother-in-law is silent for a while. Then she looks at me and breaks down.

I run to her side and hold her hand, wiping away her tears with a tissue.

'Don't worry, Ma. Everything's going to be fine,' I console her with the usual cliché.

Strangely enough, it comforts her.

'It is just that at my age, Diksha,' she whispers, 'and at times like this, you miss your partner the most. I understand Sandeep is busy. But still, he didn't even wait for the report. It is like he has shoved me in here and pushed off,' she says.

'Ma, it's not like that. He knows I am here. He knows I will take care of you. You know how he is,' I say, trying to comfort her even though the very same thought just crossed my mind. She has just spoken my thought out loud.

'Yes, I do know him,' she says wearily. 'Sadly, my son is a selfish idiot. I erred in raising him,' bitterness creeps into her tone.

I do not know what to say to that.

The nurse comes in and tells me that the patient has to be changed into a hospital gown. She requests me to attend to the many formalities that have to be completed at the hospital. I gently ask my mother-in-law if she will be okay alone while I go. She nods, saying she will be fine. The nurse tells her that she only need ring the bell by her headside and someone will immediately attend to her.

I complete the formalities in about forty-five minutes and, when I come back, I find my mother-in-law fast asleep. In the hospital attire, she appears frail and vulnerable. My heart goes out to her, even though I know hers is not a life-threatening injury and she will soon be fine.

It is only then that I remember 'my date' with Gaurav.

The day's events have completely overwhelmed me. It is already two in the afternoon.

I dial his number and he picks up on the first ring itself.

'Hey there. I am already here. Where are you?' he asks.

'I am so sorry, Gaurav. I won't be able to make it. My mother-in-law is in the hospital and I am with her,' I reply.

'Oh,' he says and I know that he is thinking I stood him up and am making an excuse now.

'She is likely to be discharged today itself or maybe tomorrow. I can meet you another day perhaps?' I ask, wanting to make it up to him. I feel bad ditching him like this today.

'Okay, fine. How about Friday, after class?' he asks

'Done deal. I will meet you on Friday afternoon then. Bye, Gaurav,' I say, as I hang up.

When I turn around, I freeze. I realise that my mother-in-law is awake and has heard every word.

I do not know what to say.

She smiles feebly and says, 'It is okay. Don't worry. I will not tell Sandeep.'

I am stunned at her astuteness and how fast she has grasped the situation. I cannot believe she is actually supporting me and is on my side.

'Ma, actually it's nothing like that. It is not what you think. I... er... I am taking these classes and Gaurav is my instructor,' I mumble.

'What classes, Diksha?' she asks.

The last thing I want is for her to presume that I am having an affair with Gaurav. It must have sounded like that from the phone call. So I pull up the chair and sit next to her. Then I tell her about all that happened in Vibha's house. About how trapped I have been feeling. I tell her about how Sandeep behaves when he is at home. I speak about how we have no conversation and how all he does when he comes back from work is watch television. I tell her I am really single-handedly parenting Abhay. I unload all that is on my chest. I also tell her about Sandeep's insensitivity in most matters. I open my heart and pour out everything. However I leave out the part about my secret wish list. I am not ready to share that with her. At least not yet. She listens patiently and understands exactly what I am saying.

'You know, I felt much the same way. I too got married to Sandeep's father, way too early. I have never ever lived my life or done things for myself. But that was okay for women of that generation. Certainly not of your generation,' she says.

It feels strange to be opening up to my mother-in-law like this. While we have always had a cordial relationship, we have never talked this way before. We now speak like long-lost friends.

This is the first time that I am seeing her as Mrs Subadhra Pandit, the person, and not just as my mother-in-law.

'I always felt you were too young to get married, Diksha. You were just nineteen. If you remember, when we first met you, I had suggested to your parents that we wait till you were twenty-one at least. We were more than ready for a long engagement. But your parents insisted so much on an early marriage, that we had no option but to comply,' she says.

I simply nod.

How can I tell her that my parents just wanted me to get married at any cost? How can I tell her how petrified my father was that Sandeep's family would call off the marriage if they came to know about my incident with Ankit. How can I tell her that I was only sixteen at that time and it was just a kiss, yet my parents acted like I got pregnant and brought shame on the family. I haven't forgiven them till date for that. How can I tell her how oppressed and sad I felt in that all-women's college that they put me into and how I longed to get out of it? How can I explain that my parents had demoralised me so much by their words that I was willing to do *anything* they wanted in order to win back their trust, which was why I had agreed to this marriage. I had no idea really what marriage meant when I had said a yes to please my parents. If my parents had asked me to walk on hot coals in order to win back their trust, I would gladly have.

But they hadn't. All they wanted for me was to get married. Most girls in my community got married before they were twenty-two anyway. If a girl was twenty-four or twenty-five, and still unmarried, she would be talked and gossiped about and all the aunties and other relatives would frantically start the matchmaking process. As far as my parents were concerned, Sandeep was a good guy, and he had excellent educational qualifications (he had done his Law and Company Secretaryship) and earned good money. Most importantly, he had 'liked' me and said a yes. As far as my parents were concerned, that was all that mattered.

How could I possibly explain all this to my mother-in-law who is so earnestly telling me I married early?

So I simply say, 'Anyway whether at nineteen or twenty-one, I would eventually have had to get married and that too the arranged marriage way. I did not mind really.'

She smiles and squeezes my hand.

'You're a good girl, Diksha. You are too good for my son really. Go learn your salsa. Don't be afraid of him. I will speak to him about it and make him understand,' she says.

'Oh no, Ma, please do not do that. I really don't want

any complications. I don't think he will understand,' I quickly reply in panic. I really do not want Sandeep to know. I am secretly terrified that he will create a huge fuss and there is no telling how he will react.

'Okay. It is our secret then,' she says and chuckles. I am happy to see her in good spirits.

I glance at the time and tell her that I will have to leave her and pick up Abhay as he would be arriving home soon. She assures me that she will be fine.

I call up Sandeep to tell him that I am leaving the hospital to pick up Abhay.

'What is it, Diksha? Can't you manage? Didn't I tell you this was important? Why are you calling?' he hisses on the phone angrily, his voice a few decibels higher that what it usually is.

I am taken aback by it. I have called him only very rarely on the phone. I never disturb him at work usually. It is *his* mother in the hospital for God's sake. The least he can do is be polite. I don't expect a thanks, but his curt attitude and tone feels like a hard slap on my face.

I really do not know what to say. While I am quite used to his insensitive nature and selfish attitude, this one really takes the cake.

'Sorry,' I mutter and hang up. I do not even have the guts to talk back to him or tell him off. I feel very small. And very hurt.

Then I hail an auto and head towards home to pick up Abhay.

I remember Tanu's mail on my way home. I so badly want to call up Tanu, but there is really no time as I have to rush back to the hospital, taking Abhay along with me.

When I reach the hospital, I discover that the reports have all arrived and everything is clear. There are no broken bones or hairline fractures which, I'm told, are common for people her age in case of a fall. There is only a twisted ankle. Dr Hooja who is attending to her says that she can be discharged and advise her to take it easy and rest for a few days.

I do not even want to call up Sandeep to tell him that his mother is being discharged. I pay up all the hospital bills, using the add-on credit card. It is a large amount. Ha! He can account for this whopping expense in his account book that he maintains. I feel a sadistic sense of satisfaction at this thought.

I then book a cab and one of the hospital attendants who has just finished his duty, accompanies Abhay and me in the cab to take my mother-in-law home. She has agreed to live with us for a few days till she is able to manage on her own.

'I am so happy you will be staying with us, Aayi,' says Abhay as he hugs her. She smiles back.

'Me too,' I add and I mean it.

Sandeep calls on my cell phone at around eight pm, when I am in the middle of serving dinner to my mother-in-law and Abhay.

'I got late as I couldn't possibly leave office before the Korean team left. So what is the scene? Shall I come to the hospital?' he asks.

'We are at home. She is with us,' I reply, trying to keep the anger and accusations out of my voice.

'Oh,' he says. Then a moment later adds, 'How did you get her home? Why didn't you call me?'

'Because you said you had important stuff at work,' I grit my teeth and answer. I think that if there is a Nobel Prize awarded for tolerance of extreme selfishness in a spouse, I would win it.

Later when everyone has slept, I log in to the computer and quickly draft a reply to Tanu.

'Hey Tanu!!

It is really me. How AWESOME to hear from you. I wanted to call you last night itself, as soon as I saw your mail, but it was too late. And then I wanted to call you the first thing this morning, but a lot has been happening.

I am married and have been married now for fifteen years. Can you believe? And I am a mother too. Yeah—don't be shocked, my son is now nine.

Sandeep works in an MNC and we stay on Artillery Road in Bangalore.

I am so excited that you are moving here! This is a real bolt from the blue, Tanu, albeit a pleasant one.

And, Oh my God, you have become a total career woman!

Are you married?

I am dying to catch up. Eighteen years is a lifetime really! Cannot believe it is that long since we connected.

I will call you first thing tomorrow.

Loads of love,

Diksha

Fifteen

SANDEEP SEEMS TO BE GROWING MORE IRRITABLE and grouchy by the minute. When I hand him his morning coffee in bed, he snaps at me saying that it is not warm enough. He seems preoccupied and generally pissed off about something. I run around, fixing breakfast, cooking and packing Abhay's and Sandeep's lunch, and seeing to it that Abhay gets to school on time, as well as checking on my mother-in-law. Sandeep exchanges a perfunctory greeting with his mother, before he disappears behind *The Economic Times*, in his usual place in the garden.

My mother-in-law quietly observes everything and, once or twice, I catch her giving me sympathetic glances, but I look away.

As soon as Sandeep leaves, she says,'It is obnoxious, his behaviour, Diksha. He is my son and all that, but I can see what's happening with a detached eye. He does absolutely nothing to help you around the house. You should talk to him about it.'

'Do you think I haven't tried, Ma? Sandeep's view is that if I need more help with housework, I can employ an additional maid. He just doesn't get it,' I reply. 'I have more or less resigned to it, really. If I bring it up, he will shred me to bits with his words and I prefer to keep peace at any cost.

'I really don't know how he turned out like this. You know, Sandeep's father was so different from him. He used to help me with everything. He was such a good man,' she says, her eyes misting at the memory.

I have only heard stories about my father-in-law. I never met him as he had passed away a few years before I married Sandeep. My mother-in-law reminisces about him and I listen to her patiently, even though all I want to do is rush to my room and call up Tanu. I really want to catch up with her.

Finally, when my mother-in-law retires to her room for a nap, I rush to my bedroom and switch on my computer. I open Tanu's mail and smile once again as I read it.

Then I dial her number. My heart is beating so fast that I am unable to focus on anything other than the ringtone, a peppy modern song that I hear often on the radio, perhaps a Katie Perry number.

She answers after a few seconds with a business-like, 'Yes?' not even a hello.

'Hey! Tanu?' I almost scream.

'OH MY GOD. Is it really, you Diksha?' The excitement and joy in her voice is clearly evident and I smile broadly.

Something really amazing happens when old friends, who you have known since childhood, come back into your life.

'You bitch, you fool, you stupid woman, you donkey!' yells Tanu into the phone.'Where the fuck did you disappear after school? Do you know how many letters I wrote you?' she demands.

It is as though we left school just yesterday and all that happened in between has melted. I am astonished by the closeness and warmth I feel towards Tanu, and by the fact that she still addresses me like she used to in school, with the easy familiarity of a deep friendship, unaffected by anything—a gap of eighteen years, a marriage, motherhood and everything else.

I am too stunned to speak. In those few seconds, everything that happened after my parents pulled me out of school, till the time I got married, flash before my eyes. I abhorred that part of my life. I didn't receive a single letter from Tanu. Perhaps my grandmother and Meera Mausi had been instructed by my parents to cut me off from all my friends. I do not know. I had often wondered why I never heard from her. Back then, I was too broken, too frightened and too supervised to try and contact either Tanu or Ankit.

Now with Tanu suddenly back in my life, demanding to know why I dropped out of hers, is forcing me, rather, transporting me back to a time and place I'd rather not revisit. I am shaking and need to sit on the bed. I am so overwhelmed with emotions that there is a tightness in my throat which is making it difficult for me to speak.

'Hello? Are you there?' asks Tanu.

'Yeah, Tanu. I will tell you everything in detail, but only when we meet. You say—what are you doing now? Where are you and when are you moving to Bangalore? How did you find me?' I ask.

'Hmmm, okay. I get by. I work with Barclays. I am now moving to take over the Bangalore operations. My career is really rocking and I love my work. I am single and live on my own. And we should meet soon,' she says.

I truly envy her at that moment. She has lived her life, made something out of it, unlike me who has got married and done nothing except produce a child. I feel worthless, like I have wasted my life. I have never had a job, never worked. And Tanu, who is exactly my age has a name for herself, is financially independent and will now head the Bangalore operations.

'Wow! You have made it, Tanu. I am so proud of you,' I finally say. I mean it with all my heart. Even though my admiration for my friend is a hundred per cent genuine, it is still laced with a tinge of regret for my wasted life.

'Listen. I arrive this weekend. I am selling off all my stuff there and buying everything from a scratch in Bangalore. You know all the furniture shops there, right?'

'Yeah, I can help you with that. Come and stay with me, Tanu. We have such a lot to catch up on,' I offer.

'I appreciate your offer, Diksha, but I have never met your husband. My company has booked me at Oberoi and it is close to work too. I can stay there till I find a home. Let's meet there. We have so much to catch up on and, while your husband may be a sweet guy and all that, I don't think we can really talk if your family is around, isn't it?'

My husband is not a sweet guy and is an insensitive jerk and I am too cowardly to stand up to him.

'Yes, you do have a point, I guess. But if you change your mind or if you need anything, feel free to treat my home as your own.'

'As though you need to tell me that!'

'And who did you manage to track down?' I ask, dying to know and unable to hold back the question anymore.

'Who do you think, Diksha?' She asks in a tone which is different from her usual excited pitch.

I hesitate to ask. I dread hearing it. It is like my worst fears are going to come true.

'Don't tell me,' I say, almost holding my breath. I want to hear it, yet I don't want to. I want to know it, yet I do not want to. It is the strangest thing I have ever felt.

'Ankit' she says.

I could have sworn I felt my heart stop.

'Fuck,' I say.

And it is the first time in eighteen years that I have sworn.

'So where is he and what does he do?' I finally ask.

'Will tell you all in good time. Meet me on Saturday for lunch?' she asks.

'Hmm, sure, let me confirm to you later. A meeting will be possible, but I think lunch may not be,' I say.

How can I explain to her that after marriage, I have never gone out with my women friends, leaving my husband and child at home. It would probably sound archaic to her. How can I explain to her that I still take Sandeep's 'permission' to travel anywhere? Even to my own years, it sounds like an eighteenth-century tradition. Yet that is how it has been for me. I wonder how marriage has changed me such a lot.

As soon as Tanu hangs up, I get a call from Vibha.

'So my lady, how did your secret date with the salsa man go? And why didn't you call me yesterday? I waited and waited. Don't tell me you got so carried away that you forgot all about me,' she says.

'Hey! Give me a chance to speak at least, before you go on like a bullet train!' I exclaim.

I tell her about my mother-in-law's fall. I tell her how Sandeep left for office, leaving me alone with her in the hospital. I tell her how she overheard me speaking to Gaurav and how I opened up to her.

'Oh my God, Diksha! You are really something!' she exclaims.

'Why?' I ask, a bit puzzled about her reaction. Is she praising me? Does she find it odd? Or does she appreciate the fact?

'Whoever heard of a daughter-in-law making friends with her mother-in-law!' she says.

'Come on, Vibha. How can you, of all the people, say that? Don't your in-laws live with you and help you look after Monu? Haven't they been supportive?'

'Yeah, but it isn't like I pour out my heart to my mom-in-law.'

'I agree, it may not be conventional, Vibha, but honestly, yesterday for the first time, I saw her as Mrs Pandit, the woman and not just my mother-in-law. And I can't tell you what a huge difference it has made to my perspective. She is really understanding, Vibha. In fact, she asked me to go ahead with my salsa. How many mothers-in law do you know who will actually say that?' I ask

'Yes, you are right of course. It is indeed a good thing you have bonded with her. So did you tell her about your wish list too?'

'I knew that was coming,' I smile. 'No, for the record, I haven't told her about the wish list. Happy?' I ask.

'I will be happy when all the items, except Number 6, are ticked off,' she replies.

The conversation with Tanu has reminded me, with startling intensity, of the person I used to be—a person with hopes, ambitions and a desire to live life to the brim. I was just like Tanu—bubbly, enthusiastic and positive.

I think about Ankit. I think about that kiss. I have replayed everything that happened on that day at least a million times in my mind through all these years. I loved him with all the purity and innocence of a sixteen-year-old heart. I was certain at that time that he loved me too. I wonder how he looks now. I wonder what I will feel if I were to ever meet him again.

It is ironic how the years change you and yet you remain the same. Even if you are married, become a parent, deep down you are still the person you were before you became all of that.

Later, as I cook the afternoon meal, Ankit dances around in my head. He refuses to go away when I serve my mother- in-law her meal and make inane conversation with her. He is still with me when I greet Abhay, back from school, and remains there when I help him with homework. And, later that night, when my husband, after his usual round of television viewing, comes to bed and squeezes my breasts and has sex with me, *he is still there*.

I lie awake a long time that night, the darkness of my bedroom punctuated by Sandeep's rhythmic post-coital snoring.

I realise with a jolt that Ankit had never really left. He has been in my head all along.

And now that the possibility of reconnecting with him has been presented to me on a platter, it makes me intensely restless. It is as though someone has poured a can of gasoline to the already blazing fire and turmoil within my heart.

Somewhere at the back of my mind, warning bells are clanging, but their sounds are very feeble, almost muffled. The voice of my heart is too loud.

When you cannot get someone out of your head for eighteen years, it has to be true love.

Sixteen

IT IS ALMOST AS IF I CANNOT WAIT FOR TANU TO arrive and for me to meet her. A part of me knows that it is also because I am eager to know about Ankit. But there is still a whole week left and all I can do is go about my daily tasks and duties like everything is the same as before. Inside my head, it feels like clouds are brewing for a thunderstorm of mammoth proportions. After all, this is the guy because of whom my life took a sharp ninety-degree turn. This is the guy I failed to resist.

Who knows what he has made of himself in these eighteen years. Perhaps he is balding, fat and potbellied? Perhaps he is married with a nagging wife and two children, or worse with a gorgeous, slim wife who looks like a model and has two wonderful children as well. Thoughts about Ankit are distracting me such a lot that I am unable to think of anything else. I just *have* to know.

So I call up Tanu again. But she cuts my call and a moment later I get a text which says, 'In a meeting. Will call back.' There is nothing I can do except wait and continue with my usual chores, pretending all is well, when in reality it feels as though there are a million questions inside me threatening to explode.

The only way I can distract myself is to focus on the salsa class which is this evening. That is when I remember that I have agreed to meet Gaurav after class today.

My mother-in-law is much better now. She says that by the end of the week she would like to shift back to her own apartment. She has a set of friends who have been calling her every single day to check on her. One couple, Mrs and Mr Prabhu even visited, bringing flowers and fruits. How lucky she is to have friends like that. I think that if I fell ill or injured myself, I would have nobody perhaps other than Vibha and now Tanu, who would bother to check on me or find out how I was.

At the bus stop that morning, with the children interacting with each other in the background, it seems as though Jyoti and Rachna seem to have made it their life's mission to tease and hound me.

'Today also you are glowing, Diksha! Do tell us the chakkar,' says Rachna, the chakkar woman.

'You guys just love teasing me!' I say with a smile.'Believe me, there is no chakkar. I have joined salsa and a have class this evening,' I say.

'Ooooh! Salsa! Where? At Dancing Shoes?' asks Jyoti.

'Yeah, how did you guess?' I ask

'That is the one closest, so it is only logical. Gaurav is an awesome teacher. My husband and I had done the basic course last summer. In fact, we have already signed up for the intermediate course which starts next month,' she says.

'Oh!' I reply.

I am surprised that all these days, ever since the academic year started, I have been meeting these two women at the bus stop and we have never talked about this before. Our conversations have mostly centred around movies and other inane stuff like school policies.

Neither Rachna nor Jyoti read, so I cannot discuss my love for books or what I am currently reading, with them. I get my books through an online library which delivers and collects books from home. Neither Jyoti nor Rachna are tech savvy and hardly go on the Internet, except for emails and so we always have a limited repertory of things to talk about. Therefore, I am pleasantly surprised to discover Jyoti's interest in salsa.

Jyoti says that Dancing Shoes is really good as it organises stage performances for its students, as well as gets them invited to salsa parties regularly. That is news to me. I had no idea they did all that. I make a mental note to check with Gaurav after class today.

My second salsa class goes off even better than the first. It is almost as if wearing those smart western clothes I bought on my last shopping spree, transforms me into a different person, much like Cinderella going to the ball. I feel happy and light-headed as I join my salsa-mates, Janie, Nitya, Gagan and others in the class. Lorraine is there along with the other instructors, but Gaurav is nowhere to be seen.

Gagan asks about him and Lorraine says that he will join us soon. My eyes keep looking for him even as I continue to do the steps that Lorraine and the other instructor demonstrate. This time, just like the last class, we have to dance with partners, using the simple steps that we have learnt. They get us to form a circle, with the women in the inner circle and the guys in the outer circle facing the women. The women and men have to face each other and mirror each other's movement. When the beat stops, the guys have to walk to the next partner and perform the same step with her.

'This way all the women in the room get to dance with all the guys and vice versa. That is the best way, else you will get too used to a single partner. The idea here is that you should be able to do the salsa with anyone,' explains Lorraine.

We start dancing and I can see that Gaurav's words have had an effect on the guys. Almost all of them, including Gagan, have made a special effort with their appearance today. His palms are thankfully no longer sweaty. We are shown how the guys have to grip the lady's hand and how the hold should not be too tight or too loose. We are also taught that the man should hold the woman under the shoulder blades gently without hurting her or feeling up her bra-strap. Lorraine says all of this without blushing, though I sense a slight awkwardness among the guys at her words, even as they try to act nonchalant. Lorraine sums up her talk by adding that we should not be shy and strained while dancing.

'The salsa is an intimate dance, but remember, it is also a very elegant dance—a gentleman's dance. Please treat your lady-partner with dignity. Do not pull her arm out of the socket when you twirl her. Be gentle. Make her feel at ease. Do not try and show off. Even if you do a few basic steps, it is fine. It is better than trying some stunning moves and leaving her feeling inadequate. There is a lot of non-verbal communication that happens in dance, so always have a smile on your face, no matter how nervous you are,' says Lorraine.

The guys exchange nervous glances, while the women grin at each other. I am thoroughly enjoying this. I love the candid manner in which Lorraine reels out the instructions and gives us a lesson in etiquette. I enjoy the atmosphere here—it is so liberating. It is like nothing I have experienced before and I absolutely revel in every moment of it.

'Come on now, let's start,' says Lorraine. 'You will soon get the groove of it, 'she reassures. 'One two three...' and the music starts again. Lorraine keeps up the count and, in no time, we are dancing in full swing. Then the beat stops and we exchange partners. I keep a watch out for Gaurav from the corner of my eye and see him entering a while later. He waves out to Lorraine who gestures for him to join in.

Gaurav does that and, in the very next round, he is my partner. It feels phenomenal to be dancing with someone who is obviously an expert. He is so smooth with his moves that he makes me feel on top of the world. He guides me with the practised ease of a brilliant dancer. We make a great pair and do not miss a single beat. I am surprised to discover just how valuable the expertise of your partner is in salsa. When the beat ends, we are supposed to stop and rotate partners again, but Gaurav doesn't stop. He continues and I pick up his cue and we dance in perfect synchronicity. He makes me feel at ease as I follow his lead. His eyes do not leave mine for a second, and, as he dances, he smiles at me. I am completely mesmerised, as though in a trance. It is the first time in my life I am dancing like this with a good-looking man who, with his moves, makes me feel like a princess in a fairy tale. Who makes me believe that I am a superb dancer. When we finally stop, the whole class which has paused to watch us, breaks into spontaneous applause.

'Well done, Diksha, you are a natural,' says Lorraine and I beam. 'And now, Gaurav, I think the other ladies deserve the same treatment too. Janie and Nitya, you can both take a turn with Gaurav and each of the guys can dance with me. You see how important it is that partners are in perfect sync?' she says.

I feel a stab of jealousy as Gaurav dances with Nitya and then with Janie.

This is crazy. I tell myself. Get a grip. He is not your boyfriend. You are a married woman and he is just doing his job as an instructor.

Yet, childish as it is, I am a little pacified to see that he does not achieve the same level of dancing with either Janie or Nitya that he did with me. I also feel smugly satisfied that it is me he has asked out for coffee and not them, despite knowing that I am a mother, though it makes me wonder why. But there is no time to dwell on it as Lorraine keeps us on our toes till the session ends. After class, I bid others a bye and Gaurav and I walk towards the café where we met the last time.

'Sorry I was late for class today. I give private lessons too, you know, and the couple I was teaching wanted to practise a bit more. Their wedding is in four days and they wanted their moves to be perfect,' he says.

'That is fine,' I smile. I am ridiculously happy as I walk beside him. I have never gone out anywhere on my own, except on family outings with Sandeep and Abhay. This little 'thing' with Gaurav is making me feel good.

'You are great at salsa, Diksha. A natural. Very few are gifted like that,' he says.

I remind him it is only because he guided me so well and that is different when I dance with the other guys.

'They are only learning. They are still not used to the concept of "guiding" and "leading" the lady. Give them a few more sessions and you will see the difference,' he says confidently.

We reach the café and Gaurav pulls out a chair for me and asks me what I will have. I settle for a iced mint tea and he says will have a burger as he did not get time to eat earlier. Would I like to eat something? he enquires politely.

When the formalities of ordering are done and the waiter vanishes, I catch Gaurav looking at me and smiling.

'What?' I ask.

'You aren't used to this, are you?' he continues smiling and looking into my eyes. Gazing actually.

His manner is making me slightly uncomfortable, but I am hugely flattered too.

'Used to what? Ordering stuff at cafés?' I tease him, even though I know he is referring to going out on dates.

'Ha ha, yeah. That is exactly what I meant,' he retorts laughing. I join in.

With that, the ice is completely broken and I instantly feel at ease.

'So why did you ask me out? Me, of all the people. There must be so many women in your classes, right?' I ask.

'Yeah, but the married ones always come with their husbands. You are the first, and a mother at that, to have come without her partner.'

'So of all the things, it is my motherhood that you found date-worthy?' I laugh

'Of course! Do you have any idea how hot that makes you?' he says with a straight face, his voice dipping low.

I really don't know whether he is joking, but I can tell he is definitely flirting. I am totally new to these dating games which single women probably play and are experts at.

I do not know what to say and, before I can respond, my phone rings. It is Tanu. Instantly my mind races to

Ankit. Even with the charming Gaurav in front of me, I am obsessed with knowing about Ankit.

'Excuse me, I have to take this call,' I say.

I rise to take my call at a discreet distance, but Gaurav gestures me to sit and leaves the table.

'Hey babes, I am with someone, but I just had to take your call. Tell me about Ankit! I am dying to know,' I say in a low voice.

'Ha, ha, ha! So that could not wait! You still have the hots for him, don't you?' she teases.

'Shut up, Tanu! What nonsense you talk.'

'Of course, it is deeper than merely 'having the hots'. Look how impatient you are,' she continues teasing.

I realise that I will not easily be able to inveigle any information about Ankit out of her in a short phone call. Besides, I can see Gaurav hanging about waiting for me to finish the call.

'Okay. Have it your way. I have to go now as I am outside with someone. Mail me, okay?' I say.

'Done. Will mail you soon,' she says and we hang up. I gesture for Gaurav to join me.

'Hey, there was no need for you to leave the table, but it was rather sweet of you,' I say.

He smiles.

He asks me what attracted me to salsa.

I tell him that it is a long story.

'I have all the time in the world. Do tell, I want to know,' he says.

I do not know if it is the sincerity in his eyes that convinces me or whether it is the high I am feeling after a superb salsa session, or perhaps it is the whole intimacy of the café, but I am deeply flattered by his obvious interest in me.

'Are you sure you really want to know? Or are you just making conversation?' I ask.

'Of course, I do. Do you think I am asking just for the heck of it? Or do you not trust me enough to share?' he looks hurt.

'No, it's not like that at all,' I reply.

'Then tell,' he says.

So I tell him about Vibha. I tell him about Mohan's sudden death. I tell him about how I got married at nineteen. I leave out the part about how insensitive Sandeep is or how discontented I feel in the marriage.

I talk about the jolt Mohan's passing gave us all and how Vibha goaded me into making a wish list. And that learning salsa was one of the things on the list.

Gaurav is all ears and listens with rapt attention, without interrupting even once. He is genuinely interested in everything I am saying.

And finally when I am done, he is silent for a few seconds.

Then he says, 'Oh my God. That is really amazing, Diksha. Most of us just talk about what we want to do. And here you are, you have actually made a list and, even more impressive, are actually carrying it out. How wonderful is that?!'

I shrug.

'You are amazing. And, trust me, I don't say this to everyone I meet, and I meet a lot of women. You are really something else, Diksha,' he says.

He asks me if I will share my wish list with him. I tell him that I will consider it. All of a sudden, I feel a bit shy at having told him so much about my life.

I realise that while I have shared some details of my life with him, I know nothing about his personal life. I ask him whether he has a girlfriend.

'Divorced recently,' he says.

'Oh, I'm sorry,' I say, not knowing how else to respond.

'Don't be. I was glad when the divorce finally came through. Fortunately no kids. It was messy enough without,' he says drily.

He doesn't want to divulge any more details and I do not press him. Instead I change the topic to movies and books. I am delighted to discover that he reads a lot and has read Milan Kundera, whose work I greatly admire. I am overjoyed to find a kindred soul. We talk enthusiastically about all the authors we love and discover that we have much in common when it comes to our taste in books.

He opens up about his passion—salsa—and tells me how he got into it. He has done courses from the World Salsa Federation, the recognised and governing body for salsa dancing and competitions recognised even by the International Olympic Committee.

'Most instructors don't really have certification. Many of them in India, in fact, have just trained under someone or the other, and not received any formal training.'

'Is that accepted? Is it valid?'

'Well, it's like this. There are institutes all over the world that offer certification. And, in the end, it is how you dance and how you are able to teach that matters, right? Most students are just looking for some basic steps to be able to do at wedding or parties, to learn a few moves and impress their friends. Very few have it in them to do it professionally. But you, Diksha, really have it in you. It is amazing, the way salsa has come so easily to you. I am really impressed and it is a joy teaching you.'

'And I must return the compliment, Gaurav. It is indeed fantastic dancing with you. It comes so effortlessly because of you.'

'Ever considered becoming an instructor?'

'Goodness, no! I haven't even thought about it.'

'But you must. I too had joined a salsa class while in

college, just to meet girls and make friends. And then I got heavily involved, won a few competitions and so on, and after that there was no looking back. And finally, I convinced my mother. I really faced hell from her as she wanted me to do an MBA. She raised me single-handedly, you see. I lost my dad when I was five.'

'Oh! She must have been disappointed then in your choice of career?'

'Initially she was. But I kept talking to her. I even took her for a few dance contests.'

'Really?'

'Yeah! That's when she saw me performing on stage, saw my passion, saw the adulation I got. She realised that I had talent and finally agreed that this was perhaps my true calling. Then I went to Miami and got my certification.'

'Wow! That is really something. No wonder you are this good.'

'Yes. In those days, I had to go all the way to Miami. But now, because of the Internet, it is so much easier. Today, you can take the test by sending DVDs of yourself dancing. The institute trainers spell out every move—the turns, foot placement, etc, and the applicant basically needs a partner to dance with. They even test if the applicant can do both parts—male and female. They have various grading systems and specify the names of the steps. It's all very organised now and, depending on your competence, they grade you bronze, silver or gold.'

'And you must definitely have got Gold, right?'

'Of course,' he smiles. 'I love salsa and it shows. And I feel delighted to have found that same love for salsa in you.'

I am fascinated by Gaurav's narration. I keep asking him questions and he enjoys answering them.

He tells me how much he desires to open his own dance studio and how he is still a paid employee in the current place.

'You must! You are such a good teacher. Your own studio will be wonderful,' I say.

He says he is saving up for it but it would take a huge initial investment, especially in real estate. Then he would have to hire instructors and, ultimately, generate enough students to break even and make it sustainable. He says he plans to, in the long run, and is slowly moving towards it.

Later, as I say my byes to him, he gives me a hug and that happy feeling stays inside me, lights me up, warms up my soul, and I cannot help thinking how beautiful life is when you have the right people in it.

I am yet to know then just how much of a tumult the 'right people' can really cause. But right now, I am happy and content to bask in the warmth of a new friendship as it makes my life worthwhile and I am so grateful for that.

Seventeen

MY MOTHER-IN-LAW MOVES BACK INTO HER OWN apartment on Saturday. Sandeep drops her off and then goes for his usual round of golf. Before she leaves, I ask her if she will be fine on her own or whether she wants me to come and help her settle in.

'I am around, am I not? I'll settle her in or do you think I'm not capable of it? What do you take me for?' Sandeep snaps at me before she even has a chance to reply. I keep quiet.

My mother-in-law doesn't miss either the exchange or the hurt expression on my face, even though Sandeep is oblivious to it.

I should be used to him by now. I really should. Yet, each time it hurts. I still haven't learnt to grow a thick skin to deflect his jabbing words.

She gives me a hug as she leaves. 'God bless you, Diksha. May you always have happiness. And come around sometime. Send Abhay also over to stay. You know I enjoy it,' she says.

'Can I go with Aayi now? Can I ? Can I?' Abhay dances around excitedly.

'No, Abhay, not today, but I will send you another day. I promise,' I say to him.

'I will,' I reassure my mom-in-law, hugging her back.

A bond has definitely been established between us, something which wasn't this strong before. I decide that, every now and then, I will definitely send Abhay to spend time with her. I can hear the loneliness behind her words and I promise to myself that I will make amends and visit her more often.

Tanu arrives in Bangalore that afternoon. And with her arrive memories. She has been such an important part of my early years that I think our personalities have crisscrossed each other and shaped us into being the people we are today. There is a bit of Tanu in me, as much as there is a bit of me in her.

When Sandeep returns from golf, I tell him that my childhood friend has shifted to Bangalore, and is temporarily staying at the Oberoi, and that I will be spending the afternoon with her.

'Who? Who is this friend? You never mentioned her before,' he says.

'Yes, I know. Her name is Tanu. We used to study together. Then we lost touch. Vibha had registered me on a reunion site some weeks back and that is how she found me. We were best of friends back then,' I tell him.

'You shouldn't put personal details on the Internet. It is not safe. Vibha should know better,' he says in a disapproving tone.

I want to roll my eyes. His ideas and outlook are really outdated. Most people would be delighted that I am reconnecting with a person who has meant or means a great deal to me, but all Sandeep can see is the danger in posting information on the Internet.

'Well, she just put my email ID online. We exchanged phone numbers through mail. It is not as if she put up my whole address and phone number,' I reply.

He does not know what to say to that.

'Uh, okay. Take Abhay with you, and... umm... by what time will you be back?' he asks.

'What will Abhay do in a hotel room, Sandeep? He will get thoroughly bored. Tanu and I have such a lot to catch up on. Besides, if he's here, he can go out to play with his friends and return at six thirty pm. It's not like he is going to trouble you or even take up your time,' I reply. I am annoyed at his suggestion of taking Abhay with me. How unreasonable is that? But I control my urge to vent my irritation. I am so eager to meet Tanu that I just want to placate Sandeep somehow and get out of the house. I do not want to confront or argue with him.

It is really these small things about Sandeep which reflect his supreme selfishness. As far as he is concerned, his needs must always come first.

Finally, Sandeep reluctantly agrees to let Abhay stay at home. And before he can change his mind, I am out of the house and in a rick, heading to meet Tanu.

I spot Tanu before she sees me. She is waiting at the entrance lobby of the hotel. I recognise her immediately. She hasn't yet seen me and, as I walk towards her, I am stunned at how gorgeous she looks. She is about four inches taller than me which makes her five eight. And she is wearing four-inch heels which make her look even taller. Her complexion is flawless and her hair is silky straight like the hair of models one sees in television ads. She sports white skinny Guess jeans and her well-fitted top is very obviously designer stuff, cut to show off her toned shoulders. Her nails are perfectly manicured and she sports a platinum bracelet studded with Swarovski crystals. She is carrying an oversized red designer bag. She could easily be mistaken for a professional model. I immediately feel dowdy in my 'Mummy clothes' which translates to a nondescript salwar kameez which I had flung on without a thought. It is probably silly, but the first thing I think of when I see her is, 'Damn, I should have dressed up a bit.' I wish I had at least worn the clothes I wear to my salsa class, but it is too late for that now.

Tanu turns around and sees me walking towards her. She looks a bit confused, then as slowly recognition dawns on her, she screams, 'DIKSHA! OH MY GOD!' She envelops me in a bear hug, almost crushing me, and I am surrounded by a whiff of her strong perfume, most probably Chanel.

I hug her right back and she plants a kiss on either cheek—a real kiss, not those fake air kisses which Page 3 people do, even though she can easily be mistaken for one herself—totally surprising me with her genuine warmth.

'God it *is* amazing to see you after so many years,' she says and there are tears in her eyes. I squeeze her hand and we go up to her room which is luxurious like any five star hotel room. I sink into the plush bed. I love these luxury hotels and all the material comforts they offer.

'Isn't this amazing, Diksha? Look at us, we're meeting after eighteen years. Our lives have taken such different turns and yet this connection we feel, it is stronger than ever.'

'Yeah, Tanu. And God, you really look stunning. You have transformed into a total model-type. I really feel like the village bumpkin who has come to visit a city cousin.'

'Thanks babes and, come on, you are no village bumpkin!' she says loyally.

'To be honest, I hate these clothes of mine, Tanu. But Sandeep doesn't like me in anything other than these mummy outfits.'

She looks at me and walks over to me. Then she hugs me again and says softly, 'Look at what marriage has done to you, babes. Even your clothes aren't yours anymore.'

She has hit the nail right on the head. It is one thing which I hate about myself—the things I do to placate Sandeep and my sheer lack of guts to stand up to him and assert myself.

'Tell me the truth, is Sandeep an asshole?' she asks directly.

'Shut up, Tanu! It is my HUSBAND you are talking about,' I say with more force than necessary.

'So? So what? What is this? Are you some kind of modern version of Savitri? So bloody what if he is your husband? You have a choice, you know! Come on, Diksha. Between us there is nothing really to hide, is there?' she asks indignantly.

'I will tell you everything, Tanu. This marriage thing, it is complicated. It gets even more complicated when kids arrive. You get pregnant and you change in ways you never thought possible. For me, having Abhay makes it all worthwhile.'

'I agree motherhood and all that is great. But tell me, are you really happy in your marriage?' she persists.

'Look, let's not talk about it now, Tanu. We will talk, but another time.'

'Ha! I knew it! I knew you weren't happy, even from your mails.'

I smile at her total honesty and the liberty that she takes with me. Coming from anyone else. I might have found it rude, but from her, I actually like it. I like how she demands to know all about my life. I like that she still cares as fiercely and as intensely as she did back in school. And I feel ecstatic to have her back in my life.

'Wine?' asks Tanu as she opens a bottle chilling in an ice bucket in her room.

'Hmm, no thanks,' I say. I have never had alcohol and I curiously read the label on the bottle. It is a Chardonnay, made in Australia. There is also a card on it is addressed to Tanu, welcoming her to Bangalore.

'It is from my office. They are being extra nice to me. I am taking over you see,' she explains.

'You know, I have never had alcohol even though I have always wanted to,' I say.

'What?!Never? Oh my God, Diksha, You really are missing the one big pleasure of life!' says Tanu.

'I wouldn't know really, would I? Sandeep never drinks and we do not have any alcohol in our home,' I reply.

'Didn't you drink in college?'

'Ha. You know how my college life was. I was watched over like a hawk. And by the time I was nineteen, I was married off. And then, I got pregnant. Once a baby arrives, it takes over your life. I have never done the normal things most young people do Tanu. I have never really 'had fun' or at least the kind of things that most people term fun, like partying, going to discos, watching movies, theatre, etc. My life has been so different from yours. In fact, this is the first time I have left Abhay at home and come out like this. He is nine now, and fairly independent. But this is only now. Earlier he needed me all the time.'

Tanu is silent for a while as she takes in all I have said.

'Hey, it's okay. We will do all the things you missed out on. We will have fun, babes. In fact, we will start right now. Here, let me pour you a glass,' she says.

I indeed want to know what wine taste like. I want to find out what all the fuss is about. But while I am excited, I am also a bit scared.

'Hmm. What if I get drunk?' I say to Tanu.

'So what if you do? Are you scared I will rape you?' she asks

I chuckle.

'Cheers!' she says as she hands over the glass to me.

I take a sip and it is not sweet. Yet it is not bitter. It is nothing like I have ever tasted before.

'How is it? Do you like?' asks Tanu

'Yeah! I like it,' I reply as I take another sip.

'Have it slowly. There are many varieties in wine. Some are sweet, some dry, some full-bodied. I did a wine appreciation course once,' she says.

We settle down on the bed with our glasses and lean against the propped-up pillows. This is something I haven't ever done—relaxing with a good friend like this. It feels wonderful.

Tanu brings me up to speed about her life. She tells me about the MBA she did in Australia. About her four failed relationships. About how she lost her virginity. She talks about sex, about being single and how she buried herself in her career to get over the pain of breaking up with a guy who, each time, she thought was 'the one'. She talks about how, now, her career is top priority for her.

I tell her about my married life. About Sandeep and his idiosyncrasies and how stifled I have been feeling in my marriage lately. I tell her about my secret wish list which I made with Vibha, and she makes me promise that I will show it to her. I also tell her about my salsa class and my 'date' with Gaurav.

I want to ask her about Ankit, but somehow I don't,

as in this moment, my closeness to her overshadows all other feelings, including my curiosity about Ankit. There is time for that later, I decide in my mind and right now all that matters is that I am here with Tanu, after eighteen long years and that we are still as close as ever. It feels incredible and I feel so fortunate for a friendship like this. My mind is full of all that she has told me about her life and all that I have shared with her. Our lives couldn't have been more starkly different.

It is only when the light outside changes to orange that I realise it is evening and the entire afternoon has passed. The colours of the sunset are beautiful. I feel light-headed because of the wine and a bit unsteady on my feet.

'Oh, Tanu. This has been truly amazing. Look at the sunset. It feels as though someone has emptied a can of paint all over the sky,' I say, gazing at it from the french windows which provide a marvellous view.

Tanu nods happily from the bed.

'Hey, I have to get back and I feel slightly dizzy now,' I say as I reach for my handbag and wear my sandals.

'I'll call a car. I am entitled to a car and a driver here. One of the few perks of slogging my butt off,' she replies.

It is only then that I look at my phone and see two missed calls from Sandeep and a text which says, **'Where are you? Why are you taking so long? Abhay is hungry.'**

I panic seeing the text. I know Sandeep is irked. I feel like a teen who has overshot the curfew time set by the parent.

'Oh no. I didn't hear the phone, Tanu. It was in my bag. And now Sandeep is upset,' I say.

She grabs my phone from my hand and reads the text.

'Come on! It is not every day that you meet your best friend after eighteen years. And you have been here just three hours, Diksha. So what if Abhay is hungry? Can't

Sandeep make a sandwich for him? Is he that helpless? Isn't he a full-grown adult?'

'Look, you really don't know him. He can be nasty.'

'Hey, let me do one thing. I am coming home with you, right now. Let me see how nasty he can be,' she says.

I giggle. I find it funny that I, a full grown woman, am taking my best friend home to avoid getting a 'scolding' from my husband.

I want to protest and tell her that I will manage just fine, but the wine is making me really light-headed and unsteady on my feet. I am happy to go along with whatever she wants to do. I am in no state to take a rick by myself, in any case.

She brushes her hair, touches up her lip gloss and calls for the car.

Then we head towards my home.

Eighteen

SANDEEP IS OUTSIDE THE HOUSE PACING UP AND down, when Tanu and I arrive in the hired hotel car. One look at him and I know he is murderously angry. The wine has really gone to my head now and I try hard to suppress my giggles. I find his angry, balding face apt to be caricatured.

He looks puzzled when the car stops and Tanu emerges. I continue sitting in the car.

'Hi, I am Tanu, Diksha's friend,' says Tanu as she extends her hand. Tanu is sober and can obviously hold her drink, unlike me, the novice.

Sandeep's jaw almost drops to the floor. He is clearly flabbergasted by how gorgeous she is.

'Uh—oh. I am Sandeep, her husband,' he says and his astonished look sends me into a fresh paroxysm of giggles that I quickly suppress.

'Where is Diksha?' asks Sandeep.

Both of them look towards the car and I realise they cannot see me because of the tinted windows. I am forced to open the door and climb out.

'Here I am. Ta-da,' I say and chuckle.

Tanu smiles and Sandeep cannot, for the life of him, figure out what has come over me.

'We just had some wine to drink and Diksha isn't used to it. She will be fine, won't you, babes?' asks Tanu as she takes my arm and we march inside, leaving a gaping Sandeep behind to follow suit.

Sandeep scuttles around asking Tanu if she is comfortable and if he can fetch her something to drink. I am seeing this avatar of my husband—the cordial host—for the first time and I am stunned at how he is meting out the royal treatment to Tanu. I have never seen him behave like this.

'Yes please, what do you have? I wouldn't mind another glass of wine, really,' she says with a straight face and watches Sandeep squirm in embarrassment.

'Uh, sorry. I don't have wine,' he says.

'Oh, then it's fine. Whatever you have, really. Vodka, whiskey, anything is okay,' she says and winks at me.

Sandeep doesn't know what to say.

'Sorry, I don't drink. We do not have hard drinks in the house, actually,' he fumbles.

'Oh is it? Such a shame,' she says, narrowing her eyes and looking flirtatiously at him, as though making a pass.

He is clearly very uncomfortable. She is thoroughly enjoying herself and I am too.

He begins to perspire now and takes out his handkerchief to dab his forehead. He looks totally lost.

'Hey, relax. I was just kidding. I have to leave now, in any case. I just came to drop off Diksha. Bye, babes, and we will catch up soon? I need you to help me choose all my furniture. I will call and pick you up, okay?' she says and with that she is gone.

Sandeep stares after her as though she is an

apparition. He does not know what has just happened. He looks dazed.

Then he catches me looking at him and quickly composes himself.

'What the hell, Diksha? Are you drunk?' he says

'Just a little wine, darling,' I say and laugh uncontrollably. I have never used words like 'darling' with him before. I cannot stop myself.

Sandeep is too taken aback to react. That amuses me no end. It is the first time in all the years of marriage that I have seen him like this.

'You look like a goldfish, opening and closing your mouth like that. It doesn't suit you, you know,' I say.

Then I feel something rising in my mouth. I run to the loo downstairs and throw up violently. I shudder at the bitter taste. I rise, rinse my mouth and gargle, but the horrid taste still lingers.

'See, this is what happens when you indulge in such nonsense. Drinking is nothing to be proud of,' says Sandeep angrily.

I have nothing to say. I wash my face and plonk myself on the sofa.

'What? It is your own stupid fault. Who told you to drink? You think it is so very cool, don't you?' he follows me and continues watching me.

It is not because I think it is cool, it is only because I have never done it and I want to know what it feels like. It is because I became a mother at an age most people go out pubbing and drinking and I had to change diapers and sing lullabies. I had a drink with a friend. Is that so wrong? Is it such a crime?

'And let me tell you, all this drinking and everything, it leads to no good. And by the way, what are we having for dinner tonight?' He continues in a smug superior, preachy tone.

'Shut the fuck up. Is dinner all you can think of?' I want to scream. I can always blame it on the wine later, I think. But somehow I don't.

Sometimes in a marriage, it is easier to just buy peace and pay the price of swallowing your ego and keeping quiet.

⚜

The next day, long after Sandeep leaves for work, I get a text from Gaurav:

'Want to join me for lunch? I will pick you up and drop you back.' It reads.

I am too overwhelmed by my little drinking adventure and don't feel like seeing him today.

'Not today. Can I take a rain check?' I text back.

'Anytime! Whenever you feel like, just text. See you in class on Friday.' His text comes promptly making me smile.

'Do you always chase all your women students like this?' I text back smiling.

'Only the married ones☺!!!' His reply makes me smile even wider.

I call up Vibha and update her on all the happenings and the adventures that I have had since we last spoke. Vibha chuckles to hear how astonished Sandeep was to see Tanu, and to hear about his behaviour around her, and how she was teasing him. I tell her that I had my first glass of wine and got drunk.

'Oh my God, Diksha! You managed to tick off one more item on your wish list!' she says.

'What?' I ask puzzled, as I try to remember what it could possibly be. Then it strikes me that one of the things that I had written (of course, purely on a whim) was 'getting drunk', and I had managed to do that last evening.

'Oh yes, I had almost forgotten. How did you remember?' I smile.

'How can you forget your wish list?! I remember everything you wrote. I had told you I will push you to achieve it. And I will do just that. You wait and see. And by the way, what is Ankit doing? Where is he based now? Did you both talk about him?'

'You know, Vibha, I am going to call Tanu right now and ask her. We talked about everything under the sun and somehow we did not speak about Ankit at all. I just have to know now. I can't wait any longer,' I say.

I call Tanu and she says she will forward me a few mails that she and Ankit exchanged. She adds that she had meant to do it much earlier, but wanted to meet me first before forwarding anything.

'Why? Why did you want to meet me first?' I ask.

'Somehow, that seemed the right thing to do. Read the mails and you will understand why,' she says.

I rush to the computer and wait impatiently for Tanu's mail.

I keep hitting the refresh button and finally, on the third try, there it is. The string of messages that Tanu has exchanged with Ankit. My heart beats increase rapidly and I scroll down to the bottom of the messages and begin to read.

From: Ankit Uttam (ankit2112@uttamhospitality.com)

To: Tanushree Dev (tanud@bib.com)

Subject: Reaching out

Hi there,

Is this the same Tanushree, better known as Tanu, who once wrote a rather bold note in a senior's book? ☺

Of course, the details of your batch year seem to match, and, as far as I can remember, there was just one Tanu in the whole school.

But, in case I have made a mistake, please ignore this mail. I have been trying hard to get in touch with someone who was in school with me, and when Blast from the Past threw up your contact, it was hard to pass up.☺

Ankit

From: Tanushree Dev (tanud@bib.com)

To: Ankit Uttam (ankit2112@uttamhospitality.com)

Subject: Reaching out

Ankit!!

You devil!

Yes, it is me.

It is Diksha you are trying so desperately to get in touch with, isn't it? Say!

Where are you based now? What do you do? Give me ALL details please. Where did you go after school?

I did my graduation from Delhi and then my MBA from Australia. I am based in Gurgaon right now with an international bank, but will be moving soon to Bangalore.

Your phone number(s) please!

Tanu

From: Ankit Uttam (ankit2112@uttamhospitality.com)

To: Tanushree Dev (tanud@bibcom)

Subject: Reaching out

Tanu!

Hey!

I knew it was you. I was 99.9% sure. But left that .01% to chance and hence wrote a 'disclaimer' line.

Yes, I have been trying hard to locate Diksha all these years. There seems to be no trace of her or Rohan (not that he will want to speak to me). I did get in touch with a few of my batch mates but they had no idea either.

I truly cannot get over what happened to her and how she was pulled out of school. I felt guilty for years. I guess I still do.

And even you stopped talking to me after that incident. And then I finished my twelfth, and we were scattered all over.

My parents sent me to Canada for an engineering degree.

Got into Wharton for my MBA. Did a dual-degree programme there (and so I have an MA in International Studies as well). Joined my dad's business. But got bored.

Diversified and started my own chain of resorts, which I now manage and head and, at the risk of sounding boastful, I must tell you, we have branches all over the world now. ☺

If you, by any chance, are in touch with Diksha, do pass me her contact details.

Ankit

From: Tanushree Dev (tanud@bibcom)

To: Ankit Uttam (ankit2112@uttamhospitality.com)

Subject: Reaching out

Are you sure you looked properly in the site for Diksha? ☺

Look again.

I am mailing her straight away.

And you never gave me your number.

Tanu

From: Ankit Uttam (ankit2112@ uttamhospitality.com)

To: Tanushree Dev (tanud@bibcom)

OMG! You are right!

How could I miss it? I swear, I looked for months and never saw her name.

In fact, even when I saw yours, hers wasn't there.

Is it the same Diksha?

Please check and tell. I don't want to mail her just yet.

A

From: Tanushree Dev (tanud@bibcom)

To: Ankit Uttam (ankit2112@ uttamhospitality.com)

Subject: Reaching out

I just mailed her. I too had searched many times earlier, but she wasn't there. She must have registered recently. Will let you know when she replies.

And I am not going to ask for your number again.

Mine are here in this mail.

Tanu

The mails ended here.

I read them again and again. It really is Ankit. *My* Ankit.

And he has been desperate to get in touch with me.

Why hasn't he got in touch with me, then?

I want to know and I want to know right now. So I call up Tanu.

When she answers, I ask if it's okay for her to talk now.

'Of course, babes. Anytime. Never too busy for you,' she says

'Tanu, I read the mails. Why hasn't Ankit got in touch with me? Why do the mails end abruptly?'

'That is because he called me after the last mail, silly.'

'Oh! You never said a thing!'

'You never asked,' she says and I can almost feel her smile.

'I wanted to but…' I trail off.

'I know. See, the thing is, I wanted to see you first. I wanted to see if you were happy in your marriage. To know if you really want Ankit back in your life, at this point.'

'What? You wanted to see? How can you take a call on that? How can you decide my life for me? What if I was perfectly content in my marriage? What would you have done then?'

'I would have told Ankit that this is not our Diksha, it is someone else and the email ID is fake.'

I know she is only teasing. I hound her to tell me all about her conversation with Ankit. I want to know all the details. How he sounds, does he still speak the same way, what did they talk about.

Tanu says that Ankit and she had talked for a long time immediately after that mail. She wanted to tell me about it when we first met, but somehow the time didn't seem right. She said that Ankit had mentioned that even though he really wants to get in touch with me, he wants to be certain that I do too.

Then after Tanu had met and talked to me, she had once again contacted Ankit and confirmed that it was indeed me and that I was now married and based in Bangalore and had a child too. She said that Ankit was quiet for a long time. She had asked him if he was okay and he had replied that he was as okay as he could ever be.

Tanu wasn't sure how to tell me all this, which was one of the reasons why she kept stalling it.

But now that I had brought it up, she had no choice but to tell me in detail.

My head is reeling with this entire information-overload about Ankit.

I do not know what to say or do. I tell Tanu that there is someone at the door and I have to hang up.

'Okay. Call me right back after you attend to whoever it is,' she says and hangs up.

I lie on the bed and I think about all of this. It is obvious that Ankit does want to contact me, but maybe he is not making the first move as he knows I am married and a mother now. I am in a dilemma.

The easiest thing for me would be to *not* get in touch with Ankit. Treat all of it like it never happened. After all, Ankit hasn't reached out.

But how can I not reach out to him, now that I know this much has happened? The meeting with Tanu has brought back all the memories of Ankit and all the time we spent together.

He seems to have taken a permanent place in my head these days. I just cannot stop thinking of him.

There is only one way to deal with ghosts of the past. To lay them to rest, I have to face them. And in order to do that, I have to speak to Ankit.

There is no doubt at all in my mind now.

I call Tanu right back.

'Hey, babes,' I say. 'Please pass me Ankit's number. I want to talk to him.'

Nineteen

IT ISN'T OFTEN THAT THE PAST COMES CALLING. And sometimes when it does, you have no choice but to answer.

Ankit—a name that has haunted me and changed the entire course of my life—a name which still has the power to give me goose bumps all over my skin and a tightness in my throat. Mostly, when memories of him had come to mind, I had not allowed myself to luxuriate in them, instead I had pushed them aside forcibly, rudely, and had continued with my mundane chores. I had convinced myself that the domesticity I had settled for was bliss. But over the years, the veil has worn thin and I know now that delusion can work only up to a point and no further.

Now, I know, more than ever before, I just *have* to speak to Ankit.

And even though I am alone in the house, I lock myself in my bedroom to make the call. The guilt is that deeply ingrained. I guess, things that happen to you when you are sixteen seep into your blood and grow with you.

When he answers, it feels as though a million butterflies have been let loose inside the hollow of my stomach. His voice is deeper, more suave, and polished now. Yet he sounds the same as he did all those years ago. I pause just for a few seconds to absorb the impact of the moment—the fact that at the other end of the line is someone who has cast his presence over my entire life, without even being there.

'Hello?' he says again.

'Ankit, it is me,' I say and am quiet.

There is silence for a few seconds.

And then he says, 'Oh my God. Is this real? Give me a minute.'

I hear him ask someone to excuse him as he needs to take this call. I hear a shuffling of the chair and guess that whoever he was with has left the room.

'Hey, Diksha,' he says. His voice is almost a whisper.

'Yes,' I say and then I am unable to say anything more even though there are a million things I want to say.

The silence between us speaks a thousand words. We sit, submerged in the quietness, holding on to our receivers listening to each other breathe. A sudden waft of breeze rattles my window panes ever so slightly. There is complete silence from his end.

I guess he is in office which is probably soundproof.

'You have no idea how much I have tried to track you down,' he finally says, breaking the silence which was screaming in our ears.

'So now that you have found me, what are you going to do?' I smile.

'I will fly soon to Bangalore,' he replies.

'You aren't serious?'

'Never been more serious in my life. I am not kidding. I want to meet you. Real bad.'

I don't know what to say, really. I too want to meet him, but I am drowning in a flood of emotions. There is exhilaration on one side, and trepidation and nervousness on the other.

'So where are you right now?' I ask

'Doha. I'll fly back to India tonight,' he says.

'To which place?'

'Mumbai. And then I will take a flight to Bangalore.'

'Wow,' I say and stop at that.

'You will meet me, won't you?'

'Have I ever said no to you, Ankit?'

'God, Diksha, I do want to tell you how very sorry I am. Back then, I was helpless, but now I am not, and you have no idea how happy I feel right now, speaking to you. '

'Me too, Ankit. Me too.'

And with that our tryst is sealed. Laced in secrecy. Shrouded in guilt.

The unfinished business between us that changed both our lives forever, has come cruising back into our lives and is begging to reach completion.

It has been eighteen long years and it is time to make amends.

And so I hear myself asking him his flight details, where he will stay? (At The Leela, no less, I note), for how many days will he be here? I hear him reply that he is flying down just to meet me and will leave the same day. I inhale sharply at that.

When I hang up, I realise I feel something which I have never felt in a very long time. At first it is so hard to recognise what the feeling is and when I finally do, it leaves me astonished.

What I feel is utter contentment and peace.

It feels as though I am complete.

It feels as though I am home.

⁂

Ankit calls me the next morning around eleven and my heart again performs its customary drum roll when it sees his name flashing. One would think it would have calmed down by now. But it has a mind of its own and I cannot control it anymore.

I answer on the first ring itself.

'Hey, how come you called without texting first?' I ask

'Is there a rule that I have to first take your permission to call?'

'What if my husband had been at home?'

'Does your husband answer your phone calls for you?'

'No, but he would have asked me who called.'

'So?'

'Come on! How can I tell him about you?'

'I know, I was just teasing you. I am really not used to this. I don't usually call up married women, you see.'

His tone changes as he speaks and I can feel a slight hesitation or perhaps shyness creeping into his voice. I imagine him blushing and find myself smiling, relaxing into that easy vibe we used to have with each other all those years ago. Funny, how some things remain the same. Here I am, connecting with Ankit after what seems a lifetime, and it feels like yesterday. All that happened in between did not matter.

'So where are you? Back in India?' I ask.

'Yes. How soon can you get out of the house?'

'What? You're in Bangalore?' I almost scream.

'Yes, ma'am. Couldn't wait. After I heard your voice on

the phone, I was impatient to meet you. I am checking into Leela in about five minutes.'

'Oh my God! Ankit! This is crazy.'

'I know. I have been trying to ask myself what the hell I am doing. I don't know. All I know is I just have to see you.'

'I have put on tons of weight. I have a double chin and I have become really fat. My arms are the size of the balloons you see at kids' parties. You are going to be disappointed, Ankit,' I say and a huge smile spreads across my face.

'Oh,' he says and pauses for a minute.

I smile even wider in the five second silence that follows.

Then he says, 'You know what, Diksha, I really don't give a damn about how you look and how much weight you have gained. All I know is that I have to meet you and I have flown directly from Mumbai just for that. Now are you coming here or should I come to your place? Where do you live?'

It is my turn to be speechless now. I know that with those words, Ankit has won me over completely. All these years I have tried to suppress my feelings for him. I have tried to immerse myself in my domestic life. Tried to do 'the right thing' by marrying the guy my parents chose. To walk the prescribed path. But Ankit has blown my cover now.

My heart has never sung the way it is singing now. It is a song I cannot stop. A perfect rhythm, a melody so harmonious and its notes are perfectly in sync and rise beautifully, making me feel more alive than I have ever felt my entire life.

It is as though all the emptiness and hurt in my heart has vanished and it is overflowing now with love, abundance, happiness—everything that had eluded me so far.

It is so strange, this feeling. It is irrational, completely illogical, and I am powerless to stop it.

'Yeah, Ankit. I will meet you. I live on Artillery Road. It isn't too far from where you are. I will see you in about forty-five minutes to an hour,' I say.

'So long? An hour? How are you coming?'

'I'll take an auto.'

'No way. I am sending the car for you. Give me your address.'

'No!'

'Yes! I can't let you travel in a rick.'

'No, Ankit. I will be fine. I will see you soon.'

'I know you will be fine, but I don't want you to take a rick. The hotel car will come and pick you up, Diksha. Just give me your home address.'

'Hey, listen. You are delaying me by arguing about this. I have to return home before Abhay comes back from school. Now let me hang up, else I will get no time at all with you,' I reason patiently. I feel so touched that he doesn't want me to take an auto and is ready to send a car for me. It is something that would never occur to Sandeep.

I take time to choose what I will wear. The fluttering in my heart refuses to die down. I realise that I have never dressed up this way for Sandeep. I apply my eyeliner and the mascara that I use only for special occasions. Then I use a sheer lip gloss that make my lips look fuller. I select one of the new outfits I had bought for salsa and, boy, am I glad I went shopping.

'Dressed to kill,' I think, as I glance at myself in the mirror, feeling childishly pleased with the overall effect. I have worn a white sleeveless top with delicate lace, skinny jeans which accentuate my legs and the Charles and Keith heels which I usually wear only to parties. I am thankful I am slim and haven't put on weight even after having a child. I am so glad that I look so much younger than my years and I feel so too.

And as I step out and get into the auto, there is a text from Ankit.

'**Hurry. I am waiting at the coffee shop**' it reads.

'**Coming. See you soon**.' I text back.

⁂

When I finally see him, he is bent over his smart phone, both legs stretched out, a half-finished iced tea on the table, fully absorbed in his task. He looks as handsome as he did when he was seventeen and I can see that he has really looked after his body too. He is toned and fit, his short-sleeved electric-blue T-shirt showing off muscular arms which must have pumped iron for hours in a gym. His hair is stylishly cut with slight traces of grey at the sides, which makes him even more appealing in my eyes. I note that he wears glasses now, the rimless kinds. He looks every inch the rich (everything about him seems to scream money), well-dressed, well-travelled business tycoon that he now is. He has transformed, amazingly well, into a gorgeous man from the lean lanky lad he used to be.

I stand and stare at him for a few minutes, taking in every detail about him.

Then I walk up to his table and say, 'Hey.'

He looks up and his gaze meets my eye. The look of startled surprise changes into slow recognition and then his eyes light up in pure joy as a million-watt smile flashes across his face.

'God, you're beautiful,' he says.

The next moment I am enveloped in a bear hug. The feeling is electric. I feel as though someone has jolted me with a live wire. He is so tall and he has hugged me so tight that my face is crushed against his chest. His arms around me feel wonderful and I savour the moment, enjoying every bit of it.

I love his perfume, I love this feeling, I love the warmth. Heck, I realise just how much I love all of him. Nothing has changed.

When he finally breaks away and smiles at me, I know that my life from now on is going to be different. This connect that I feel with him is exhilarating, giddy and nothing has prepared me for this. Every nerve, every fibre, every cell in my body seems to be resonating with joy. Even though this is so wrong, it feels *so right.* I struggle at first to understand it. But I soon give up—the force is too powerful, too overwhelming.

He asks me what I will have and I am unable to speak.

And without warning, tears start rolling down.

He reaches out and grips my hand and says, 'Shall we go upstairs to my room?'

I can only nod.

We go to his room in silence, his arm protectively around me. The entire thing feels like a dream. I cannot believe this is happening to me. I am taken aback at how comfortable I feel with him, how completely I trust him.

He guides me inside the hotel room, and it reminds me of my other reunion—with Tanu—and the time I went upstairs to her room.

I do not trust myself to speak and so I say nothing. I just enjoy every bit of this moment and lean on his arm around me.

Once we are inside, he shuts the door and I do not

know what to expect. He cups my chin in his hands and plants a kiss on my forehead.

'Oh, Diksha. You are so gorgeous. And the way you look now, you are killing me,' he says, looking into my eyes.

I smile and look away.

'Thanks,' I say and blush.

I am sixteen again.

'Did you know I was teasing you when I said I had put on tons of weight and have a double chin?' I ask as I kick off my heels and sink down comfortably on the double bed, propping up the soft pillows.

Ankit sits on the chair opposite the bed.

'I wasn't sure if you were teasing or not. All I knew is that I had to see you,' he says.

'Why are you sitting there? Come and sit on the bed,' I say, surprising myself with my boldness. I feel like a new person in his presence. The caution and timidity which I usually cover myself with seems to have fallen off like a cloak, and underneath is this bold new woman who knows what she wants.

Ankit comes and sits next to me. I take his hand in mine. His hands are so much bigger than mine and I suddenly realise that holding hands is something I have never done with Sandeep in all the years that we have been married. With him, there has never been tenderness, never been this feeling which am I now experiencing with Ankit. Ankit lifts my hand and kisses it and begins stroking it.

I move closer to him and he lies down next to me, facing me, and draws me into his arms. We lie in silence for a long time. I place my ear on his chest and listen to his heartbeat.

'Isn't this surreal, Diksha?' he says

'So totally. You have flown so many miles just to see

me. We haven't even talked and here we are—lying in each other's arms. We are really acting like the teenagers we were.'

'I know. I just want to hold you, Diksha, and never let you go. I have lost you once. I don't want to lose you again.'

'You already have me, Ankit. I am all yours,' I smile as I kiss him on the lips.

He kisses me back and a blaze of fire rushes from my belly to my throat. I melt in his arms and surrender completely.

He unbuttons my top and I can feel myself holding my breath. I am glad I have worn lacy lingerie. He kisses the top of my breasts and I sigh. He goes back to kissing me on my lips, as he buttons my top right back.

'What happened?' I whisper. I so want this guy now. I want him to make love to me, slowly, languorously. It is a hunger I have never felt before. With Sandeep, the lovemaking has been functional, hurried, quick and I have never enjoyed it. With Ankit, I am, for the first time, beginning to realise why all those women in romance novels, swoon when their lover kisses them. All the clichés described there are so true, I think.

'Nothing,' he smiles as he props himself on one arm and looks at me. 'You are beautiful.'

'Yes, you have told me that three times already.'

'Are you tired of hearing it?'

'How can I ever be?' I smile.

He is truly driving me crazy now. I am mad with desire for him. He looks irresistible propped up like that, so close to me, with his head resting on his arm.

I feel like unbuttoning his shirt, tearing off his clothes and insisting that he make love to me, right there and right then.

I draw him towards me and hug him as tight as I can and kiss him with ferocity and urgency. He slips his hand under my shirt and strokes my back.

I slowly unbutton his shirt and then unzip his trouser. He smiles in pleasure.

'You can't wait, can you?' he teases.

'No! I want you. Now,' I say.

'How badly?' he asks and smiles.

'Let me show you,' I say as I yank down his trousers and nip him on the ear.

It feels as though I have been starved of sex all these years. With Ankit, it is as if a new version of me has emerged. I so badly *want* to make love to this man. I want to please him. I want to make him happy. And I so badly want him inside me. This is very different from the functional married sex which I am used to. This is wild passion with all caution thrown to the winds. This is madness. This is frenzy.

And this is scarily the new me.

Ankit, I discover, is gentle, caring and he really wants to please me too. He makes love like an expert, knowing exactly when to take me to a pinnacle, when to ease and when to linger.

And when I finally come, all I can do is moan and call out his name repeatedly and dig my fingernails deep into his back.

Ankit cuddles me after he comes. I like that. Again, it is something Sandeep has never done.

We lie in silence, hugging each other for a long time as our breathing slowly returns to its normal pace. Then he turns around and traces a line with his forefinger on my cheek.

'God, Diksha, you are amazing,' he says.

'You too, Ankit. You too,' I reply.

I have never felt this complete before. Ankit completes me, he really does.

He glances at his watch and asks, 'What time do you have to go back?'

'Three thirty is when the school bus reaches home,' I reply.

'I so wish you could stay longer,' he says.

'Me too, but I have to be home,' I say.

'I will drop you home. You aren't taking any more autos. Not when I am around,' he says.

I kiss him again in response.

We are ravenously hungry and he orders food while I shower and get dressed. I am amazed at how easily I have slipped and committed adultery and gone from being a 'good housewife' into a 'cheating adulterous spouse.' I don't even feel guilty. I wonder where my conscience has vanished.

As we eat our meal, Ankit and I talk. I ask him about his relationships.

He tells me about his brief engagement to the daughter of his father's wealthy friend, which he broke off (much to his parents' fury). He tells me it was more a business deal for his dad than anything else, and while the girl was pretty and pleasant, he felt nothing at all towards her. He also tells me about the large number of women he has had sex with, some of whose names he does not even remember.

'And don't worry. It was all safe sex. I never ever do it without a condom.'

Strangely, I don't feel jealous at all.

'No wonder you are so good at it. You have had so much practice,' I tease him.

'You know what, Diksha, it is the first time in ages I have felt this peace that I am feeling with you,' he says.

'This thing I feel for you, it is so strong, I am powerless, Diksha. I truly am.'

I am amazed that I feel exactly the same way.

Somewhere at the back of my mind, I do know that what I am getting into here will be a tangled mess. But it feels so wonderful and so very right that I am unable to stop it.

All that matters at this moment is that Ankit is back in my life and I feel ever so happy about it.

Twenty

THERE IS A SONG IN MY HEART AS I COOK DINNER that night. I smile constantly to myself as I recall how Ankit pulled me towards him and kissed me hard in the backseat of the hired hotel cab, as he dropped me home, even as the chauffeur probably got a nice look through the rear-view mirror, and how very glad I was for the tinted glasses.

'Will see you again soon. Take care, Diksha,' he had said.

'Bye,' I had replied looking into his eyes and there was so much said in that one single word. I knew he understood. It was the secret language of lovers, of two souls who understand each other intuitively and who are in perfect sync.

I miss Ankit like crazy even as I stir the dal.

'Ma, why are you smiling so much today?' asks Abhay, jolting me back to reality. He is perched on the kitchen counter, watching me cook. He loves doing this. He sits and swings his legs while I cook and is usually the most communicative at these moments, and we discuss and talk about various things.

'I just remembered a joke,' I lie.

'What joke? Tell me?' he insists.

'Why is an elephant large, grey and wrinkled?' I ask, telling him the first joke that comes to my head.

'I don't know. Hmm... Because they evolved that way?' he asks. He is my little geek, my little Darwin.

I smile.

'No, because if it was smooth, round and small, it would be a headache tablet,' I say and smile.

Abhay chuckles.

'That's a good one, Ma,' he says. I am relieved that I have thought of something to tell him which explains my mysterious smile.

Sandeep has an announcement to make that night and he chooses to do so at dinner.

'I will be going to Korea for about a week. If things work out, I will probably have to be there for a month or so. I have been chosen to spearhead a project and my visit will be crucial for the deal,' he says. He looks triumphant. As though he has won a war. I know this is really important for him and I am happy he has got what he wanted.

'Oh. Glad you got to head it. When will you be leaving?' I ask.

'Day after tomorrow. I have to be there as soon as possible,' he says.

'Oh, you will miss my science fair, Papa. I am making a robot, a real robot. And it moves,' says Abhay.

'I can't help it, son. Mummy will be there for you. This is a very important project for papa,' replies Sandeep.

'So? This is an important project for me, too,' says Abhay as he pushes away his plate of food angrily and stands up. The plate knocks over the glass of water which floods the table.

'ABHAY. How DARE you? Sit down right now and behave,' Sandeep yells at Abhay.

I hate it when he does that. His booming voice echoes across the room making my ears hurt. I am very scared when Sandeep is like this, though I mask it. But Abhay is unfazed.

He sits down, but does not touch his food. He crosses his arm over his chest and sulks. 'You are never there, Papa. I was chosen to display my robot. I beat all the older kids,' he says. All his pent-up frustration at Sandeep for not spending time with him comes pouring out.

I am so afraid of how Sandeep will react. I am certain that he will crush Abhay's spirit with his harsh words. Sandeep is quite insensitive that way.

'Abhay, it is okay, sweetie. We will video-tape the whole thing and send it to Papa. He will see it from Korea,' I quickly intervene before Sandeep can say anything, creating a truce between father and son.

Later, I cannot help thinking how right Abhay is. Sandeep is never around to witness and appreciate any of Abhay's accomplishments at school. It is always I who attend all his events and everything he participates in. I recall how Abhay, while in kindergarten, many years ago, was participating in a function on his school day, where he was a rabbit and had to hop across the stage in a bunny costume. Sandeep had taken off to play golf as usual, saying he could not attend, as he found such events boring and had no interest in seeing a bunch of kids prancing about on stage. I had felt bad, but quietly accepted. Over the years, it had become a pattern. Sandeep would wash his hands off anything to do with Abhay, and I was always the ever-present parent. Abhay too had quietly accepted it and today was the first time he was speaking out. My little boy is growing up and standing up to his father. Secretly I am proud of Abhay.

Of course, I say nothing.

Later that night, when Sandeep wants his usual dose of loveless sex, I shudder and clench my fists as I lie quietly while he pounds away, oblivious to the turmoil inside me. I hate Sandeep now. I do not want to be touched by him anymore. I recall how magical and how different it was with Ankit. I grit my teeth as he comes.

Then I leap out of bed and go into the bathroom feeling defiled, polluted and completely miserable. I wait until I hear his snores. Then I stand under the shower for a long time, the hot water soothing my body.

I slowly realise that everything between Sandeep and me has changed from this moment onwards. This is perhaps the last straw, the breaking point. It had been heading towards this all this while, but I had refused to accept it. Ankit entering my life all of a sudden has been the catalyst too. It has very clearly shown me just how much I have put up with, all these years. I feel that I cannot bear to live with this man anymore. I do not want to be touched by him again.

I wonder how I can break it to him

Darling, I met my old flame and we had awesome sex and now I want a divorce.

How in the world would I explain this to Sandeep? I realise too that, deep down, the coward that I am, I am actually scared of him as well. Telling him I want out will take a lot of courage. Also, I realise with a kind of helplessness that financially too, I am totally dependent on him. I have never worked and never earned anything in my life. How in the world will I manage if I break away? I know nothing about divorce and child custody and alimony. I have only read about and heard of people going through these difficult and painful issues.

Perhaps that is also one of the reasons I have never

stood up to him. It is easier to just go with the flow and give in to all that he says.

I am suddenly glad that he is going to Korea. If nothing else, it will at least give me some time to sort out the tangled mess that I find myself in.

⚜

Tanu calls the next day.

'Hey, babes, want to go house-hunting with me? I have to finalise my apartment soon. The real estate agency that my company hires has some houses. I am going today and tomorrow to see them. Would you like to come?' she asks.

'What time, Tanu? I have to be back here at three thirty as Abhay comes back then.'

'Tell your mother-in-law to keep him for today. I am sure she won't mind.'

'Yes, Tanu, but I haven't told Abhay to get off at the other stop, and neither have I informed the school. I can do that only tomorrow as he is already in school now,' I explain patiently. It strikes me how clueless Tanu really is when it comes to children and organising their activities. One's life totally changes when one has children. Every single thing that you do revolves around them, their schedules, their meal-times, their nap-times. I sometimes forget how inexperienced Tanu is in all of this.

'Oh, okay. Never mind then. I will drop you back at three thirty, and tomorrow you make the arrangements, okay?' she says.

I readily agree.

I debate and think to myself whether I should share what happened between Ankit and me with Vibha and Tanu. It is something so amazing, so powerful and so incredible that I want to hug it all to myself. I am not ready to share it just yet. I know I will eventually, but for now, it is all too new, too raw and I am overwhelmed by it all. Also, I feel what I have with Ankit is something magical. I want to preserve it as a secret for as long as possible. It is very special and I want to protect it and hold it close to my heart.

I keep glancing at the phone for messages from Ankit. He does not disappoint. He is in the midst of meeting clients at Goa. But any break he gets, he texts me. I immediately reply back.

He tells me about the deal he is finalising.

I tell him what I am cooking.

He tells me how much he misses me, that he wants to see me real soon.

I reply that I just can't wait either.

It is only when I suddenly get Gaurav's text asking if I want to encash that rain check today after class, that I remember his previous texts and also that there is a salsa class. My head is full of Ankit now. He seems to have overtaken everything. Every single thing really.

I feel bad about turning down Gaurav a second time. The last time he asked, I had postponed it. So I text back saying that we could grab a quick cup after class.

I get another text from Ankit.

'**Doesn't your phone have an IM**?' it reads.

'**No. Mine is an ancient outdated phone. I can't even access the Internet from it.**' I type back and hit send.

The phone buzzes after a few seconds.

'**What? I don't believe this. I am gifting you an iPhone when we meet next,**' Ankit writes.

'I don't care about the"I"-phone. I just want "U' with or without the phone,' I type.

'Soon, *meine liebe*. Soon,' he replies.

I run to the computer to google what *meine liebe* means and when I know that it means 'my love' in German, I beam with happiness.

I tell Ankit over text that I am going for my salsa class and will text him when I get back. He says he didn't know I learnt salsa. He asks me to teach him some moves.

I promise him that I will the next time we meet. I want to know when that will be.

'In about four days, will see you again,' he replies,

I truly can't wait.

As I hurry to the salsa class, I think about just how much my life has changed in a matter of forty-eight hours. Three days back, there was no Ankit in my life. Now it seems as though I cannot live without him. It all seems so strange, so surreal. I had never really thought of extramarital affairs before this. But now that I am embroiled in a full-fledged one, I realise I want to know more about it. Are there more couples like us? I think of every married couple I know. Who knows how many secrets their married life holds? Perhaps they have all cheated on their spouses at some point or the other?

Today in class we are learning a step where the guy has to do a double-handed turn which also involves a crossover step, where the guy has to turn the woman after he takes a turn himself and comes back to his initial position. The whole thing is done in quick succession and the movement of the guy as well as his partner has to flow seamlessly. It is a slightly complicated move. We begin by practising what we have learnt in the first two classes and for the first half hour, Lorraine ensures that we all get whatever steps we have learnt so far perfectly.

Lorraine addresses Gagan as well as Pavan.

'You both need to practise your steps, guys. You have to practise, practise and practise hard. Unless your basics are perfect, how will you be able to do this move?' she gently admonishes them, as she and Varun display the step perfectly.

'Diksha and the others, you are all doing great. Good going,' she says and I bask in her praise.

'Okay, let's start now. We do one round and then rotate partners. Come on,' says Lorraine and turns up the music.

All of us have got into the rhythm of the dance. I thoroughly enjoy this particular lesson. Now that we have conquered the basics, we all feel more confident of trying a slightly more complicated move. We finish a round and then we rotate partners. We have all now got used to the idea and have become good at it. We know what to do now, without being told or prompted. While I enjoy dancing with Pavan or Gagan, it is when Gaurav dances with me and I am able to move perfectly. In salsa, I discover, a lot depends on your partner. If your partner is good, then it becomes that much easier, as men always 'lead and guide' the women in this dance.

I am fully absorbed in dancing with Gaurav when I sense something is very wrong by the expression on his face. He looks startled and stops dancing.

The music too suddenly stops and I hear Lorraine say,'What the hell is happening here?'

I turn back and I freeze. It takes me a few seconds to register that the person stomping wildly into the dance floor is Sandeep. The stonefaced look and cold rage on his face makes me shudder. I feel sick to the pit of my stomach. My hands turn icy-cold as I clench my fists involuntarily. My heart sinks.

'DIKSHA,' he thunders. There is so much force in his

voice, something I have never heard before. 'WHAT THE FUCK IS THIS?' he asks.

I don't know what to do and I feel like a trapped animal. I want the ground to swallow me up. It feels as though somebody has shoved a stick down my throat and I cannot utter a word.

Everybody's eyes are on me, as if to ask who is this guy and what is my relationship with him.

'Excuse me, what is happening here? You cannot enter the dance floor like this. You are disrupting a class,' says Lorraine stepping forward.

'FUCK your dance class. I am talking to my WIFE,' he says as he charges towards me and yanks me roughly by the hand and drags me. I lose my balance and almost fall.

'Hey, watch how you treat a lady,' says Gaurav as he steadies me.

The next thing I know, Sandeep has swung out and punched Gaurav on the face with his right hand. With his left hand he grips me so tightly, it hurts.

'BASTARD, you stay out of this. You asshole. HOW DARE YOU? You will fucking stay out of this.' He spews profanities. His voice is loud and I am very frightened.

Gaurav is too stunned to react.

Sandeep drags me across the dance floor. I am ashamed, embarrassed and too terrified to protest or react. I go with him meekly.

He shoves me roughly into the car.

'What the fuck, Diksha? What the fuck is this? You go around shaking your tits with other men, like a cheap whore? Have you forgotten you are married?'

Each word feels like a slap on my face. Which century is Sandeep living in? I was only dancing, something I love doing, something I am good at. How can he be so narrow-minded? How dare he do this? Treat me like I am his personal slave.

How did he find out where I was? And what is he doing away from work?

All these questions reel inside my head. But I am unable to speak. I sit quietly like a statue made of marble, even as Sandeep drives like a maniac, in a fury.

'Why are you sitting there quietly now? Are you not going to speak?' he snarls.

I want to ask him what is wrong in my wanting to learn the salsa. I want to tell him that even his mother knows about it. I want to point out to him that there is a huge gap in his thinking and mine. I want to tell him we were never really made for each other and I have never been happy with him.

But I continue sitting in the car, tears streaming down my cheeks, too humiliated, too stunned too battered and too frightened to speak out.

Sandeep, with this act of his, has crushed my spirit. I never knew he was capable of violence. His hitting Gaurav has shaken me up completely. I realise, I don't even know the man I married, anymore. We have grown so apart.

I feel defeated, broken, and very vulnerable.

But more than anything, I feel so trapped.

Twenty-One

THE SHAME AND HUMILIATION I FACED IN FRONT of everyone in the salsa class hurt me more than anything else. I hadn't really talked about my personal life with anyone there and only Gaurav knew I was married and had a son. I had let the others presume that I was single. It wasn't that I was ashamed of being married, it was just that I did not bother to clarify really. Perhaps, at some level, I enjoyed the deception too. I was there to learn salsa, and I had made a friend in Gaurav. I hadn't really got to know the others in class. But what Sandeep did has completely spoilt it for me. I know that I cannot ever go back and face the others after this shameful episode. I will not be able to stand the looks of pity and more than anything, I am so ashamed to be married to someone like Sandeep now.

I see three text notifications from Gaurav. But I am too terrified to open and read them in front of Sandeep, lest he snatches the phone from my hand and reads my messages. So I hide in the bathroom later and read them. The first one asks if I am okay. The second one, sent after a while, says: **'Hope things are fine. I am really upset**

with your husband; this is no way to behave. I fear for your safety.'

The third one reads: **'Please, please text back to let me know you are fine.'**

I hurriedly text back saying that I am fine and that we will speak tomorrow.

Sandeep doesn't utter a word to me while I serve the family dinner. We pretend it is just another usual day. If Abhay notices that something is amiss, he is too diplomatic a child to say anything. He pretends there is nothing wrong at all.

I dread facing Sandeep in the bedroom. I cannot even stand the thought of sharing a bed with him. Sandeep watches his usual round of television and when he finally enters the bedroom, I feel cornered and trapped, like a fly stuck behind a glass-window.

'So, how long has this been going on behind my back?' he asks. I can feel the anger in those calmly uttered words. A cold rage.

Sandeep accuses me as though by learning salsa I have committed a huge crime. I have had extramarital sex and I am in love with another guy. Yet, of that he has no clue and is behaving like he has 'caught me out'. The irony of it strikes me hard.

I say nothing.

'You will answer me when I talk to you, you stupid bitch!' he says as he walks towards me and jabs his fingers into my upper arm. His words, more than the physical abuse, make me wince.

I am really frightened now. I know he is furious. Of late, even the slightest of things seem to irk him. I am so scared that he might hit me. After the way he has behaved today, I know he is capable of anything. I realise that the best way to ease the situation is to just give in to him.

'I am sorry, Sandeep,' I hear myself say in a voice I do not recognise. Tears sting my eyes as I say it, and I cower in fright.

'How dare you? And how come all the neighbours know about it and I don't?' he says.

That is when it dawns on me that the chakkar woman must have fed him the information. Sandeep must have come home early for some reason and she must have somehow seen him and intervened. From his words, it is evident that it had to be one of the mothers at the bus stop. He couldn't have got the information from anywhere else.

'I just meant to go for a demo class. It's always been my wish to learn salsa,' I say.

'And this wish emerged all of a sudden, is it? In all these years we have been married, you never had this wish. And who was that bastard you were shaking your tits at?' he spews out.

'Please don't talk like that,' I plead. I truly cannot bear his language.

'You really have loose morals. Look at you. You forget you are a wife and a mother.'

No, I am fully aware of it. I have never neglected my duties as a wife or as a mother. I have done everything for you these last fifteen years. I have been your subservient, faithful wife who has kept house and raised a child. You have never once appreciated or even noticed me. Have you once spoken a kind word to me? Have you ever told me I look beautiful? Have you even thought of what I might like and enjoy? You have always made decisions for me and you have presumed I am happy. It is you who forgot that a mother and a wife is also a woman and a human being, just like everyone else, and deserves to be treated right.

'Sorry, Sandeep. I will not attend any more classes,' I whisper, detesting myself for saying the words.

He switches off the light and tears off my clothes.

This time the love-making is animalistic, rough, and savage. It is as though he wants to punish me and claim his ownership of me. He does not even notice that I am crying and sobbing as he thrusts and thrusts.

Or perhaps he does and it gives him a kick. I do not know the man I married anymore.

I continue sobbing long after he had dozed off. I want to call up Ankit and tell him the reality of my marriage. I want to call up Tanu and tell her what has happened. I want to reply to Gaurav's text. I know I cannot be a silent martyr in my marriage anymore. I have had enough of this. I know I must do something, but I really have no clue where to start, what to do or how I am going to do it. All I know is, I want to be free of this man, the father of my child. I am done with enduring all of this. I am done with trying to please my parents, my husband and society at large.

It is about time I started living my life, doing what I want to do.

The next morning Sandeep pretends as though everything is fine. He packs his clothes meticulously for his trip to Korea.

I go about all my chores, cooking breakfast, lunch, sending Abhay to school, and keep mum most of the time. I speak only when he speaks to me. He is mostly busy packing his stuff, ticking off the things on his list and answering phone calls and mails on his smart phone. I hear him talking to his mother, telling her that he will be in touch from Korea.

I hear him talking to his colleagues, giving them instructions and discussing something related to his project with them.

Finally his cab arrives.

'Don't do anything stupid. Bye,' are his parting words as he finally leaves for the airport.

I wait and watch till the cab disappears round the bend. Then I come inside the house. I make sure that I double bolt the door. I turn up the music really loud. The song 'Are We Human' by Killers, streams across the room.

'Close your eyes, hear your heart, Cut the cord.' The words seem to be speaking to me.

I dance and dance and dance. I dance like I have never danced before. It feels wonderful, exhilarating—to be doing something that gives me so much joy.

Sandeep's departure has made me feel as though a huge burden has been lifted off my chest. I am actually celebrating his leaving. I am happy to see him go.

And, finally, when I have exhausted myself dancing, I take a quick shower and finish the day's cooking.

I want to tell Vibha all that has happened, but I am not ready to speak to her yet. So I sit at the computer and draft a long mail to her, updating her with all that has been happening so far, leaving out the part about my involvement with Ankit or even meeting him.

Then I call up Gaurav and tell him I want to meet him.

'Now?' he asks

'Yes, now, unless you have a class.'

'I was in a class when you called.'

'Oh, I am sorry. You shouldn't have picked up my call then.'

'How could I not? I finish in about twenty minutes. Where do you want to meet?'

'At Ajanta, near Brunton Road, in about thirty minutes?

'Sure. I will be there.'

'And Gaurav—I am calling one of my close friends too. There is something I want to talk to you guys about. I hope you don't mind.'

'Of course not, Diksha. A friend of yours is a friend of mine,' he says.

Then I call up Tanu.

'So all set, babes? Shall I come and pick you up? You have made arrangements for Abhay to get dropped off at your MIL's place right?' Tanu asks, as soon as she answers the phone.

'Yeah, I have. Listen, Tanu, something happened last evening. I am really shaken. I need to talk to you. In fact I have called another friend too. I am meeting him at Ajanta, in about thirty minutes. Can you come?' I ask.

'Sure, babes. I will be there. Are you okay?' she asks

'Yeah, sort of. I guess. But I am terribly shaken,' I reply.

When I reach Ajanta, I find Tanu already waiting. I hug her and I cannot stop tears from rising to my eyes, clouding my vision.

The waiters give us curious stares, but I am past caring. I explain to her all that happened last evening.

Tanu is aghast. She is shocked and angry.

'You must leave him, Diksha. What the hell are you doing sticking around in that marriage?' she asks.

'Look, it isn't so easy for me,' I reply.

Before she can answer, I see Gaurav walking towards us.

I can tell that, like most men, he is very impressed by Tanu. But then he conceals it quickly and recovers. I watch Tanu too and I know she likes his manner, his poise, his good looks and his stylish clothes.

'Hey Gaurav, meet Tanu, my best pal. Tanu has just

moved to Bangalore and heads the Bangalore division of Barclays. And Tanu, this is Gaurav, my salsa instructor,' I say as they both shake hands and say their hellos.

'Hey, I thought I was your good friend more than your salsa instructor! And you never told me you had such a great-looking friend,' smiles Gaurav.

'She did not tell me about you either,' smiles Tanu and I know they already like each other.

'Yeah, yeah, now you have both met, so you can't complain,' I say, secretly pleased that he asserted he was a good friend. Somehow it matters to me, these small things.

We all order mini-idlis and filter coffee which is the speciality of this restaurant.

My phone rings and it is Vibha. I cut her call and text her, telling her that I am out and will call her back later.

As the waiter scuttles off to get us our order, Gaurav looks at me and raises his eyebrows, as though to ask whether Tanu knows what happened and what it was that I wanted to talk about.

'I told Tanu about the incident at the salsa class and she was just telling me that I should leave him and, hey, I am really, really sorry that he hit you,' I say, laying out the topic in the open.

'Well, you don't have to apologise for him. I was really shocked. This has never happened to me in class before and I was taken totally by surprise. And, ouch, it still hurts. From now on, I must make sure that the spouses sign a no-objections clause and a consent form before I let married people join a class,' he says half-joking, rubbing his jaws and making an exaggerated comic face to show extreme pain.

Tanu laughs.

I am unable to.

'Hey, Diksha, relax, It is really not your fault that you are married to an asshole who is stuck in the dark ages, pardon my language,' says Gaurav.

I tell them that I really want their advice. I explain that Sandeep is in Korea and will be there for the next few weeks. I truly do not want to stay in this marriage anymore.

But the problem is I have no financial means to fall back on. I have never worked and have a nine-year-old son whom I dote on, to take care of. I am actually filling in the void for a father as well in his life as Sandeep is never there for him. I tell them how much it meant to Abhay to have his father at his science fair, but Sandeep couldn't care less. I explain how difficult it is to walk away from a marriage when a child is involved.

'Child or no child, ending it and going through a long-winded divorce is always messy, Diksha. Trust me, I speak from experience,' says Gaurav.

I reach out and squeeze his hand. I can feel the pain behind those words.

'I agree. Not the divorce bit, but ending relationships,' says Tanu.

Our steaming-hot mini-idlis arrive and we eat in silence.

'Hey guys, you both are truly the only real friends I have and I am so glad you are with me in this,' I say.

'Anytime. We are with you, Diksha. We will sort this out. There are no easy solutions, but that does not mean there are no solutions at all,' says Gaurav.

'Yes, I agree. You have time for now, Diksha. At least till he returns. We will figure out something,' says Tanu.

And sitting in that café with Gaurav and Tanu, I am really glad I have these two people in my life. I feel grateful to have someone I can speak openly to, without fear of judgement. Someone who understands the situation fully. Someone supportive and someone who genuinely cares for me. I feel good about my friendship with Gaurav and Tanu, who have unexpectedly come into my life and are now there when I need them most.

But I still hide my involvement with Ankit from them.

Somehow, even though I have shared so much, I am not ready to share that yet.

My phone beeps and I smile when I see that it is a message from him. I quickly put it away, like saving a treasure for later, to be savoured in secrecy when I am by myself.

No matter what has happened in my life, even the mere thought of him is enough to make me smile.

'So what are you going to do now? Will you be coming for dance class or no? Personally, I think you have great potential and you should continue,' says Gaurav.

'I want to, Gaurav. But I do not feel like facing the others now. How can I after Sandeep behaved the way he did?'

'Hey listen. Let us get one thing very clear, you are not responsible for his behaviour, okay?'

'I agree,' says Tanu. 'You should continue your class, Diksha. It would truly be a pity if you stopped.'

'And, you know what? She is really one of the best students I have had. She should, in fact, do the intermediate and advanced levels too. Salsa comes naturally to her. Do convince your friend,' he tells Tanu.

Tanu replies that she will do her best.

Gaurav hugs me and tells me that I can call him anytime. He tells me to take care and assures me not to worry and that everything will be all right. We bid a bye to Gaurav, who has another class soon.

And then we go house-hunting.

Tanu is very clear about what she wants. It has to be something modern, swanky and upmarket. She wants round-the-clock security and amenities such as a good gym (a must, she insists as she works out every single day) and a swimming pool.

We are not happy with most of the properties that the agent shows us. Some have interiors that are too dark, some are too far away from her place of work, some are very poorly constructed and some just have terrible floor plans. We find one which seems okay, except the road that leads to it is terribly narrow.

I tell her that there is a new construction, just a few metres away from my home, that she could check out. She is keen to do so.

'Your home is really close to my office. So I am already inclined towards this place. Let's go and see it,' she says.

We finally reach my lane and have a look at it. It is like a dream home.

The project has eighteen exclusive penthouses, each with its own private terrace garden. Added to that, it is a space full of extraordinary amenities like a bowling alley, a putting green, a swimming pool. There is a round-the-clock power back-up. The whole area has wi-fi and, apart from all this, there is also an amphitheatre. The entrance to each home is through an electronic key and finger-print scanning. There is wooden flooring in the master bedroom and beautifully landscaped gardens surround the area. The balconies all have transparent fibre-glass. The whole effect is very urban, posh, classy, in short exactly what Tanu wants.

'Wow, Tanu, this is awesome!' I exclaim.

'Yeah, isn't it just?' She is as delighted as me.

'Why didn't you mention this one before? We could have saved the whole morning.'

'Aaah, then you wouldn't have appreciated it so much. It is only when we go through bad experiences that we recognise the good ones,' I say.

'So right about that. But don't tell me we went all over town even though you knew this one existed, just for the experience?'

'No, Tanu. I knew this was there but I never expected it to be so good. I had only seen it from outside. I've never been inside this complex.'

Tanu goes to the site office. Many of the homes are unoccupied as the project is just getting completed. There are plenty of options available for rent as many of the owners live abroad and have bought apartments here purely as investments or to move in at a later date.

Tanu finalises a beautiful three-bedroom penthouse which overlooks the pool. Since it is going to be leased by her company, she passes on all the details to the property manager who manages all this stuff. I am very impressed.

'One of the perks of being in this organisation, babes. We don't have to worry about any of this. In fact, at very senior levels, they have these personal concierge services, where everything they want is taken care of. Can you believe one of the senior executives wanted some particular drink flown in from Australia and they arranged for it?' she says.

'Wow, what luxury,' I exclaim.

'I agree, but then they slog off their butts too. These are small ways in which they can retain people.'

I think about how different Tanu's world is from mine. I am happy about her success and how far she has come in life. But it once again painfully reminds me that the only thing I have really to show for my life, in these past years, is a well-raised child and perhaps a well-kept home. I am not even proud of my husband anymore.

Tanu drops me off and tells me I will have to accompany her over the weekend to go furniture shopping. She intends to move in that weekend itself.

'And the best part about this property is that it is just a stone's throw away from your home. I feel so good, we are now so close to each other. Bring Abhay over anytime. He would love to use the pool and bowling alley,' she says.

I too am very happy to have her live so close by.

Ankit calls almost as soon as I enter the house.

'And, *meine liebe*, how are we this morning?' he asks.

'Not so good, really,' I answer him honestly.

'What happened?' I ask.

'Will fill you in, face to face, when you come here. When are you coming?'

'Tomorrow. You know what? I am planning to start a business hotel there. I have a meeting with some people tomorrow. It will give me a legitimate reason to move base to Bangalore. I want to be closer to you.'

I am stunned that he is actually contemplating moving base to Bangalore. I ask him about his current living arrangements and about his parents. I learn that they are divorced now. His mother lives in Mumbai and his father is still in Chennai.

Ankit travels the world over and has no fixed place that he can call home. The business group that he has set up has service apartments, resorts and hotels in major cities in India, as well as a few locations abroad and, at all these places, he has an exclusive presidential suite just for himself, which is where he stays when he travels.

'It is high time we had a presidential suite to ourselves in Bangalore too. I am kind of bored with Leela,' he quips.

I marvel at how easily Ankit deals with millions of rupees worth of business, as though it is child's play. To me, it all seems extraordinary and amazing. For him, it is just business as usual. I have only read about such go-getting business tycoons in newspapers like *The Economic Times* and business magazines. I have never personally encountered anybody from that circle. And here is one, madly in love with me, an ordinary housewife.

When I mention this to Ankit, he says, 'You may call yourself ordinary, Diksha. But you fail to see your own qualities.'

'And what qualities are those?' I persist, hungry for his praise.

'Beauty, intelligence, smartness, but, most importantly, empathy and a kind heart,' he says.

I know he genuinely means all of it and I glow in the warmth of his words.

'For how long are you here?' I ask.

'Three days, maybe four. Depends on how the discussions go. I am looking at properties too,' he says.

'And in between all this, will you still have time for me?'

'You forget that you are the reason I am doing this whole deal. I am doing it to have more time with you. That's how much you mean to me, Diksha.'

'We could meet at my place this time, Ankit. I want you to see my house and also meet Abhay.'

'And what about your husband? How will you explain to him?'

'He is out of town. He won't be back for a week or maybe even a fortnight. There is a lot I have to tell you.'

'Hmmm, okay. In that case, let me finish my morning meetings. I'll be there by noon. Is that fine?'

'Perfect. I can hardly wait.'

'Me too, Diksha. You know, any moment that I am not working, I am thinking of you. You are a song playing inside my head continuously in auto-loop.'

'I think about you all the time, Ankit, all the time. I myself wonder how it is even possible that the auto-loop is forever on, 24 X 7.'

I feel that I have to 'prepare my home' for his visit. I want it to look really nice. I instruct the house-help to give all the bathrooms an extra scrubbing as I am having guests over. I tell her that everything should be spotless. I shift a few plants from the garden to the living room. It gives the room a cozy and welcoming look.

I tell Abhay that an old schoolmate, called Ankit, is coming home for dinner and that he is a successful businessman who has a large chain of hotels and resorts.

'Oh, does Tanu know him?' he asks. Tanu has specified that Abhay call her by name and not 'Tanu Aunty' or 'Aunty Tanu' as is the norm.

'"Tanu Aunty" makes me feels so old. I am not an aunty yet, am I?' she had smiled.

She and Abhay had got along really well. She had showed him a few tricks with his favourite video game, 'Super Mario Bros', when she had dropped in one evening and he had been thoroughly impressed with her ever since.

'Ma! Tanu is so cool. She knows all the video games. And she is your age. How come you do not know anything?' he had asked.

That is because I was busy raising you, feeding you, taking you to school, teaching you the alphabets, teaching you to ride a bike, and there was no time for video games in my life. She hasn't had a child yet.

'What to do? Your mummy is a *buddhuram*.'

'No, that isn't true. My mummy is very smart too, in a different way and I love her very much. She's the BEST,' he had said and given me an enormous hug. I had smiled broadly and hugged him back.

✣

And this is how Ankit and I meet at my home. He texts me as soon as he lands in Bangalore.

'Landed. Meeting them in the morning. See you at twelve thirty?'

'Can't wait. Come soon!' I text back

'Do you want me to cancel the meetings?'

'No way! You meet and finish your work. Work comes first, romance later.'

'You're a darling. Loads of love. Mmmmuah. See you soon.'

It is funny how a few words typed in an electronic medium have the power to affect emotions this much. I truly feel on top of the world after I read his texts. It is like I am flying, like I am invincible. Love is a drug that gives a natural high. No wonder it has been an eternal subject of thousands of poets, artists, writers. I wonder if everyone in love feels the same way—that theirs is an exclusive emotion which nobody else can understand.

I go about fluffing up the cushions in the living room as the radio plays on. All the mushy love songs on radio have taken on new depth now. I smile at my own silliness as I listen to the lyrics of the song that is now playing:

When I look in your eyes
You're all I ever wanted,
I always want you to be mine
Let's make a promise till the end of time ,
We'll always be together,
And our love will never die.

I would earlier not pay much attention to lyrics or even bother about music. But now I find myself looking up love songs, searching for their lyrics on the Internet so that I can send them to Ankit. It is as though no matter how much I express my love for him, it isn't enough.

And finally, Ankit lands up at my doorstep. I open the door and see his eyes light up and his whole face transform before my very eyes. He looks a carefree, happy and besotted man.

I draw him inside, bolt the door and he pulls me to him. We hold each other tight. He strokes my hair and our embrace seems to go on forever. When we finally break away, I lead him to the drawing room.

He is interested in every single detail of my home. Things which I have long forgotten because they have become so much a part of my life that I hardly even notice them. He looks at the framed photographs on the chest of drawers. I haven't looked at them properly in years. Strange, how we become so used to our surroundings that we stop noticing.

One of the frames has a very old photo of Sandeep and me clicked when we had just got married. Sandeep has his hands on his hips and I am half-smiling, half-scowling in the picture. I remember we had visited his relatives in Mysore and they had insisted on clicking a picture and later mailed it to us. The other frame has a photo of Abhay as a baby.

'He is cute, your son,' says Ankit.

I smile. These words are music to any mother's ears.

'Were you ever happy with Sandeep, Diksha? Look at you in this picture. The smile looks so forced,' he says, studying the other photo intensely.

'In the beginning I did make an effort. I tried hard to get over you. After all, I was just sixteen. I guess that was what my parents had gambled on too, when they married me off.'

'But why did you agree, Diksha? You were just nineteen when you got married, right?'

'I did not have a choice, Ankit. The all-women's college in Kerala they sent me to felt like prison after our school in Chennai. My grandmother and aunt monitored everything I did. I was dropped to college and picked up as soon as the bell rang. I used to feel sick, really. I hated it there. I longed to get out. I hardly spoke to anyone or made any friends. It is so hard to assert yourself when you are nineteen and weighed down by the guilt and parental pressure imposed on you.'

'I know, Diksha. I wrote to you every single day for three months. But I had no address to post those letters to.'

'Yeah, I wish we had the Internet and smart phones back then.'

'Then we would have probably eloped. We would have never lost touch. Incidentally, I have a gift for you,' he says. He opens his carry-bag and whips out a packet which is beautifully wrapped in white paper tied with a golden bow.

'What is this? Perfume?' I ask.

'Open it,' he smiles.

I do and I gasp. It is an iPhone. There is a tag tied to it, which has a handwritten message from Ankit:

'U phone, I phone—doesn't matter. All I want is to be always connected. For meine liebe, with all my love, Ankit.'

'Oh my God! Ankit!' I say.

'What?' he asks as he comes up from behind and hugs me, planting a kiss on my cheek.

'This is really nice of you, Ankit, but what will I tell Sandeep?'

'Tell him Tanu gifted it to you. And who pays your mobile bills? I am guessing it is Sandeep right?'

'Yes, and he checks every single thing in the itemised bill. He is finicky that way about money.'

'I guessed as much. Which is why this phone has a sim card which enables the bill to get automatically debited from my account.'

'Oh my God, Ankit! You are too much!' I say and kiss him.

I lead him to the spare bedroom and we lie on the bed and listen to classical music. We play *Poudre d'Or* by Erik Satie. As the music fills the room, we lie close together and look into each other's eyes and smile.

We do not make love.

Instead we talk. And talk and talk.

With the music softly playing in the background.

I tell him about how Sandeep created a scene at the salsa class and how shamed I felt. His blood boils listening to it. He says he feels like killing Sandeep. He says he fails to understand how a man can be so old-fashioned, possessive and jealous. He wonders how men can treat women like that.

We talk about old times and how we had got caught kissing. We talk about parental aspirations. He tells me how he joined his dad's business and how quickly he got bored and wanted to branch out on his own. He talks about how he raised funds for his first resort, how hard he worked and how he got it up and running from scratch. He talks about how it led to the second one being opened and then the third and how the others followed.

He says, 'I had turned into a total workaholic, Diksha. I was like a man possessed. It felt as though by burying myself in work, I could forget about you. I truly haven't had time to even breathe all these years, let alone have a relationship. Yes, I did have meaningless flings. Woman after woman after woman. I used to change girlfriends the moment they got clingy and demanded a bit more of my time. Heartless, I know, but I never really felt anything for them, Diksha. There really was no place for anyone in my heart but you.'

I kiss him softly on the mouth and say, 'You're really a specimen—you know that, don't you? Whoever heard of "true love" at seventeen? Whoever holds on like that?'

'I do. And you do too, Diksha. You know it. And if I am a specimen, so be it. You are in love with a specimen,' he smiles.

I kiss him again.

'And you know what, Ankit, I can be content just lying here and gazing at you. This isn't even about the sex. Look, we haven't had sex now and we are perfectly content.'

'I know, Diksha, I know. This connect, this bond I feel with you is really something extraordinary'.

'You know what they say, Ankit—if you cannot get someone out of your head, maybe they are supposed to be there.'

He draws me into his arms and we lie there hugging each other, fully clothed, two souls who have at last found home.

Later when Abhay arrives from school, I introduce Ankit to him. Ankit is genuinely interested in everything that Abhay has to say. In no time at all, they are chatting with each other like old friends. Abhay has already offered to show Ankit his room and I overhear him telling Ankit all about his science project. Ankit has a lot of suggestions to make and Abhay and he discuss the project in detail. Ankit is surprised at the depth of Abhay's knowledge.

'I hope you know, Diksha, your son is a little genius. I am amazed at just how much he knows. He is an awesome little young man. Do you know, he is able to explain all that stuff about robots in detail to me?'

'I know. And I don't even have to teach him anything, Ankit. He just researches and finds out everything on his own. He borrows books from his school and local libraries, gathers information from the Internet – and reads and reads! But he is zero in sports,'

'See, Diksha—this is the problem with most parents. Here you have a child who is bordering on genius and yet look at the way you are downplaying it by saying he is zero in sports. Most parents do that. They just want their children to live according to their expectations of them.'

'Tell me about it, Ankit. *You* know I even got married to placate my parents. Come on. I wasn't downplaying Abhay's achievements. I was just telling you how geeky he is as a person. '

'It is okay. It is okay to be geeky and nerdy,' smiles Ankit.

'I really don't care. I just want him to be a good, happy, well-adjusted human being who contributes something to the society.'

'He will be. You are indeed raising him well.'

Later Ankit, Abhay and I watch a documentary on television, something that Abhay insists Ankit 'must see'. It is a programme about surviving in the wild. Abhay animatedly describes in detail the exploits of Bear Grylls, adventurer, writer and television presenter, who stars in the show. Ankit listen patiently to everything Abhay explains and I can see he finds it fascinating too.

Later, after dinner, Ankit leaves for his hotel and Abhay promptly brings his blanket and comes to my bedroom. Whenever Sandeep travels, it is an unwritten rule that Abhay gets to sleep in my bed. He cuddles up with me, his leg flung over me. I so love it when he still needs his mama.

'Ma, you know what?' he says in the darkness.

'What?' I ask as I snuggle up to him, smelling his hair, remembering his baby smells, my heart overflowing with tenderness towards my son who is no longer a baby.

'If Papa was here, we wouldn't have been able to watch Bear Grylls because Papa likes watching only his programmes all the time.'

'I know, baby. Sometimes it is nice to watch something you like, right?'

'Yeah and Ankit is really cool, Mummy. I really like him.'

I want to say, 'I do too' but I refrain. Instead I pull him closer to me and smile in the darkness as Abhay drifts off to sleep in my arms.

Later I think about how well Ankit seems to have blended into my life, with Abhay, how interested he was in his science project, how we watched television together like a family. This is indeed bliss. I realise that this is something I have never experienced with Sandeep—this feeling of completeness and contentment. This feeling of functioning as a single team, of being a family unit, and experiencing the warmth only a family can bring.

I think that perhaps this was what my parents had hoped I would achieve with Sandeep when they married me off, trying to get me away from Ankit.

How ironic that it is Ankit who has shown it to me. And now that I have tasted it, I want it for ever.

Twenty-Two

ONCE TANU MOVES INTO HER NEW APARTMENT, our life improves dramatically. She gives me a key to her apartment as she works late most days, and I have a free run of her place. Soon as Abhay comes from school, I take him there and he swims for an hour. He totally digs the pool. We carve out our own little routine and both of us love it.

Ankit's visit this time has resulted in a bond between Abhay and him. While I am indeed happy at this development, I also wonder what I am really doing. Will this behaviour of mine impact Abhay in anyway?

My 'moral mind' reminds me that I am having an extramarital affair and questions whether it's right to introduce my child to my lover (I wince at the word) and do things which are irrevocable. My moral mind says it is wrong. It says I should be happy and content with my husband. That my husband, after all, hasn't run behind any other woman or cheated on me. It is me who has had an affair and cheated on him. My moral mind is really the voice of my mother and perhaps of society at large.

But, I think of the numerous times when Sandeep had a chance to create a happy family. It would have taken very little to have kept me happy. A dinner in a nice restaurant once in a while, a movie on a weekend, or even a trip to the mall – would have been good enough. Instead, his weekends are reserved always only for golf, TV and a visit to his mother's house. We don't even have anyone that we can call our 'family friends'. He socialises after work with his colleagues and on weekends with his golf buddies. We attend office-dos where I have to play the 'good corporate wife' and I have always done that. But as a 'family' we truly have never bonded or connected.

Is that reason enough to have an affair, my moral mind asks.

I think of the forced sex, I think of the humiliation at the salsa class, I think about how different I am as a person when I am with Sandeep, I think of the countless instances of supreme selfishness and a taken-for-granted attitude when it comes to me. I think of his mother's words and I think of all that he has brought to the table in this marriage and all that I have.

Then I tell my moral mind to sod off and that it is indeed reason enough.

I have lived my life according to the diktats of my mother and of the society. I have really tried hard to make a happy family.

Fact is, I do feel complete only with Ankit. There is no refuting it after his visit this time. And I know his visits will continue.

Ankit truly makes my life worth living. I know I want him more than anything else. But I lack the courage to say this to Sandeep. I am terrified of the repercussions and I am terrified of facing his wrath.

And so I settle for the clandestine meetings. It is truly these meetings that keep me going. Apart from the happiness that I feel when I am with Ankit, there is also a small ego-kick I get from being lavished attention by such a successful business tycoon for whom I mean the world. He travels a lot on business, but messages me the moment he lands from wherever he is. I feel as though I am with him. We are constantly connected. His resort-hotel has branches in Goa, Trivandrum, Delhi, Pune and Chennai in India, and the Maldives and Mauritius abroad, and he travels to all of these places.

I sometimes still cannot believe that this is indeed happening to me. Ankit and I, after the first two meetings, have become almost inseparable. I message him using the Instant Messenger App on my iPhone, and send him photographs of me or Abhay when we aren't on the phone with each other. There is such a lot I want to share with him.

I still say nothing about Ankit to either Tanu or Vibha. I know that I will have to tell them at some point, but for now I hug my secret and keep it to myself.

There is a phone call from Sandeep after a week. I am now so involved with Ankit and so busy living my life that it really makes no difference to me whether or not he calls. I debate with myself whether to mention Ankit's visit to him or not. But he does not give me a chance to do so.

His tone is curt, brief and to the point. He says his

company has bagged the deal and it makes sense for him to extend his stay. Even if he comes back, he might have to rush back for a month or maybe even two, he isn't sure. He asks if all is well and if Abhay is okay. I reply that he is. He asks me to tell his mother too.

I ask him why he cannot call his mother directly. In an exasperated tone, he says that international calls are expensive and, besides, there is really nothing to talk about, so could I pass on the message. Then, abruptly, he says he has to go and will call or email if there are any further developments at his end. And then he hangs up.

I call my mother-in-law to pass on the message. She sighs.

'I really cannot understand him. He has changed so much after his father died. It feels as though he has gone into a shell, for he is certainly not the boy I raised. He could have easily called me, all it takes is one measly phone call.'

'You know how he is when it comes to money. He counts every penny,' I find myself making excuses for him.

'I know only too well, Diksha. We have come up the hard way. In fact, he took care of his higher education all by himself, paid off his educational loans, and all that. But, today, he is in a position where he does not have to count the pennies. He seems to have forgotten that. It seems as though he has got stuck in a time-warp. Gosh, in some ways, I am more modern than him! And I am sixty-five.'

'I know.'

I know she is referring to his views. I want to tell her about how he behaved with me at the salsa class, and how humiliated I still feel when I think about it. That I haven't had the nerve to face my classmates ever since. But I do not mention it to her. There isn't anything she can do anyway. It will only add more misery to her. In a funny way, even though I am hurt myself, I feel this compelling need to protect her.

She asks me how Abhay is doing in school and when I will send him over. She says that she misses him.

I realise that ever since Tanu moved into her apartment, Abhay hasn't really bothered to ask if we can go to Aayi's house. Earlier, the swimming pool in her apartment complex was an attraction for him. But now that he has access to one, like all children, he has been immediately distracted. Children live in the immediacy of the moment. For them, there is only the near future, never the far future—they live from day to day.

I apologise to her and tell her that we will soon pay her a visit. She says she will be more than happy to have him over and I thank her for it.

Ankit is in Bangalore for two more days. He isn't able to meet me the next day as he is in meetings. His responses to my messages are much delayed.

'Sorry, meine liebe. This deal is important. In meetings whole day. Will call you the moment I get free.'

He types and there is also an emoticon, a kiss which sends my heart racing again.

It is as though I have turned into a teenager overnight after meeting Ankit. He says that he feels the same way.

'It's okay. I'm right here waiting for you. Do your work well,' I type back. I do mean it.

I do not mind when he is busy with meetings. He in talks with a group of investors who want to collaborate with him to open a hotel in Bangalore which will have super-luxury service apartments instead of just rooms. They plan to offer studio apartments as well as two- and three-bedroom apartments with the unique comforts of home, the ambience of a corporate guest house or a five star hotel, and the exclusive facilities ideal for both a short-term and extended stay.

I feel proud just thinking of his achievements. I am amazed that he has still held on to a love that he felt when he was seventeen. I cannot get over the fact that he loves me so much. He must have met scores of attractive women, smart women. Yet, he wants a relationship with *me*. But then, I think about my friendship with Tanu and how we still feel the same way towards each other. And I realise that some bonds forged during the early years are eternal.

I have a salsa class that evening and I am increasingly certain that I do not want to go back and face the others in class. Gaurav calls me up to enquire if I will attend.

'Listen, Gaurav. I love salsa, and I really do want to learn it. But let me be honest with you. After what happened that day, I cannot face my classmates. I simply do not have the guts. I had let them believe that I was single and in-between jobs. And after that crazy scene Sandeep created that day, I am ashamed to even show my face there.'

'I know, Diksha. But you have already paid up. 16K isn't exactly a small sum. And the institute has a policy of non-refund. If I owned the institute, I would have gladly refunded you the full amount. But I get audited for it. I feel bad about you not only losing money, but more so about you losing out on learning salsa. You are really talented. It would be a shame to let that talent go waste.'

'What can I do, Gaurav? Like I said earlier, I do want to learn, but it's awkward for me to come to class. I really cannot.'

'Hmm, how about I shift your timings? Put you in a new batch?'

That idea had not occurred to me at all. While I had wanted to very much continue learning salsa, I hadn't seen a way out of my current predicament. Gaurav's solution seems ideal.

'Wow! Can you do that? That would be just perfect,' I say.

'But it will have to be late evening. What will you do with your son?'

'That will be a problem. If Sandeep isn't in town, there won't be an issue, as I can leave Abhay with my mother-in-law. But if he is around, then he will definitely ask and create a fuss if he comes to know I am continuing to learn.'

'Diksha, I have the perfect solution for this,' he says.

'Which is?' I prompt him.

'Have coffee with me today and I will tell you,' he says.

I know that Ankit will not be able to meet me as he is busy for the day, so I readily agree to have coffee with Gaurav.

'Same place, same time?'

'Yes, I will be there.'

While Gaurav is a great guy, I know all I feel for him is fondness as a friend. I do not know if he feels anything more than that for me. And I do not want to take any chances screwing up a great friendship, just in the remote case of him wanting a relationship. I know it is too early and even perhaps ridiculous of me to think he might want something more, but I value his presence so much in my life that I do not want to take even the smallest risk. I decide that I will tell him about Ankit.

We meet at the usual place and he greets me with a hug.

We now talk with the ease of old friends and I feel that I have known him all my life. By now, I am used to his good looks. He is really attractive and is as well-dressed as usual. I see women turning around to look at him, trying to catch his eye and checking me out as though to say, 'What does he see in *her*?' I feel a kind of vicarious pride when he is with me.

I tell him that I really appreciate all that he is doing for me.

He says, 'Hey, that's what friends are for. Don't even mention it.'

'I wouldn't know, Gaurav. I really haven't made any good friends other than you.'

'Really? I am surprised. But you do have Tanu, right?'

That gives me the opening I am looking for. I tell him about my friendship with Tanu. How close we are. I tell him about all our escapades in school.

Then I ask him, 'Do you remember you had asked me what rules I had broken and I had told you I will tell you later?'

Of course he remembers he says and still wants to know.

So I tell him about the night Ankit and I were caught kissing. I tell him about how miserable my life became after that—the new school, new city, the monitoring, the pressure, the constant reminding of my wrongdoing, the pressure to get me married which I eventually succumbed to, thinking, in my naivete, of it as an escape route. But, unfortunately, it didn't quite turn out that way, and I tell him what it's been like all these years with Sandeep. I tell him about how Tanu and Ankit came back in my life. And I tell him about how much Ankit means to me and how we have been meeting in secret.

He listens to all of it patiently. Without any interruptions. And finally when I finish, he says, 'Oh my God, Diksha. I truly would have never guessed. What a life you have led!'

'Yeah, I know. It is like leading my life in reverse. Most people go through relationships and finally settle down with someone they like, have a baby, etc. Here, I have had a baby and now I am going on dates, as though to compensate for what I have missed. It is crazy.'

'No, no, Diksha. I never looked at it that way. What I meant was, when you first came to the salsa class, I could have never imagined that you came from such a conservative background and how hard it must have been for you to join the class, and how many internal barriers you must have broken to follow your heart. Looking at you, I would have never guessed all of this. So when Sandeep stormed in that day, I was indeed shell-shocked. But now it all makes sense.'

'Anyway, now you know my whole story, Gaurav. This is the first time I have opened up like this to somebody.'

'I am honoured, Diksha', he says and cups my hand. It is the touch of a good friend as though to say, 'Don't worry. I am with you through and through.'

Then I ask him what was the brilliant idea he had.

He says that he wants to offer me private salsa lessons. They will be exclusive lessons, just for me. I cannot believe what he is offering. It is like a dream come true.

'But the money, Gaurav? I can't afford private lessons, you know. My cousin, Vibha, paid for this course.'

'Did I ask you for money, Diksha? Come on! How can you even talk about money and belittle our friendship. This is truly the least I can do for a friend. Please! If I wanted money, do you think I would have called you out and spent time with you? Wouldn't I have simply suggested this over the phone? What a silly goose you are, Diksha. I *like* you! You're my *friend*. And if I cannot do this much for a good friend, what is the use of friendship?'

The generosity of his offer takes me completely by surprise.

'Wow,' I say, my voice almost a whisper. I am speechless.

Gaurav smiles.

'I knew this was the perfect solution. So will you come to the studio? When shall we start?' he asks.

I tell him that I will let him know. All of this has happened so suddenly. I thank him and tell him that I definitely want to learn and that we will work out the timings and other details.

Once I am back home, I know that I have to speak to Tanu. I have just told Gaurav about my relationship with Ankit and it seems unfair to hide it from Tanu anymore. But somehow I am still reluctant to share it with Vibha.

I call up Tanu, telling her that I am coming over to her place to spend the night and that I want to talk.

'Anytime, babes, anytime. I am only delighted to have you. You know that well,' she says.

Next, I call up my mother-in-law and tell her that since I want to spend a night with my old school friend, just chatting and catching up, would she be okay to have Abhay over? She is thrilled by the idea and suggests that I drop him off at the earliest and leave him till the weekend or even longer if I want.

This fits perfectly with my plans. I know Ankit will be free to spend the next day with me. If Abhay isn't around, who knows I could perhaps even spend the night with him? The very prospect excites me.

⚜

Tanu and I sit on her balcony overlooking the pool. The lights in the swimming pool shimmer and the reflections dance on the dark bobbing waters. There is nobody in the pool at this time of the night and it is so tranquil just to sit there and gaze at the water.

I tell Tanu that I have a confession to make. It reminds me of the time all those years ago when I had cycled to her home to tell her about Ankit. Strangely after so many years, I am once again confessing to her, and it is once again about Ankit.

Tanu says that we will talk over a glass of wine.

I laugh and say that this time it is okay even if I get drunk as I am staying over and Sandeep isn't around to pass moral judgements or be shocked. Tanu opens a bottle of Sauvignon Blanc and pours it into long-stemmed flute glasses and hands over one to me.

As we sit sipping our wine on her balcony, I find myself relaxing more and more.

Tanu is so easy to talk to and she has been such a loyal and devoted friend. I tell her about Gaurav's offer to teach me salsa. I tell her about how my marriage really is and how sex in my marriage leaves me feeling raped. I tell her about how I am unable to stand up to Sandeep, and how subservient I have always been, and how I am unable to find the courage to break free. I tell her about my meetings with Ankit and how we have now got into a relationship and become inseparable.

Tanu listens without judging me and I am grateful for that.

She tells me about all the men she has been in a relationship with in detail. 'I am thirty-four, Diksha. I head a business unit. But I am still single. I really don't think I will ever find Mr Right,' she says. She talks about her last relationship with an investment banker who really broke her heart.

'It was just a relationship for sex, Diksha. But he led me to believe otherwise. I was a naïve fool to have slept with him. He finally left me a week before he got married, can you believe? He had hidden all of that from me. He is happily married now, but I still burn with the memories. What a bastard he turned out to be. And the sad little pathetic fool that I am, I still wait for him secretly. I know she is so wrong for him, and one foolish little part of me still hopes he will come back to me. How stupid is that?' she says as she takes a last gulp of wine and pours herself some more.

'So you see, we all have our little secrets. Our little burdens to carry. We should just make choices that bring us happiness. We have only one life, Diksha. We should follow our heart and do what gives us joy. Learn salsa. And you know what, if you think going to the studio at a late hour is difficult, just use my apartment. It is anyway large enough. This way, you will be close to home and can bring Abhay over too. When Sandeep gets back, you can always say you are popping over to my place and he will not suspect a thing.'

I smile. It is indeed the perfect solution. I am happy about it. I immediately call up Gaurav who says it is ideal too. He then speaks to Tanu and thanks her and tells her that this will give him an excuse to see her more often as well.

Tanu laughs and I know she likes the idea of seeing him as well. I am happy.

'What have I done to deserve such marvellous friends? First Gaurav, then you,' I ask her.

'I don't know. You bring comfort and joy to people. You are sincere and true and honest, and that's what attracts others to you. You don't find such qualities anymore. It is as though you have been untouched by time. There is something pure and innocent about you, Diksha. Anyone who gets to know you is immediately struck by this.'

I don't know if it is the wine which is making her say all this. But I know she means it.

'Ha, ha, ha. You say I am so innocent and pure, and here I am cheating on my husband and having an affair. Some kind of purity it is,' I laugh.

'But you see, that is precisely the point. You have never really loved your husband, Diksha. You have always been faithful to only Ankit. It's not about physical infidelity, if you want to call it that. It really isn't about sex—even a blind fool can see that. Your love for Ankit—it is so pure. It is untouched by time and it is strong and true, Diksha. You have no idea how rare that is. And how very fortunate you both are to have found it.'

Later that night, I think about Tanu's words about my relationship with Ankit. I am not able to reach any conclusion about it. All I know is that I feel so totally complete when Ankit is with me. I need him. Now that I have found him I will do anything to be with him.

I text him saying so. He replies back almost instantly. He feels exactly the same.

Twenty-Three

Ankit calls me up the next noon.

'Hey listen, are you sure you want to spend a night together?' he asks.

'Why? Are you having second thoughts?' I tease him.

'Of course not. Why would I? You are the married one, remember?'

'Ha, ha, yes. But you know what the adultery laws in India say?'

'What?'

'Firstly, in Indian law, adultery is defined as sex between a man and a woman without the consent of the woman's husband. And since I do not think you will ever get my husband's consent, what we are doing is definitely adultery.'

'Hmmm, don't make it sound so cold.'

'Secondly, only the man is prosecutable and can be sentenced for up to five years, even if he himself is unmarried. And the married woman in the affair cannot be jailed.'

'What? Don't tell me! That is so unfair,' he says.

'Ha, ha, yes. In fact, the National Commission for Women has strongly opposed this archaic law set in the British times. It *is* really gender discrimination, as it implies that women are the property of the husband. They have recommended that this law be rescinded and they want it reduced to a civil offence. But that is yet to happen. In fact, most European nations have decriminalised adultery, but you know India. We are still stuck in ancient times in some matters.'

'Wow, Diksha. How do you know all this? I am so impressed. I hadn't even thought of adultery and its implications and what the law says. That angle hadn't even occurred to me.'

'Well, you have been busy signing multimillion dollar deals while I have been busy reading up and contemplating the possible consequences of my actions if this ever comes to light,' I say.

'It won't. But I know that I want you. Leave Sandeep, Diksha. Walk out. And let us make a life together.'

I do not know what to say to that. I don't even have the guts to face up to my husband when he treats me badly. How in the world will I have the courage to walk out of my marriage? I am indeed terrified of Sandeep's rage. Besides, fifteen years of being with him has made me emotionally dependent on him—something that I am slowly trying to break away from now that I have Tanu and Gaurav and Ankit as my support systems.

'I don't know, Ankit. I have been married so long, I have forgotten how it feels to live on my own and make my own decisions.'

'Who says you have to live on your own? You will live with me.'

'And your parents? You think they will accept it? Your social status, the circles they move in—what will people say? That you married a woman with a child?'

'Look, Diksha, my parents are divorced themselves.

They really don't care. My mother is having an affair with an industrialist. My father is seeing someone who is younger than me. Ours is a crazy mixed-up family. You think they will really care?'

'Ankit, we will talk about making a life and all that later. You tell me what time will you come home today? And tonight you can stay. Abhay is at his grandmother's.'

'Diksha, you come over. I will drop you back in the morning when I leave for the airport. Let me not spend the night there. You never know if the chakkar woman is spying on you from her balcony,' he says. He is only half-joking, but he does have a valid point.

I spend the night with Ankit at The Leela, a super-luxury hotel. It is the best night of my life. I have never stayed away from home on my own my entire life. I love every little thing about the hotel. I love the extravagance, the luxury and all the comfort it brings.

Ankit smiles at my childish joy at discovering the handmade chocolates with rum at the centre. He laughs when I go to the bathroom and quickly strip and emerge wearing a bathrobe with nothing underneath. He pulls me towards him and we make love slowly this time. He kisses my forehead, my nose and my lips. He traces slow circles on my bare back, driving me wild, and I press my body against him. His touch sends seismic waves through me. The unhurried manner makes it even more intense and finally when I come, I scream. It feels like a volcanic explosion has taken place inside of me. I have never known such intense pleasure, such joy, such absolute contentment.

'Ankit, I love you,' I say later as we lie next to each other wrapped up in a cozy duvet. I am so glad that Ankit holds me after sex and actually makes conversation. So glad that he isn't one of those men who roll over and go to sleep.

'I know, *meine liebe*. I do too. Imagine having this for the rest of our lives.'

'A marriage ruins everything, Ankit. It brings familiarity. Right now all this is exciting, maybe because it is rationed, measured and clandestine. Maybe it is because we cannot have each other when we want, that it is so intense. Maybe we will get bored of each other if we spend just three days together, who knows.'

'No way. A lifetime with you won't be enough for me.'

'I would be content with just three days. Three days – just you and me and nobody else. I would be so happy to get that,' I smile.

'Let's do it' he says.

'What?'

'Spend three days together. Just you and me, without anyone else. Let us go to the Maldives.'

'What? Are you crazy? How can I? I have never done anything that wild.'

'So? Have you ever slept in a hotel room before with another guy? You are doing it so easily now, right?'

'But the Maldives, Ankit? How? Don't you need a visa?'

'You need a visa, but on arrival. It is a wonderful place, Diksha. Ethereal, out of the world. We have a superb presidential ultra-luxury water villa there, in the middle of the ocean. I promise you, it will be unforgettable.'

'And what will I do with Abhay?'

'What you did with him today. Leave him with your mother-in-law. Come with me, Diksha. It will be a memory to cherish for life. Wait, let me show you what I am talking about,' he says and leans over to the side table where his Mac is resting. He flips it open and types in the address of the website of the resort. What I see blows me away.

It is stunningly beautiful. The water villa is right in the ocean, which is a myriad shades of blue—cobalt, aquamarine, Prussian, sky blue—all of which have mingled to create a scene straight out of a painting. The villa itself is luxury personified, done-up beautifully and tastefully.

'Oh my God, Ankit, this is so out of the world,' I say, gazing dreamily at the photos.

'Why else do you think I am asking you to come away here with me? It is indeed amazing, Diksha. We can create our memories. Make our dreams come true. Let's do it,' he says.

'Hmmm. We will plan something. But not immediately. We will do it at some point,' I reply.

'Yes, that's my girl,' he says as he pulls me towards him and cuddles me. I run my hand through his hair and inhale his smell, a delicious male scent that is his alone mixed with an expensive designer cologne. It is something I love.

Sandeep comes back two weeks later.

And with him comes back the life I have now grown to hate. Earlier, if there was a growing sense of discontentment, now it is full-blown anathema.

Sandeep has not noticed anything new about me. I am having an affair right under his nose and he is completely oblivious to anything that might give him an inkling of it. One part of me is angry about that. How can he be *that* indifferent to me? But the other part is strangely relieved as it is because of this very indifference that I am able to continue meeting Ankit clandestinely and to continue learning salsa with Gaurav in secret, at Tanu's apartment.

Sandeep is so involved with his work that it is as though he is lost in his own world. This new project has him completely occupied. He comes home very late these days, sometimes long past eleven pm, when I am almost ready to sleep. There are reports to be sent, data to be analysed and, even on weekends, I find him working furiously. It is as though the project has completely taken over his life and everything else has ceased to exist for him. He goes for his usual round of golf on weekends, but as soon as he comes back, he is at his laptop working. He is so busy that he does not even watch television any more. But more than anything, what elates me is that he is too tired to have sex.

Sandeep's preoccupation with work has also given me the freedom to pursue my salsa classes. Gaurav is an excellent teacher and now that he is teaching me exclusively, my progress takes a fast-track. I have mastered the basics now. He tells me to keep practising my 'shines'—the term for a specific footwork step in salsa, and the 'turn patterns' which I can do by myself. He has given me a CD which has all the salsa music, and the moment Sandeep and Abhay leave, I quickly finish my household chores for the day and put on the CD at top volume. Then I stand in front of my full-length mirror in the bedroom and practise my shines over and over again. Whenever I take a break, I message Ankit.

He replies when he takes a break. We keep sending each other messages throughout the day.

It is as though my life is finally coming together, except in secret. Sandeep has no idea at all about my progress in salsa. I keep Vibha updated through our usual phone calls, but I am not ready yet to tell her about Ankit. Only Gaurav and Tanu know about Ankit and I want it to stay that way. Gaurav is delighted with my progress in salsa.

Sandeep keeps travelling to Korea on and off. In these nine weeks, he has made at least five trips. He travels so often that I lose count. I no longer bother about his comings and goings. It is almost as if we lead parallel lives now, despite living in the same house.

Ankit travels to Bangalore just as often and I have lost track of how many times we have met now. He has integrated so well in my life that I cannot imagine how empty my life used to be earlier.

I have no option but to take Abhay with me to Tanu's house whenever I have a class and he either watches me dance or goes to the apartment park area and plays with the kids there. During some of my classes, Tanu is around and sometimes she is working late.

She enjoys the music and loves watching Gaurav and me dance. I can see that she and Gaurav are hitting it off well and I feel delighted for them. After class, Abhay and I walk back home and on some days Gaurav walks with us and on others stays back. I can see that Gaurav and Tanu truly enjoy each other's company. Perhaps they fill a void in each other's lives, I think to myself.

'Mama, Papa does not know about these dance classes of yours, right?' Abhay asks me after one such class as we walk back home. Gaurav is with us.

'What do you think we should do about that?' I throw the question right back at him.

Abhay is a very smart child and I know he has guessed what is going on.

'I think it is best if he doesn't know. I won't tell him as long as you buy me soft drinks whenever I demand.

And, oh yes, you can buy me chocolates too and throw in a game of GTA as well,' he says with a chuckle and runs off ahead.

'Come here, you little pirate of the Caribbean, you blackmailer,' I say and pretend to chase him round the park.

Gaurav bursts out laughing.

'He is really smart,' he says. 'What if he tells Sandeep?'

'He won't. He is my son. His loyalty is towards me. Do you know he has even met Ankit?'

'Oh my God. Really? And he hasn't mentioned it at all to Sandeep?'

'No. He knows a lot of things intuitively. It is as though he is wise beyond his years.'

In about ten weeks, I have mastered the twelve-turn-pattern moves as well as all its variations. There is a move called cucaracha and I have nicknamed it the cockroach. There is the mambo, basic back and opening out and cross-body lead. When Gaurav teaches me, all of these come to me almost effortlessly.

'Diksha, at this rate you can soon be my dancing partner at competitions. Your progress is awesome,' he says.

'Really?' I ask, pleased at his praise.

'Yes, I can see you have been practising really hard. That is the key and what counts most, apart from the inclination and basic talent that you already have. You are a natural.' he says.

As the weeks roll by, Gaurav starts staying back after class and spending more and more time with Tanu. Tanu enjoys his company immensely now and I know she tries to come home early from work on the days I have class just so she can meet Gaurav.

I ask her over the phone if there is anything brewing

between them.

'It's really early days, babes,' she replies, adding with a wicked laugh, 'but he is good in bed, I can tell you!'

'What?! What? Oh my God! Tanu, are sleeping with him?' I shriek.

'No, he leaves after sex,' she says solemnly and we both laugh hysterically.

❦

Sandeep announces that he is once again travelling to Korea for a week. His travels make no difference to me now. It is as though I have found my niche and carved my space. I am happy with my dance classes, helping Abhay with his homework, meeting Ankit, spending time with Tanu and leading a full life.

I visit my mother-in-law every now and then with Abhay.

'I am so glad at least you come and see me, Diksha. I am tired of expecting Sandeep to,' she says frankly.

'Aayi, it is okay if Papa is busy. Mama and I will come and meet you,' says my ever-gallant, mature-beyond-his-years son, and my mother-in-law hugs him.

'I wish your Papa had half your sense,' she says.

'I agree,' I say and we both smile.

I tell my mother-in-law about my private salsa lessons, and how much progress I have made. I tell her that Gaurav feels I can take the qualifying exams. She is delighted for me.

'You must take the qualifying exams,' she says.

'That is what Gaurav says too. He is confident that I will easily pass them.'

'He is right, of course. No knowledge is ever wasted.

Do it. Go for the exams. I will keep Abhay.'

'Thank you,' I say and mean it with all my heart.

Ankit comes to Bangalore that week. I tell him that I really want him to meet Tanu and Gaurav.

When I ask my mother-in-law over the phone if Abhay can stay over as I want to go out for dinner with Tanu, she is only too happy to oblige.

'Let him stay for two-three days. I really do not mind. And yes, if you want to take your exams, leave him with me for more time.'

'You are a darling,' I tell her.

'But that is only because you are too,' she replies.

I cannot help thinking how different my mother-in-law is from my own mother. My mother really hasn't bothered much about me or ever offered me help with Abhay. She has always lived with Rohan and done everything for him, including looking after his children. I do not like dwelling on my mother. Her relationship with me is a complex tangled web of love and hate. And so I push it aside.

We go out that night, Tanu, Ankit, Gaurav and I. Ankit has made reservations at an upmarket posh place (with Ankit you can expect nothing but the best) which specialises in Italian cuisine. We have a wonderful time chatting, sharing anecdotes and laughing.

Gaurav praises my dancing skills and Ankit is really proud of me.

'You know what, Ankit? It is all because of Gaurav. He is an excellent teacher. His dream is to open his own dance academy some day,' I say.

'Yeah, you should,' says Ankit.

'Hmm, some day I will,' replies Gaurav.

I feel elated being with my friends. For most people it is an ordinary experience, but for me it means the world.

It is something I never did in college and something I never had a chance to do after marriage.

It is little things like these, which Sandeep denied me, that matter so much to me. Now that I am getting it all, I revel in the moment, cherish it and enjoy it.

After we drop off Gaurav and Tanu to their respective homes, Ankit decides to stay over at my home as Abhay isn't around.

'Somehow, Diksha, I don't like staying the night when Abhay is around. It just doesn't seem right, you know. He is a growing boy, after all,' says Ankit.

'I know. Even I would feel very uncomfortable if you stayed over when he was around. Coming over for dinner is one thing, but staying over is another thing entirely. And I do hope the chakkar woman hasn't spotted you.'

'Do you think she spies on people long past midnight?' All the lights are off and there really is no sign of life on the street.

'I highly doubt it. Let us not worry about it,' I say

Later that night, Ankit has a surprise for me. It is a plain white envelope that he drops on my chest.

'What is this, Ankit?' I ask.

'A love letter,' he smiles.

'Really? You wrote me a love letter? Last time you did that, we were in school,' I say and open it eagerly.

'Well, this is a grown-up version of it,' he says.

And when I open it, I am stunned at what I see. I am so taken aback that I am unable to speak.

It is a printout of a plane ticket to Maldives with both our names.

And the flight leaves next morning.

Twenty-Four

'WHY ARE YOU SO SILENT NOW? DIDN'T YOU SAY you wanted three days with me, alone, far away. Well, here is our chance,' he says smiling.

'Oh my God, Ankit. How can you book tickets like this? That too for tomorrow.'

'So?'

'It's all so sudden.'

'So?'

'I haven't told Abhay. I haven't packed. I just am not prepared!'

'What is there to prepare? Request your mother-in-law tomorrow to keep Abhay for three more days. We will be back on Friday. This is really a fantastic opportunity, Diksha. We may not get another, let us just do it. I so want to show you Maldives.'

'I want to see it too, but...'

'What "but"? Don't you have the guts? Scaredy Cat!'

'Am not!'

'Prove it,' he challenges.

'I will. See, I have to speak to my mother-in-law first and I also have to keep Tanu in the loop. Plus, of course, I will need to tell Gaurav that I am taking a break from salsa.'

'And here I thought I was the busy businessman,' he jokes.

'Yeah, it is easy for you. You are free bird, you can fly wherever you like. I have so many things to arrange.'

'I know, *meine liebe,* I was only teasing. I can't wait to have you to myself for three days.'

'Me too,' I smile as I hug him.

We leave for Maldives the next morning. I have taken Tanu into confidence and she is thrilled at my planned escapade.

'Wow, just do it, babes. Tell your MIL that you want to spend some time with me and that we plan to go out every night. She won't mind, will she?'

'Not at all. In fact, she loves having Abhay over. She has been encouraging me to take my salsa exams and has offered to keep Abhay for as long as I want.'

'What is the problem then? Just go,' she says.

We leave for the Maldives in the morning. I have spoken to my mother-in-law and told her I want to spend some time with my friend. She is only too happy to have Abhay stay over.

'Have a good time with your friend and don't worry about Abhay. I will look after him,' she says.

I feel a prick of guilt when she says that. She has no idea obviously, that the friend I am planning to have a good time with is Ankit and not Tanu.

I call up Tanu from the airport just to mention this.

'Hey, look. Haven't you slogged and done everything for your family for the past so many years? What have you really done for yourself? Think of this as a gift to yourself. Just go and don't even think about it. You truly are too much. This is your chance, Diksha, and it has come to you on a platter. Where are you going to travel after this, tell me? Has Sandeep ever taken you on a holiday?'

'Yeah, we went to Nagpur once and once to Delhi, but both were family trips. We had gone to visit Rohan when he was based in the two places and Abhay was much younger then. We haven't been anywhere of late. Sandeep has just been too busy,' I answer her honestly.

'God, Diksha. That doesn't count at all. This is a *real* vacation. If you don't want to go, ask Ankit if he will take me,' she laughs.

We go through immigration and it is only when the plane finally takes off, that I begin to relax as I lean on Ankit's shoulder and fall asleep, the excitement of it all finally catching up with me.

Maldives is heaven. We land at Male which is the capital city. The visa on arrival takes just ten minutes, as promised by Ankit.

There is a private limousine waiting to take us to the hangar from where the sea-planes take off for the atolls. Maldives is made up of a double chain of tiny islands called atolls. Each atoll houses a resort. And each one is a world unto itself.

I am so dazed by all of it and cannot help staring in wonderment. I have never seen sea-planes, let alone travelled in one. The waters in Maldives are a dazzling mix of various blues. It is nature in all its splendour. The sea is lovely, tranquil and serene. It feels out of the world.

When our sea-plane lands, there is a boat waiting to take us to the dock. The resort which Ankit's company owns is impossibly elegant, with about thirty beach and water villas in an intimate location of pure lagoons, sandbanks and tropical surroundings.

The resort manager and the staff are there to greet us with warm towels and a welcome drink. They treat Ankit and me like royalty. I am flabbergasted by the whole experience. Ankit asks me to give him fifteen minutes with them while he takes care of business, and I am escorted to the presidential water villa. There is a wooden bridge, almost a kilometre long, which leads to it and an eco-friendly buggy takes me to our villa which appears to be bang in the middle of waves. It is constructed on wooden stilts and the ocean view takes my breath away. It is miles and miles of tranquil blue ocean. The villa itself is plush and luxurious with every little detail taken care of.

There is caviar arranged attractively on a porcelain plate and a bottle of champagne chills in an ice-bucket next to it. There are fresh flowers too.

When Ankit returns, I tell him, 'Ankit, this is the BEST experience in my life so far. I truly cannot believe there are places like this on earth. I think one lifetime will not be enough to spend here.'

'What did I tell you, *meine liebe*? I knew you would enjoy it,' he says softly as he takes both my hands in his and kisses them.

Ankit says that snorkelling is an activity we must try out.

'But I do not have a swim suit,' I say.

'The resort has a shop where you can buy one. Just charge it to the room,' he says.

I explore the shop. It has beachwear, swimming equipment, necklaces made of sea-shells, sarongs, sun glasses, suntan lotions, in short, everything that one needs for a beach.

I look at the swimming costumes for a long time. Then I remember my secret wish list and I smile as I pick a deep-blue polka dotted bikini in my size.

Ankit whistles when I try it on.

'You are so hot and I am already hard,' he says and I blush.

'Shut up,' I say.

'Why? It isn't anything I haven't seen before,' he winks and I throw a towel at him.

We spend the whole day snorkelling.

The resort also has snorkelling equipment for the guests to borrow. They have deep-sea diving courses which have to be pre-booked. I feel strangely liberated as I prance about in my newly bought bikini and wear my snorkelling gear which Ankit shows me how to use. There is the snorkelling mask and fins and it isn't too hard to learn how to use it.

We snorkel for hours and admire the beautiful and abundant marine sea-life. The water is crystal-clear in the lagoons. There are multicoloured fishes, coral reefs and sea-shells. The hundreds of stunning colours take me by total surprise. Ankit laughs at my delight and teaches me how to identify the various fishes. I soon learn to tell the difference between Dogtooth Tuna, Tuna, Trevally's, Jacks, Sweetlips, Butterfly Fish, Mating Octopus, Wahoo and Fusiliers.

Later, we sit on our deck and watch the sunset, a stunning beautiful blood-red, mingled with golden orange, and sip our drinks.

'Oh Ankit, I wish Abhay could see all of this. I so miss him. He would have loved it,' I say.

'We will bring him next time. It isn't so hard,' he smiles.

'Let me call my mother-in-law and check on how he is doing,' I say as I reach for the phone.

'Oh, your mobile will not work here. You won't get a signal. Your service provider probably doesn't have a tower in Maldives.'

I look at it and discover that there is indeed no signal.

'Does yours work?' I ask

'No. Mine too is an Indian mobile like yours. We

will have to use the hotel line to call. Do you want to?' he asks.

'No, the number will show, right? My mother-in-law will wonder about that then. I would have called from my mobile. But it is okay. Connect me to Tanu, I want to tell her,' I say.

I describe the whole place and my experience so far to Tanu. It is as though I want to drag everyone I love to this place and make them enjoy it too. I love it that much.

Tanu is happy for me. 'I am so glad you made that trip, babes,' she says.

'Me too. I feel so lucky,' I reply.

The next morning, Ankit has planned an all-day excursion on a boat with a fibre-glass bottom which will take us into deeper waters. The fibre glass will allow us to see the marine life without snorkelling.

It turns out to be an extremely relaxing cruise and I am filled with a kind of contentment and happiness I haven't felt ever before. We watch wild dolphins frolicking in the water against a spectacular sunset over the Indian Ocean. Maldives is home to several species of dolphins and they can be seen gracing the waters around. We watch them jump and do their friendly tricks as they swim alongside our boat. This is one of the most fun-filled and moving things I have ever experienced.

'How I wish Abhay were here, Ankit,' I say.

'We will come back with him and do it again, Diksha,' he says.

When we finally head back, one of the staff, a young man named Majid, comes hurrying.

'Excuse me, sir, sorry to disturb you, but there is a call for madam from India and it is urgent. The person has called twice, but we couldn't reach you,' he says again.

I am surprised.

Nobody except Tanu knows where I am. Why is Tanu calling and why is it urgent?

I look at Ankit and he shrugs. We hurry to the reception area to take the call.

My heart almost stops at what Tanu has to say.

'Hey, babes, Sandeep has come back.'

'Oh no. When?'

'This noon. He came back unexpectedly and apparently went ballistic to find the house locked. He turned up at my flat and asked for you.'

'Oh my God,' I say and sit down.

'Is Abhay okay? What happened?' asks Ankit.

I tell Tanu to speak to Ankit and I hand over the phone to him.

'Hmmm, okay. Hmmm, okay,' is all I hear at intermittent intervals while Tanu talks to Ankit.

'Okay, okay, don't worry. We will take the first flight home, but it will probably be only tomorrow morning,' he says finally.

'God, Diksha, I am so sorry about this,' he says.

'What has Tanu told Sandeep?' I ask.

'She did not know what to say. It was all of a sudden. She said the first thing that came to her head. That you had gone for a school reunion in Chennai. He demanded to know why Tanu hadn't gone, as his mother had told him that you were with her. She cooked up a story about a last-minute board meeting she had, but he seems to be unconvinced.'

'I am terrified, Ankit. What do we do?'

'I am going to meet your husband tomorrow and tell him you no longer want to be with him.'

'No, Ankit. No. I don't want you to do that.'

'What is the alternative?'

'I don't know. Let us get back home. We will see,' I say.

I am quiet and subdued for the rest of my stay with Ankit. Ankit tries to cheer me up. But I am deep in thought. I tell him to give me some time by myself. I sit on the deck, facing the miles and miles of ocean. The gentle waves make a comforting lapping sound.

I think about how my life has changed. I think about my salsa classes. I think about that fateful day with Ankit, all those years ago, when I had got caught. And that, once again, so many years later, I have got caught with the same guy. How can the same thing happen twice? Perhaps there is something called destiny and perhaps freewill works only up to a certain extent in our lives.

The secret wish list that I made on Vibha's insistence comes back to me. Sitting there on the deck that day, staring into the ocean, it feels as though the secret wish list that I had bottled-up inside me has finally broken free and is now spilling out.

I recall it in vivid detail and remember what I had written.

1. *Take a vacation alone, without family, but with a friend.*
2. *Go snorkelling.*
3. *Get drunk!*
4. *Learn salsa.*
5. *Wear a bikini.*
6. *Have sex with a guy other than husband, just to know what it feels like!*

I realise I can strike off every single thing on the wish list now. But, has it got me what I want? Has it got me my heart's calling? I keep thinking about all of it and finally, after a very long time, I know what I must do. I hope to God I will have the courage to do it.

The sea-plane which brought us to the island arrives

and this time I am not excited to take a ride in it. It is like Sandeep's unexpected arrival has cast a long shadow over the happy sunshine and all I see now is gloom and doom. As though to match my mood, it starts drizzling and the usually blue sky is now a smoky grey.

I do not know how I will face Sandeep, but I know I have to. There is no running away anymore. Ankit keeps trying to convince me that he will come with me and we will face Sandeep together. But I refuse. The flight back home is delayed by two hours, adding to my misery.

We finally land at Bangalore. Ankit once again tries his best to get me to change my mind about taking him home with me. He says he cannot bear to let me face Sandeep alone.

'Trust me, Ankit, your presence will only complicate things. Look, allow me a chance to handle this my way,' I say with a bravado I am not feeling.

It is with a heavy heart that I say a bye to Ankit as I drop him off at Leela and the cab speeds towards my house.

I dial Sandeep and tell him I am on my way home.

'Okay,' he says curtly and hangs up. I can feel his wrath already.

He is pacing up and down the garden when the cab arrives.

He waits till I enter the house with my suitcase.

'Where were you? Where did you go gallivanting to, you *bitch*?' he says.

'Don't use language like that with me,' I say quietly, my heart in my mouth. I am so afraid, so scared that he will hit me. But I do not show it. I fake a tone of confidence.

'I asked where you were. Don't give me that spiel about Chennai. I called up your mobile and it said it is unreachable. And you haven't gone with Tanu. Who were you with and where had you gone?' he asks.

I do not know what to say. I am unable to think of any lies. I have had enough of lies and pretence. I have had enough of this lifetime of suppression. I have had enough of hiding and doing things behind his back.

And so I say in a quiet and calm voice, 'I was with the guy I am in love with and we have just returned from the Maldives.'

Sandeep looks at me like I am a demon. He doesn't know what to say or do. I can see that I have paralysed him with my words. I can see that he has no idea how to handle this.

I feel a kind of sadistic satisfaction as I see his breath quickening and anger and confusion flooding his face.

He says nothing for a while.

Then he says, 'Do you even realise what you are saying? Is this some kind of a joke?'

His eyes are pleading with me to tell him it is a joke and that I was playing the fool. Sandeep has been propelled out of his comfort zone. His timid wife is no longer the doormat she was. She has finally found a voice and he does not know how to react.

'I am not joking, Sandeep, I am serious,' I finally say.

Sandeep is silent for a while. Then I hear him march outside and I hear him make a phone call. I have no idea whom he is talking to.

I myself am in a state of shock at what I have done.

I am shaken out of it only when my phone rings. It is Vibha.

'What is this I hear, Diksha? Sandeep just called me. What is this nonsense you have told him? Where were you?' she demands to know.

I tell her calmly that whatever I have told Sandeep is indeed true. I tell her that I have just got back from the Maldives, where I have had the best time of my life.

Vibha does not know how to react either.

'How could you do this, Diksha? How could you?'

'How can you suddenly sit on a moral high-horse, Vibha? You know my whole situation. You know how Sandeep is. Weren't you the one urging me to follow my heart and do everything on my wish list? Guess what, with this, the last item on the wish list is ticked. Happy?' I say.

'It is not sitting on a moral high-horse. This is just plain wrong. You have taken your wedding vows with him.'

'I was pushed into it. At nineteen. Don't forget. How can that be valid for a lifetime? And yes, I now want to make amends. You know what? I am leaving him,' I say with an air of finality and hang up.

I am very upset with Vibha. How can she *not* be on my side?

I hear Sandeep's phone ring again and I hear him say, 'Yes, yes. There is no other option. We will have to tell her family.'

Then I hear him dialling another number and telling my brother what I have done and asking him to take the first flight to India and sort out this mess his sister has created.

Twenty-Five

MOTHER ARRIVES LIKE A ROYAL QUEEN, ALONG with her entourage consisting of my father and brother who has thankfully left his wife and their two children back at Dubai.

My mother-in-law rushes to receive them as does Sandeep.

I am the convict here, the sinner, the wrong-doer and as such am relegated to the background. The fact is, this whole explosive situation has been caused by my behaviour. I, it seems, have shamed everybody. I have brought dishonour to the family by 'eloping with another man' as mother termed it on the phone when she spoke to me.

'I did not elope, Mother. I merely went on a trip,' I tried telling her.

'With another guy, without your husband's knowledge. And what do I tell Sandeep when he calls and asks us to come to India to sort out matters? You have truly given us nothing but trouble right from school. We are taking the next flight to Bangalore.'

And I had been dismissed. Just like that. And they have landed up at our place.

I wait in the drawing room now. I am shocked at how old and pale my father looks. He has lost so much hair since I last saw him and looks painfully frail. Perhaps the treatment for prostate has taken its toll. Rohan helps him up the low stairs which lead to the drawing room. 'Careful, Dad, there is one more step,' he says, as my father places one shaky foot after another. His movements are deliberate, slow, weighed down with his age.

I rush out to help him. I cannot bear to be a silent spectator anymore.

'It's fine. We can manage,' says Rohan curtly. He does not even look at me.

My father turns his face towards me and looks away with contempt. And that is how he greets me.

There are no warm hugs or hellos here.

I am the condemned one, the black sheep who has brought them nothing but disgrace.

Abhay rushes to my mother's arms and she hugs him and asks about his school and friends. She too looks very old. I am stunned and saddened to see how much they have aged.

My mother-in-law urges them to sit and asks me to make tea.

I call Abhay aside and gently explain to him that his granny and grandpa have come to discuss an important matter not meant for children. I request him to go to his friend's house and play there for a while.

'Oh, so you don't want me to hear, eh, Ma? I want to be on your side. I like Ankit, Mama. I really do,' he says.

I hug him. I wonder how much his little nine-year-old brain has assimilated. I wonder just how much he knows. I feel touched and surprised that my son has somehow intuited that this is war, with Ankit and me on one side and the rest on the other. He has chosen sides and is trying to assure me in his own way that things are going to be okay.

'I like him too. But let us not talk about it now, okay?' I tell him.

'Do you promise to tell me what happened in detail later?' he asks.

'Have I ever hidden anything from you?' I placate him. 'Now go and play.'

Abhay knows nothing about my Maldives trip with Ankit. All he knows is that something serious is happening and that the world as he knows it will probably change forever. But that really does not affect or bother him much. I am thankful for that.

Sandeep has fortunately not created any scenes in front of Abhay.

But I had not expected Sandeep to call up my parents or his mother and tell them about it. I had expected him to rant and rave at me. And had he hit me, it would have given me a legitimate reason to walk out. In fact, I was hoping for a confrontation where I could leave, he having driven me to it. But he has truly bowled a googly by summoning my family as well as his mother. He has slandered my character, making me out to be a nymphomaniac who first had an affair with a salsa instructor and now with some other guy.

I really do not know how much of it my mother-in-law believes. I know my parents have lapped up every word that Sandeep has said about me. It has confirmed their worst fears about me—that I was a rotten egg all along. Nothing had 'cured' me, not pulling me out of school, not getting me married, not even motherhood. As far as they are concerned, I am Diksha the trouble-maker, who has brought them nothing but dishonour, despite their best to 'bring me to the right path'.

As I take the tea to the drawing room, I have made up my mind. I cannot be a silent martyr anymore. I have been treated like a football all along—kicked first by my parents to Sandeep's court, and then kicked around by Sandeep all my married life. Now that I have finally found my voice and my grounding, it has created a furore. Neither my family nor my husband can accept it. It has created a tumult in their comfortable life. And they do not like it at all. But I cannot help it. They want a confrontation and, by Jove, they are going to get one. The events of the last few days have only strengthened my resolve. I know now, so very clearly what I want and where I want to be. My parents have no choice but to accept. This is my life and I am determined now to really live it, to follow my heart's urging which I have ignored and tried to suppress for so long.

I serve the tea and continue standing. Nobody asks me to sit. Not even my mother-in-law.

'Firstly, I really want to apologise to you both for my daughter's behaviour,' says my mother.

I see Sandeep nodding and his mother turns to look at me. I guess they expect me to hang my head in shame and express remorse.

'Ma, you really do not have to apologise for my sake, I am truly *not* sorry,' I say.

There is a collective gasp from the room.

I pull up a chair from the dining table and sit down.

'Look, Ma, you really do not know anything. And Sandeep, if you wanted to sort matters out, you should have talked to me, not dragged my parents half-way across the world,' I say.

'HOW DARE YOU talk back like this, DIKSHA?' thunders my father with all his strength. 'Is this how we raised you?'

'I am sorry, Father, but all this trouble has been caused precisely because I haven't spoken out. I have complied with all your wishes. You pulled me out of school, you sent me to another city, to a strict women's college and you forced me to marry early. I really did not have a choice.'

I am speaking from a place of strength that is coming from all the years of suppression. I speak out with courage and conviction. I speak out because I now know the alternate choices that life offers me. I speak as a responsible adult now. I have made my choices and I am no longer the old, terrified mouse I used to be. I know that if I do not speak out now, I will be squished and my dreams will be trampled. And it is taking a humongous effort from my side. I am nervous, but I know I have to say everything that I am longing to say.

'You very well know the circumstances that led us to do that. It was your fault,' my mother's voice quavers and her eyes glaze over with rage, perhaps recounting the unpleasant memories that loomed over all the choices they made and also inflicted on me.

'Ma, I was sixteen. It is normal for boys and girls to fall in love at that age.'

'Oh, really? Don't teach me. We have also been through that age. And we have not gone berserk trying to have a physical relationship,' says my mother.

'What? A physical relationship at sixteen?' Sandeep is shocked.

'No, Ma. It was not a "physical relationship" as you say.' I use air quotes to emphasize my point. 'It was just a kiss, and it wasn't the crime that you made it out to be. Had you left it, it would have probably died down on its own. It wasn't a big deal really. But the way you people twisted it, pulled me out of school, treated me like a leper, and the way you made it hang over my whole life, like the sword of Damocles, the way you never really listened to what I wanted, *that* was what has brought all this about.'

'Are you making excuses for your abominable behaviour? You had an affair with some guy after marriage because we made a big deal out of something you did when you were sixteen?' My mother is boiling with rage. She knows how to hit where it hurts. She has always been an expert at that.

But this time I am prepared.

'He is not *some* guy, Ma,' I say calmly. 'He is the same guy. He is Ankit.'

There is a stunned silence in the room after that. It is as though I have dropped a bombshell and my family is reeling in the aftermath of the debris that the explosion has caused. They had no idea up to now about the identity of the 'friend' I was out with. Now that his name is mentioned, it is as though they have been jolted by an atomic bomb. They have no idea what has hit them.

They squirm and I realise that I am sadistically enjoying the discomfort and shock that I have caused.

'I have an announcement to make. I no longer wish to continue in this marriage. I know I have tried for fifteen whole years. I have done everything that a good wife and a mother is expected to do. I have never once failed in my duties. I have raised my child well, I have kept the house well. I have cooked and cleaned and served. I have supported Sandeep in all that he has wanted to do. I have never once protested, grumbled or complained. In return, I have been constantly reminded by Sandeep that it is he who earns, and therefore everything is justified. When Abhay was smaller, it was fine. Time just went by without my realising, but now that he is older, I have time on my hands and I want to make something out of my life. I have found my calling in salsa. It is something I yearn for, something I am good at and something I want to pursue as a career. And guess what? I am going to go ahead with it. Gaurav and I are opening our own academy, as equal partners. And hey, that does not mean I am having an affair with him. Ankit understands this fully. In fact, he understands me completely and is ever-so supportive. Support and understanding is something I never got from any of you. Most of all you, Sandeep.'

It is a long speech and I pause to catch my breath.

Sandeep is looking at me, stupefied. So is my family.

They truly do not know what to say or how to react. That softens me a bit.

'There is really nothing as terrible as being misunderstood. I never intended to fall in love with Ankit all over again—but I did. I am sorry, Sandeep, I did it behind your back. That I admit was wrong on my part. I make no excuses for my behaviour, but I do want to end this marriage now. It is nothing but a farce. I want to make my own life. I will always have regard for you as the father of my child and there will always be place for you in his life. But, as far as I am concerned, I really don't want to have anything to do with you anymore.'

Sandeep slumps back in his chair and I sense he has given up.

My father, mother and brother look at me as though I am an evil witch with some mysterious powers that can turn them into frogs. They look frightened of me now. I too feel like someone possessed. I have never spoken this much and this emphatically in all my life.

'I did try hard, Papa. I tried to be happy in the life you wanted me to lead. I tried to do all that you wanted me to do. All I wanted was acceptance from all of you, which I never got. I yearned for you, Ma, to take me in your arms and to tell me that it is all going to be okay and that all of us make mistakes. But you never did anything like that. I know you acted in my best interests, but the fact is each of us has to decide what is good for us. Parents forcing down decisions on their children, especially when it comes to marriage, using subtle pressure-tactics to do that, backfires. It really does. But it took me fifteen years to learn that. I finally know what I want and what I want is to spend the rest of my life with Ankit.'

I feel like a public speaker talking to an audience which is in darkness. But now that I have said everything, it feels like a boulder that I have been carrying all these years has dropped off. I feel light. I feel like dancing. Finally I have broken free of a million chains that were tying me down.

My mother-in-law is the first one to finally break the sepulchral silence that has enveloped the room after my long monologue.

'Diksha has no doubt been a good wife and a mother. I have been witness to all that she has done and, I am sorry to say, my son too has been at fault here. Sandeep has indeed been totally absorbed in his work. So much so that Diksha has indeed raised Abhay almost single-handedly. She has been very sweet and kind to me and been there for me even during the times that my son hasn't. In fact, I knew about her salsa lessons, and I really think my son should broaden his view a little. Sandeep has been looking at this whole thing in a very narrow vision. Perhaps, if he had paid a little attention to what Diksha had wanted, and trust me, it was not much, this marriage could have been saved. But it is too late now. Diksha has made up her mind and I think, as parents, if you all do not support her at least now, you risk alienating her forever.'

I am so overwhelmed by her words that I get up, walk up to her and hug her.

'Thank you,' I whisper and I mean it with all my heart.

She hugs me back. 'I have seen the whole picture. I cannot blindly support my son. I know all that he has put you through. In some ways, he is responsible for being in the position he finds himself in. He has dug his own grave.'

My parents look at me in a new way now. I know my mother-in-law's words have had an impact on them.

I walk towards my mother and I am overtaken by a rush of emotions. I hug her. I feel her frail bones and realise how thin she has become over the years. A flood of tears is streaming down my face and I am having a very difficult time holding it back.

She stands like a stone statue, stiff and unyielding, for a very long time.

'Ma, please forgive me. This is what I want,' I whisper in her ear.

And gradually, ever so slowly, after what feels likes ages, her hands go around me.

And then she hugs me really tight and I know that she is crying too.

Epilogue

TEN MONTHS LATER

Diksha walked out of her marriage and moved in with Ankit. Ankit gave her the option of having a home wherever she liked, and she chose to live in Bangalore.

She has also got a gold certification as a salsa instructor.

Ankit funded the setting up of a dance studio for Gaurav and Diksha who are equal partners in it. They have started their classes and business has taken off really well. They hope to break even the following year and pay back Ankit his initial investment with a handsome return. Diksha and Gaurav are practising hard to compete in the World Salsa Federation championship and they hope to win.

Gaurav and Tanu are officially 'in a relationship.' Tanu says laughingly, 'I never knew that I, a hot-shot banker, will fall for a salsa instructor.' But hey, opposites attract.

Sandeep has taken a three-year assignment in Korea. Shell-shocked by what has happened to his marriage, he has submerged himself in work, the only way he knows how to cope with it all.

Abhay is writing the entrance exam for Doon School

which takes boys in at Class 7 and is very confident of clearing it. He loved the trip to the Maldives he made with his mother and Ankit, and wrote about it in his school magazine. It was chosen as the 'best essay' of the month.

Vibha has re-joined her company after her sabbatical. She is still miffed with Diksha and does not speak to her. Diksha hopes she will come around some day.

Mrs Pandit, Sandeep's mother, still dotes on Abhay and Diksha and is friendly with them. They meet every now and then.

Rachna, the 'chakkar woman', and Jyoti continue to be spotted at the bus stop every morning.

Diksha's parents have finally made peace with her. They have accepted her decisions and choices in life. They have slowly begun the process to mend bridges and though there is still a long way to go, it is at least a start.

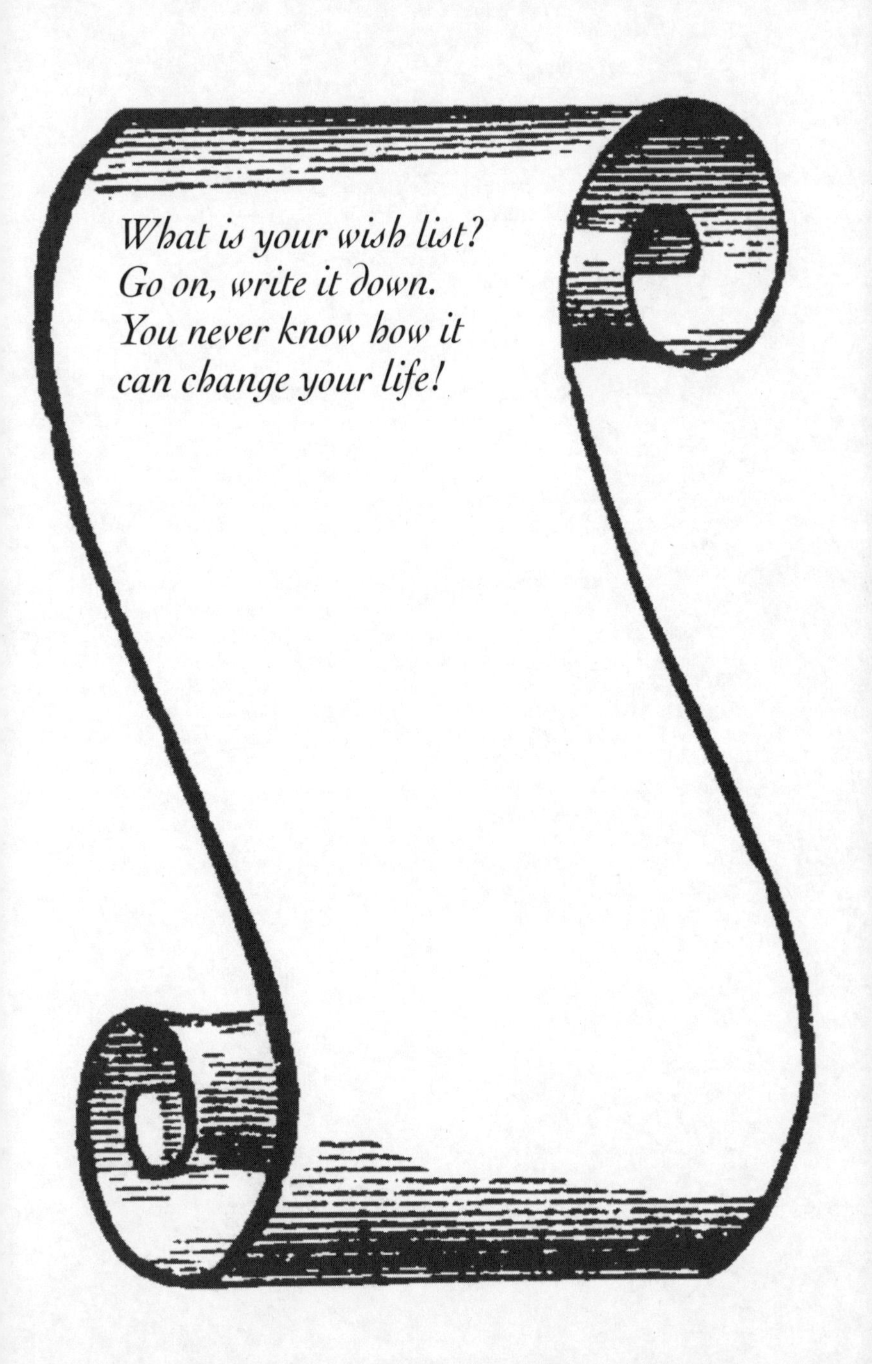
What is your wish list?
Go on, write it down.
You never know how it
can change your life!

Acknowledgements

Any story is really an amalgamation of a lifetime of experiences, a million little moments that made an impact and contributed to it in some small way or the other.

To mention all those who were a part of this journey would be an impossible task. But there are a few who just have to be mentioned, as they played a big role in shaping this book, directly or indirectly.

A huge thank you to all who read my previous books and loved them, as well as to my blog readers who shower me with so much affection.

A thank you to my mother who was the first to hear the story. She loved the idea when I first narrated it to her.

To my dad who continues to be my inspiration and who continues to live on within me.

To Satish, my husband, who I am fortunate to have in my life.

To my children, Atul and Purvi, who are very proud of all that I do.

A big thanks to Suresh Sanyasi who gave the book a different direction and who patiently read all my drafts in between his very busy schedule and was brave enough to be honest with me.

To Rathipriya who believes in me.

To Shabina, for all the love and support.

To Mayank Mittal, for all the phone calls and inputs.

Thank you to K Ramesh for the incisive inputs and for being a great support.

To all the friends in my life.

Thanks to Keshrie who kept my home neat and tidy and patiently listened to the progress of my word count on a daily basis.

Thanks to the team at Westland—Gautam Padmanabhan, Paul Vinay Kumar, Aradhana Bisht, Ahlawat Gunjan and the others for all their support. It was truly a great pleasure to interact with you. All of you are awesome to work with.

And how can I leave out Lostris who greets me every single day as though she hasn't seen me in twenty years. She is such a stress buster and has no idea how happy she makes me.